THE
VALLEY
AT THE
CENTRE
OF THE
WORLD

'Life-affirming . . . [Tallack] is a careful and precise writer . . . Given that Mackay Brown and Crichton Smith were two of the best Scottish writers of fiction in the second half of the 20th century, a first novel that sits comfortably alongside their work is a considerable achievement'
Allan Massie, *Scotsman*

'Tallack's concern here is with the push and pull of larger forces – love, grief, guilt, need, the idea of home itself. They're potent themes that could, but rarely do, overshadow characters about which he writes with palpable tenderness'
Daily Mail

'In this intense debut novel Malachy Tallack takes us to an isolated world inhabited by a community of utterly believable folk. He is great on the nature of work, how it is done, how it exhausts, how it shows our humanity. And when he gets this right other things naturally follow – like love and empathy and understanding. This book leaves us wanting his next'
Bernard MacLaverty, author of *Midwinter Break*

'Captures the emotional journey of a man who returns home to remote Shetland and the viewpoints of the people who live there'
Guardian

'Meditative, merciful and quietly moving – Tallack asks what is place, and who we are within it, all the while summoning pathos out of time past and time passing. A debut of uncommon assurance'
Paul Lynch, author of *Grace*

'Tallack brilliantly evokes both the environment and his cast of characters with understated charm and real insight'
Doug Johnstone, *The Big Issue*

'Malachy Tallack is clearly an islander through and through. In his debut novel, island life is deftly and warmly drawn'
Radio Times

'Portrays Shetland's rugged landscape and harsh backdrop with a serenity that works in tandem with Malachy Tallack's clear passion for the overall setting . . . [His] debut novel explores identity, community and the innate desire that exists within us all to feel some sense of belonging'
The List

'Evocative . . . The dilemmas and emotions of the characters we encounter are beautifully and realistically realised. Through them the book achieves moments both life-affirming and bitterly sad . . . Readers may be drawn to compare the book to an all-time classic of Scottish literature: *Sunset Song*. And this is a comparison in which Tallack holds his own'
Shetland Times

'This is a novel about love and grief, family and inheritance, rapid change and an age-old way of life . . . gives the impression of having been long pondered and matured in memory'
iNews

THE
VALLEY
AT THE
CENTRE
OF THE
WORLD

MALACHY
TALLACK

CANONGATE

This paperback edition published in 2019 by Canongate Books

First published in Great Britain, the USA and Canada in 2018
by Canongate Books Ltd, 14 High Street, Edinburgh EH1 1TE

Distributed in the USA by Publishers Group West
and in Canada by Publishers Group Canada

canongate.co.uk

1

The author acknowledges the support from Creative Scotland

ALBA | CHRUTHACHAIL

towards the writing of this book.

British Library Cataloguing-in-Publication Data
A catalogue record for this book is available on
request from the British Library

ISBN 978 1 78689 232 4

Typeset in Bembo by Palimpsest Book Production Ltd,
Falkirk, Stirlingshire

Printed and bound in Great Britain by Clays Ltd, Elcograf S.p.A.

MIX
Paper from
responsible sources
FSC® C018072

For Thea and Malin

SHETLAND GLOSSARY

athin	within
blyde	glad
bonxie	a great skua
braaly	very
bruck	rubbish
caain	rounding up animals (sheep into a pen, for instance)
caddy	a hand-reared lamb
clerty	dirty
da day	today
da moarn	tomorrow
da night	tonight
dan-a-days	in those days
doot	used to express a lack of doubt. 'I doot it'll rain' means 'I think it will rain.' However, the expression 'nae doot' means, literally, 'no doubt'.
du/dee	you (subject, object and plural forms)
dy/dine	your/yours
een	one (wan is also used)
eenoo	just now
fae	from
fairt	afraid
fantin	starving

flankers	thigh waders
gansie	jumper
giud	went
ivver/nivver	ever/never
mind	remember
muckle	much/large
noost	a boat shelter, usually cut into a bank
ollick	ling
peerie	small
piltock	saithe/coalfish
selkie	seal
shoogle	shake
skerry	rocks protruding above the sea's surface
toonie	someone from Lerwick
Up Helly Aa	'Viking' festival invented in the late nineteenth century. It involves a torch-lit procession, fancy dress and alcohol. Many rural areas have smaller, more inclusive versions of the festival, but in Lerwick only men are allowed to take part.
wadder	weather
wark/wirk	work (noun/verb)
yon	that

THE VALLEY

The Red House

THE ROAD

Flugarth

THE BEACH
PARK

THE BEACH

Gardie

BURGANESS

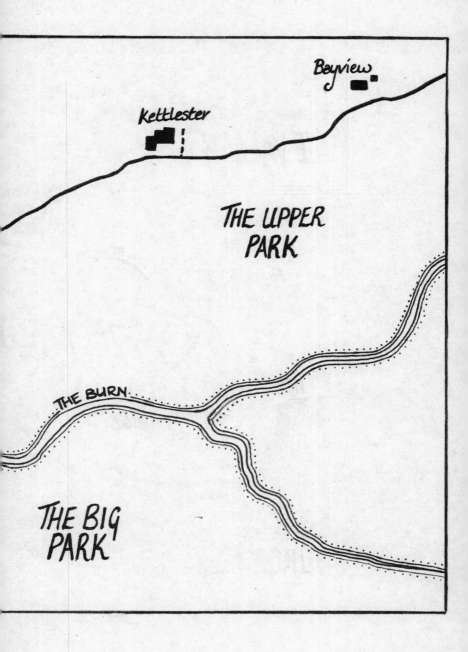

SATURDAY,
31ST OCTOBER

This morning, Sandy had to help Emma's father with the killing. The lambs were ready, and the day was dry. Last week, he'd promised he would be there to lend a hand, to do what needed done. But he hadn't known then that Emma would be gone.

He poured a bowl of cereal and boiled the kettle. He ate at the table, then stood by the window to drink his coffee. From there he could see the valley laid out in front of him, the brown thread of the burn unspooling through the crook of the land. Starlings squabbled on the stone dyke in the corner of the garden. Sheep grazed and gossiped in the nearest field. Outside Maggie's house, at the end of the road, a cockerel announced itself to the world. Beyond, the valley slipped into the sea. A glaze of salt on the glass made everything look further away than it ought to be.

Yesterday, Emma left, with a bag of clothes and a few things from the bathroom. Her toothbrush was gone. Her shampoo and conditioner. The hairbrush from their bedside table. The little stick of lip balm. She'd be back next week for the rest, she said, and after that, who knows? She would look for a place on the mainland – Edinburgh again, most likely – and in the meantime she'd be staying with a friend in Lerwick.

The timing had been a surprise, but the leaving had not. They'd talked about it for months, on and off, until Emma had tired of talking. In the end it was hard to say whose decision it had been. The thread of those conversations had grown increasingly tangled and incoherent, until it seemed the only escape was to cut loose. And though Emma had made that cut, it was Sandy who had pulled the tangle tight. He had engineered his own abandonment.

After packing her things, Emma had driven the few hundred yards up to her parents' house to tell them she was going. She'd been dreading that, he knew. The weight of their disappointment loomed. Sandy was uneasy for that hour, as her car sat in the driveway at Kettlester. He wanted to be there to defend himself, to explain things from his side. But he wasn't sure that he *could* explain. And it wasn't his place to do so. So he just waited, rubbing his palms together, glaring at the floor.

In the kitchen the clock was ticking – an American ogee, with a sailing ship on the front. Once it had belonged to Sandy's grandfather, now it belonged to Sandy. Emma always hated the intrusion of that noise, but he liked to hear it. Sometimes, when his thoughts were elsewhere and the sound had been erased, Sandy would stop and listen just to find it again, as though it were new. It brought him right back to where he was.

He shifted himself, then tried to loosen his shoulders. He rolled them a few times, moved his head from side to side. The night still clung to him like damp wool, but a walk up the road would help. It would make him feel awake. He set the mug on the draining board and took a boilersuit from the back of the door. He grabbed a coat, too, just in case. Outside, the air was calmer and quieter than he'd expected. It was one of those mornings when you could hear someone talking on the other side of the valley, if there'd been anyone there to talk. Sandy's boots clopped on the tarmac, and the sheathed knife in his pocket chafed with every stride.

'This is home,' Emma had said, the first time she'd brought

him here to meet her parents. Her arm had motioned all around, taking in everything they could see, and she'd laughed. This was the place she was brought up, the place she knew best, and the place she wanted to come back to – though she hadn't told him that yet. But that first time, as they'd stood together in front of the house, with the smell of her mother's cooking behind them, he couldn't see what she saw. Hills, fields, sheep, birds: that's all there was in this valley, and he'd felt no tug of connection to it. 'Let's go in,' he'd said. 'It's cold.'

His own home might have been twenty-five miles away, in the grey ex-council house in Lerwick where he'd spent his childhood, and where his father still lived. Or it might have been the flat he shared in Edinburgh. He'd never thought that much about it. The question just didn't seem important.

He and Emma first met in their mid-twenties, when both of them were living in the city. They'd been in different year groups at school, and they'd had different friends. He'd heard her name before – that's how it was with this place – but he didn't know anything more than that. She was a tiny part of a picture he no longer cared that much about. Until, having met, the focus of his care was dragged towards her.

'We're tied to da islands by elastic,' she told him once. 'Du just has to decide how du lives wi it. Either du goes awa and stretches that elastic – gradually it'll slacken aff and du can breathe easier – or else du just gives in. Let it pull dee back. Let it carry dee hame.' He'd laughed at her then. He'd never felt that pull since he'd moved south. Not once. The pull, always, had been in the other direction, away from the place where he began.

But two years after his first visit to the valley he had been carried back here, together with Emma. This had become his home, and for three more years it had been *their* home. And now she was gone.

David was standing at the entrance to the shed, a basin of hot, soapy water in his hands. Setting it down on the workbench, he turned and nodded at Sandy.

'I wis up early, so I got da lambs in afore brakfast.'

'That's good,' said Sandy. 'Hoo mony have we to do?'

'Juist eight da day. I hae things ta be gettin on wi later. We can dae da rest da moarn, if du's able. Else I can manage mesel, if du haes idder plans.'

Sandy shrugged. 'Tomorrow's fine.' In the stock box, the animals shuffled nervously. 'Ready to start, then?'

'Aye,' said David, walking towards the trailer. He paused, as if he'd forgotten something, then laid a hand on Sandy's shoulder. 'Ah'm sorry, boy,' he said, and nodded again. 'Ah'm really sorry.' Turning, he undid the catches and lowered the ramp to the ground. 'Ah'm ready when du's ready.'

David stood aside as Sandy pulled open the gate and stepped into the box. The lambs were six months old now, stocky and strong, and they huddled against the back wall, their eyes all turned to him. There was no panic at first, just a wire-tight expectation that hummed as he moved forward, waiting for the choice to be made. One step more and they broke. A stubby-horned ram dived to Sandy's right side, trying to escape. He reached and caught it by the shoulders, then hauled it to the gate. There, David took a front leg in each hand and walked the animal towards the shed, while Sandy turned around for another. A ewe this time.

With the second lamb held tight between his knees, he came out of the trailer and closed it behind him. He stood and waited for what was coming. Somehow it felt wrong not to watch, as though by looking away he would be dodging a guilt that was rightfully his own.

There was a carefulness to David's actions, a deliberate regard for each step along the way. Everything was laid out where he needed it, everything was ready. Leaning over, he picked up the bolt gun and held the lamb against himself. Sandy turned the head of the animal he was holding and covered one eye with his palm, as David had told him to do. 'Du nivver kens,' he'd said, in explanation. 'Du nivver kens.'

There was no hesitation in what happened next. David's hand closed over the trigger and the gun cracked, no louder than the pop of a champagne cork. The lamb, then, became a different thing. It tensed solid and shook as its nerves spasmed, back legs belting the air. David drew his knife deep through the animal's throat, then gaped the head back to let it bleed. Sandy realised he'd been holding his breath, and he relaxed as the gush of dark blood fanned out across the concrete. When the spilling and the shuddering stopped, David cut deeper and removed the head, placing it just behind him on the ground. He lifted the body clear of the mess.

'Okay, next een.'

Sandy shuffled forward, aware that the living, breathing creature in his hands had only a few more seconds to live and breathe. He was not sentimental, but nor was he immune to the gravity of what was happening. It was better done here than dragging them to the abattoir in town, David always said. And he was right. Everything was calmer and more honest this way. But still, there was a weight in Sandy's stomach as he passed the animal to David, then stood back to watch.

When both lambs were lying dead, the men took one each and carried them into the shed, front legs gripped in one hand, back legs in the other. They set them down on the curved, slatted benches by the doorway, feet pointing at the roof. David shook his knife in the basin of water, then wiped the blade and washed his hands. Sandy removed his own knife, turned it over, inspecting it.

'Is he sharp enough?' asked David.

'Should be.'

Though he'd done this job before, Sandy did not feel confident. There was a lot to remember, and he waited until David had begun before he started himself, watching and following the older man's movements. He removed the feet and lower legs. The joints split with a crunch, like the first bite of an apple. He washed the blade, then lifted the skin around the breastbone and made an incision, first one way, towards the neck, and then the other, towards the belly. Lifting the flap of pelt that faced towards him, he pressed the knife beneath, separating the skin from the flesh, like a label from a parcel. He laid the blade down, then put his right fist into the space he'd created, running his knuckles back and forth against the join, gently at first, then harder, forcing it back, widening it, until his whole hand could fit inside. It was hot and clammy in there, beneath the fleece, and Sandy felt he was entering some private, forbidden space, the heat a kind of warning. He felt the shape of the ribs against his fingers, the firm curve of the body. And as he reached further, soft-punching towards the stiff ridges of the spine, he tried hard to think only of what he was doing, not what he had done.

One side complete, he walked around and began from the other, loosening the lamb from itself until his hand met the space he'd already made beneath. His knuckles were stinging with the effort, and he paused a moment before continuing, slicing and stripping until the cloak of skin had been completely removed and the animal lay unwrapped on the bench.

Sandy looked over at David, watching the quick, perfect movement of his hands. He tried to copy, lifting the thin membrane that covered the stomach cavity, slitting it carefully, holding his blade away from the bulging gut below. A fatty, fetid smell erupted from within, and the coiled mess emerged, delicate and horrific. This is where it can go wrong, he thought. Everything you don't want to break is here: a full bladder and intestines. He cut a line from the groin up to the sternum, then cut deeper, towards the neck, splitting the rib cage. The animal came apart.

David had never taught Emma how to kill and gut a lamb. Nor had he taught his older daughter, Kate. He was not a traditionalist in every way, but he was in this one: men taught their sons, so he taught Sandy. Perhaps he had imagined that knowledge being passed on further, to his own future grandson, though he never spoke such a thought aloud. But now, today, the severing of that unspoken thought was apparent to Sandy, and perhaps to David, too. Today, they were only neighbours. The understanding of that change stood between them as they turned around their tables in silence, like lonely dancers.

'Is du feenished?' asked David.

'Almost. I'll be wi you in a moment.'

David walked to the cupboard on the side wall and fetched a handful of metal hooks. He punctured the hind leg tendons of his lamb and pushed one hook through each. Sandy stood beside him and took hold of the metal, then lifted the lamb as high as he could manage. David reached his hand in and cut away the dark liver and the heart, setting them aside. He sliced the diaphragm, cut the windpipe and oesophagus, then pulled the insides out, flopping the guts into a plastic bucket at his feet. Finally, the kidneys were removed, with an ivory nugget of fat congealed around them.

'Okay, hang him up,' David said, 'and we'll start ageen.'

When they were done, there were eight bodies suspended from the rail that ran along the side wall of the shed, each marbled pink and purple and white. All warmth had gone from them now, and all hints of the life so recently ended. They were solid and stiff. In a few days they would each be in pieces, stacked in David's chest freezer. Sandy's too, he hoped.

The two men cleaned the mess, bundling skins and guts and heads into black bags, scraping the jellied slick of blood from outside and brushing detergent over the blotched floor. They stood together in the doorway, then, looking out over the croft and the valley as an arrow of geese came wing-striding overhead, the air whimpering through their feathers. They watched the birds go, south towards Treswick.

David turned to speak. 'Is du wantin ta tak een o yon heads hame?' he asked. 'Fir company, lik.'

Sandy let the joke hang between them for a moment, enjoying the awkwardness of it. Then he laughed.

'No, I'll likely be aaright.'

David nodded solemnly. 'If du says so.'

Sandy noticed a spatter of blood on the older man's face, and he felt an urge, then, to tell him, or to wipe it off with the sleeve of his jumper. But it didn't matter. He was the only one who would ever see it.

'So du'll be back da moarn?' David asked. 'Just a few left noo, but I could dae wi dy help ageen.'

'Yeah. I'll be back.'

'Good. Ah'll ask Mary to mak extra fir denner. Du can eat wi wis. Come alang aboot ten, if it suits dee.'

Sandy smiled and picked up a polythene bag with two livers and two hearts inside, the clear plastic clinging to his greasy hands. 'See you tomorrow,' he said, then turned and walked back up the driveway and out onto the road.

★   ★   ★

'Darlin, I'm just putting the tatties on. Make sure you're back in twenty minutes, okay?'

'Aye,' David shouted. He was rummaging for something in the porch cupboard, then he was gone. The front door opened and closed. A bustle of cold air arrived in the kitchen, and Mary stepped closer to the stove. Her husband had a way of hearing without seeming to listen. It used to irritate her but not any more. She knew he'd be back in time to eat.

The sounds and smells of food filled the room, and Mary was there at the centre of it. She stood with her hands pressed into the pocket of her apron. Everything was in or on or ready. There was nothing left to do but wait. Five minutes, ten minutes, maybe more, she could just be still.

For most of her life, free time was something she never had. Bringing up two girls, working, feeding everyone: no time had ever felt free. And if she did pause, which of course sometimes she had to, those moments were always tainted with guilt, as though they were not rightfully hers but were stolen from someone else, someone more deserving. Stopping to sit down, with a cup of tea in her hands, she would be assailed at once by the thought of everything she could and should be doing instead. A list wrote itself around her. The living room needed hoovered, the bathroom needed cleaned, food needed cooked, laundry needed washed. She never resented the work she had to do – she had chosen this life, after all – but she hated the way it directed her thoughts, like a policeman inside her.

When she married David, they'd agreed: he would work the croft, she would work the house. It wasn't a business deal, exactly, but it was an understanding. Both of them had their own jobs besides that – he at the oil terminal, she at the primary school in Treswick, ten minutes' drive away – and that suited them fine. The animals didn't interest her much. Not while they were alive, at least. She helped in the vegetable garden when she was needed, lifting potatoes or whatever it was that had to be done, and she tended to the plants in the flowerbeds. But otherwise, most of her work had been indoors. And for twenty years or so it had seemed endless, a list from which nothing ever could be crossed.

Then Kate left home, and Emma moved south for university, and everything changed. Unclaimed time sneaked up on her, as though it had been hiding in the house all along. Without warning, she would find herself with nothing in particular to do, and she would search, then, for something useful to occupy her. The house became cleaner than it had ever been. The garden more free from weeds.

But when Mary retired, last summer, the shape around which her life had turned dissolved. Her days became broad spaces in need of filling. She was still learning how to do that, learning how to enjoy it. Perhaps she was happier now than she'd ever been, it was difficult to say. She couldn't remember how she'd felt when the children were younger. Maybe she'd been too busy to feel much at all. She was just there, living, being the things that she did.

The potatoes began to bump and rumble in the boiling water. Mary reduced the heat, then sat at the table, chewing at her fingernails. She was thinking about Emma, her thoughts swooping and circling around this brand-new absence. Until last night, her daughter had lived next door. She had been *right there*. Now she was in Lerwick, and soon, it seemed, she would be much further – a flight, a sea-crossing away. The thought of Emma gone was difficult. The thought of her unhappy, alone, was difficult. Emma's sadness was indistinguishable from her mother's. Mary wanted to reach out and hold her as though she were six years old again, as though she'd fallen and hurt her knee, as though there were something, *anything*, that a mother could do. But there wasn't.

Her daughter was not a little girl, and she didn't need Mary's assistance. Not now. She made her own decisions, her own mistakes, and her mother had to sit back and watch, as helpless as a child beside a sobbing parent.

Mary had seen Sandy arrive this morning, but she hadn't gone out to say hello. She'd stayed inside all the time he was there. Not because she was angry. But because she was afraid, somehow, to involve him in her sadness. The sympathy she felt for him hadn't yet extricated itself from her own sense of loss, and there were questions of loyalty still to be answered, or at least to be asked.

She stood up to check the potatoes again. She was worrying too much. She always worried too much. She took it all on, these doubts and fears. David would shake his head when he saw her like this, frowning, fretting, wasting her time. She was always fearing the worst, he said, and perhaps he was right. The worst hardly ever came to the worst. Today was a bad day, and tomorrow might be too. But there would be better days soon, she knew that.

The front door closed again, and she heard David in the porch, taking off his boots, hanging up his jacket, unzipping his boilersuit. Now he'd be rolling up the sleeves of his jumper in preparation for washing his hands. She heard him sigh, then the bathroom door closed. She took the potatoes off the hob and drained them into the sink.

They didn't speak much during the meal, and they didn't say a word about Emma. They just ate and were grateful for each other's company. They would talk later, Mary knew, when the day was over and tiredness drew them closer together. She stood up and took the plates away. David sipped at the glass of water in front of him.

'Do you want tea?' she asked.

'Aye, dat'd be splendid.'

Mary set the kettle on and opened the fridge. She paused, gazing in the door, bothered by something. It took a few seconds to return to her. 'Oh shite! I forgot! Maggie phoned at lunchtime. She was running out of milk, and I promised to take a pint down to her. That was hours ago. She'll be cursing me now.'

'No lik dee ta forgit,' said David.

'No, it's not.' Mary shook her head and grabbed a carton of milk from the fridge. 'I'll go now,' she said. 'I won't be long. Can you do the washing up, please?'

David nodded. 'Aye. An Ah'll put da kettle on ageen when du gits hame.' Mary smiled and headed for the front door. She picked up her gloves from the table in the porch, then went out to the car. The night was clear and cold, and as good as could be hoped for at the end of October. An ocean of stars turned above the valley as Mary drove down towards Maggie's, at the end of the road. Her headlights carved through the darkness, hiding everything beyond their reach.

Maggie was old – she was coming on for ninety now – and had no family close enough to look after her. A sister, Ina, lived in New Zealand, and a niece, too. But she'd had no children herself, and her husband, Walter, was long dead. She did well for her age. Her health had mostly been good, and she didn't need much help day to day. But she was not as independent as she wanted to be. David had taken on her croft more than fifteen years ago, when she lost the heart and the strength for it. He'd known Maggie for as long as he'd known anyone. He grew up in the valley, as she had done, and he looked on her not exactly as a parent, Mary thought, but as much a part of his own life as if she had been, in fact, his mother. Most days, one or other of them would look in on her, check that she was okay, see what she needed. David kept her updated with his work on the croft, and Mary related any gossip she could find worth sharing. Maggie still liked to hear 'da news', as she called it. She liked to know that lives were encircling her own.

With her thoughts still elsewhere, Mary didn't notice until she pulled up outside the house that something wasn't right. Usually it was lit up like a ship after dark, since Maggie never turned anything off as she went from room to room. But tonight it looked empty. Mary was relieved when she stepped out of the car to see a single lamp glowing through the living-room window. Maggie would be there, she thought, asleep in her chair beside the fire. But when she opened the front door and went in, shouting, as she always did, 'Hi aye, it's only me,' she found the living room empty. She turned on the main light in the hallway and climbed the stairs. She knocked quietly on the bedroom door, then opened it to look inside. The room was empty, the covers turned neatly down. She went through the house, opening each door in turn, but Maggie wasn't at home.

Mary tried to think of the possibilities. When they'd spoken earlier, everything had been fine. There had been no talk of anyone coming to pick her up, and no car had driven down the road in hours. Maggie herself gave up driving years ago, so she couldn't have gone anywhere herself. It seemed inexplicable. Mary went out the front door again and looked up towards Terry's house. The light was on there, and she drove the hundred yards or so, knocked and walked in. As she entered, Mary realised she was panicking. Terry was in the living room with Sandy, drinking beer, and at first she just looked at the pair of them, then around the room, as if the old woman might be there somewhere, crouching in a corner. When she spoke, she felt her lungs clutch.

'Have you seen her?' she said. 'Maggie, I mean. Have you seen Maggie?'

'Not recently,' said Terry.

'Nor me,' Sandy added. 'Well, not since this afternoon.'

'This afternoon? When this afternoon?'

'Aboot three o'clock,' Sandy said. 'She was in the park by the beach, not far fae the hoose.'

'And you didn't see her coming back?'

'No, I just happened to look at that time. I didn't see her ageen. I just assumed she'd gone hame.'

'Well she's *not* at home!' Mary's voice was louder than she'd intended. 'We need to look for her,' she said.

'Is du sure dat's necessary?' Terry asked.

'No, I'm not sure,' Mary said. 'I don't know. But I think so. I'm going to call David.'

The two men put their boots and coats on and followed Mary outside. She shivered as the cold air clawed at her cheeks and hands.

It was only a couple of minutes before David's pickup came down the road, and the three of them stood beside the gate in silence, waiting to be told what to do. Mary could smell the alcohol from them, and though it made no sense, she found she was angry at their irresponsibility. Drinking! Tonight of all nights!

David pulled up alongside the house, shut off the engine and opened the door, but he didn't get out. Sam, his old Border collie, sat in the footwell of the passenger seat, mouth open, ears up. David grabbed three torches, clicking them on then off again, one after the other, just to check. 'Well,' he said, 'let's hae a peerie look. She's likely geen oot wi a freend somewye, but we're mebbie best ta see. An if shu's no hame afore twelve, Ah'll gie da coastguard a ring, see whit dey think.'

He turned to Sandy. 'So, du saa her in da beach park?' he asked.

'Aye, she was mebbie halfway across the park. But, dat was four or five hours ago.'

'Okay, well, if wan o wis haes a look alang da beach, da idder twa can geing trow da park and up oer ta Burganess. We'll juist hae a wander and see whit we can see. Mary, mebbie du should sit in da hoose, in case shu comes back fae whariver shu's been. Dere's nae use wis wanderin ower da hill if shu's at hame in front o da TV.'

David looked out in the direction of the sea.

'Okay, Terry, if du goes alang da beach, startin fae dis end, dat'll wirk. If du needs wis, try me mobile, or else flash da torch a few times and we'll come doon.'

He reached out and pressed his hand to Mary's cheek as Sandy got in beside him, then they were off down to the end of the road. Mary watched as the men got out of the pickup, went out through the gate and into the dark field, the dog running on ahead. She could hear them for a while – the scuffling of their waterproof jackets and the thunk of their boots on the soft ground. There were no voices, though. Once he'd said what he needed to say, David would be quiet.

The two torch beams scraped this way and that across the field, then crossed the burn and began moving up the headland – Burganess. She could see the third light swinging somewhere on the beach behind Maggie's house. She didn't trust Terry with much, especially when he'd been drinking, but she hoped he could take the task seriously. She drove back down to Maggie's house and went inside. From the west window in the living room she could still see the torches shifting, the strange unnatural movements puncturing the night.

This valley had been Mary's home now for almost thirty-five years, and in all that time Maggie had been part of the place – as much a part of it, in fact, as the fields, the burn and the road itself. Mary thought back to the first time she'd been in this house, shortly before she and David married. She'd been brought to the valley to meet everyone. She was taken from house to house like an exhibit or a circus act, so that everyone could see her and speak to her and then discuss her with each other once she was gone. They came to meet Jimmy and Catherine, David's parents, then Maggie and Walter, here, then to the Red House to meet Willie, and Joan, up at Kettlester, where she and David now lived. Lots had changed in this house, of course. They'd fixed it up in the late eighties, modernised it, with a brand-new kitchen and another bathroom. But it was still recognisable beneath all of that. The same pictures were on the wall, the same furniture, the same ornaments. It was even the same smell she remembered from that first day: a thick, comforting smell, of hand cream and dust and soap and soup.

When the door opened, Mary jumped, her heart thudding inside her. It was David, his coat and hat and boots still on. He looked at his wife and then turned away.

'Well, did you find her?' Mary asked, trying to sound hopeful. David shuffled, looking at the floor, then finally back at Mary.

'Aye, we found her.'

SATURDAY,
23RD JANUARY

A lice looked up from her desk and out of the window at a snow-covered corner of the garden and a white stretch of hill beyond. This was the first proper snow in almost a year, and it didn't look set to stay. It never seemed much at home here in Shetland and rarely lingered for long. But its presence, sometimes, felt like a blessing. This had not been a cold winter, but it had not been an easy one either. It had arrived in early November. The morning of Maggie's funeral brought an angry fit of gales and horizontal rain, and looking back it seemed hardly to have let up since then. Week after week of wind and water, grey on grey. Now, near the end of January, this burst of clear, cold weather felt like a relief. Spring was still months away. Any brightness was welcome.

A car went past, heading out of the valley. From where she sat, Alice couldn't see the road, but she recognised the sound of the vehicle, the whine of a loose fan belt. Terry, she thought, then went back to her work. She was distracted, trying to inspire herself to write by going back over what was already written, rereading her own words. The book in front of her was not really a book. Not yet. It was a stack of paper two inches thick, each page covered in black type, some overlaid with vermicular scrawl in two colours: red ink for edits, blue for additional notes and ideas.

She flicked through the pile, stopping at random, cutting it like a deck. She read a few lines aloud to herself – a paragraph about the carnivorous sundews that grew in the damp ground near the burn, *Drosera rotundifolia*, with their sticky red tendrils and lollipop leaves – and then she flicked further. This time she stopped on a passage about the social impact of the Crofters' Holdings Act of 1886. Dry stuff, she thought. Important, but dry.

The book had started small. A few notes and observations about the valley made on scraps of paper. At one point Alice thought it might become a short history of Shetland. That would have been a simple job, really, which no one had yet bothered to do. Alice was no historian, but the details were already out there, they just needed to be thrown together over a few hundred pages. She could do that, no problem. But that wasn't what happened. In the three and a half years she'd been working on it, the book had become something else, something bigger in scale and yet narrower in focus. Those initial notes just kept growing, but her attention hardly shifted beyond the confines of the valley. It wasn't necessary to expand her view at all, she realised. This place was the story she wanted to tell.

The history, for the most part, had been easy. She had read everything she could find about the valley and the surrounding area, spoken to those who knew it best. She'd invited archaeologists out to walk with her along the edges of the burn, around the crofts and up over to Burganess. They had told her all they could tell her without digging the place up, and they had told her plenty. She trawled through the archives in Lerwick, noting down everything of relevance, filling files and folders with dates, names, events, causes and consequences. She began to see a picture of the place stretching backwards, rich and generous in its detail.

But the story of the valley couldn't be told just like that, she understood. The story of the valley was much more than the chronology of what human beings had done here. It was everything that happened in this place, everything that belonged here and lived here. So she'd begun to learn, too, about the *natural* history, reading books on the islands' birds and plants, then trying to find them for herself, describing and photographing them. And the more she learned, it turned out, the more there was to know. The book kept growing.

For a long time, she feared it would never be finished. There was too much to find out, she thought, too much to explore. She had taken on an impossible project. But now, finally, the end was approaching. The pile of papers no longer felt beyond her control. Most of the chapters were complete. The book had a shape; it was just a little blurred around the edges. Another six months, perhaps, and it would be done.

This was the first time Alice had attempted something like this, something *real*. It was also the first time she had written something for *herself*, without any other readers in mind. Crime novels: that's what she used to write. That's what she was known for. Those other books, five of them in total, she knew who'd be reading them. She could picture her readers as she wrote, and she had met them, too, at book signings and at festivals, back when she lived in York. Back when everything was as it used to be. They would tell her how much they loved her work, how much it meant to them. She couldn't understand that. Not really. But that's how it was. She was somewhat well known for a while, somewhat respected. She wrote stories of lone detectives: obsessive, flawed, angry and successful – at least in catching criminals. Gritty: that was the label they gave her, and that was fine. She enjoyed writing those stories, found it satisfying, mostly. She liked shaping the characters, moulding them, then pushing them around, moving them in their various directions until they reached the destination she had chosen, the fate she had decided.

She felt, not powerful, exactly, but something like that. She had control, and she liked it. But then she stopped liking it. When Jack, her husband, became ill, everything changed. She had just begun her last book, *Beggar Man*, with a deadline in front of her, and a mortgage and bills and a reputation. She kept working, kept getting up each day and going to her desk, a cup of black coffee in front of her. But it was different. She no longer cared what happened next in the story. She no longer cared what her characters had done or what they were going to do. She no longer cared how the pieces fit together. None of it was real. It was all make-believe. What was real was Jack, and Jack was dying.

She finished the book, of course. She had to. She'd already been paid for it in advance, and paid pretty well. But it was hard. It took longer than usual. She missed her publisher's deadline, then missed another. They were understanding, encouraging. They didn't push too hard. Take your time, they said, we can wait. But she didn't want to take her time. She wanted the book to be done and out of her way. What had once felt like her life now felt like an impediment to living. Each day was an uphill trudge. And then, when she reached the top of that hill, there was nothing to see. The path behind her had disappeared, and if there was a path ahead she couldn't find it at all. She groped her way forward, stumbling with every step. She finished it two months before Jack died.

The book was a success. The reviews weren't as positive as they once had been, but that didn't matter. People still bought it. And the reviews were right. In fact, they were kinder than Alice would have been had she been asked for an honest opinion. She wasn't embarrassed by what she'd written; she just didn't want to think about it again once it was done. She refused the interviews and the public appearances. She needed some time out, she said, and nobody argued. Alice took the money and ran. She ran as far, almost, as she could think of going.

She found this house online a few weeks after Jack's death, when she was searching for something that might make sense. She put in an offer, and that was that. She and Jack had come to Shetland on their honeymoon, at his insistence. He loved walking, loved the ocean, and neither of them had enough money back then to go any farther. Both of them had been entranced by the fortnight they had spent here, and they came back again three times in the years that followed. They talked, now and then, of coming here together, to live. This could be their place, they said, their home. But it never happened. There was always some reason not to go, some excuse to stay put. The distance, the inconvenience, the weather. So they talked about Shetland, thought about Shetland, but stayed where they were. And when Alice did finally move, she went alone. She boxed up Jack's things, put them in storage, and shipped her own belongings north.

Their house in York sold for almost three times as much as this one cost, so she didn't need to think about money again for a long time. It was a blessing not fully anticipated. It made everything easier. Sometimes the best decisions are made like this, she thought, in the weeks after her arrival. Just heart and gut and nothing more. This was a good decision. This was the right place to come.

The valley had fascinated her from the very beginning. She'd had a lot of time on her hands back then and spent much of it just walking and looking out of the windows at the place around her. She didn't write at first. Not for several months after coming north. The urge had left her, and for a while she hoped it would not return. It seemed, in those months, an entirely false thing – a tragic distraction from the business of being alive. The hunger she'd always felt to put words on the page, to make stories, was replaced by a different kind of hunger, a different kind of need. Alice wanted to know this place in which she'd landed. She wanted to feel part of it and to belong to it. She joined clubs and went to meetings in town, she got to know her neighbours and made herself visible. She read and looked and learned.

Eventually, though, the words did come. But her appetite for invention did not. This time, when she started to write, the story was not one that Alice could control, only observe and record. It was an extension, a natural development of her need to understand where she was.

The thing about an island, she'd thought, as this project first began to take shape, is that you feel you can know it. You feel your mind can encompass everything in it, everything there is to see and to learn and to comprehend. You feel you can contain it, the way that it contains you. And a small valley on a small island . . . well, that's what she was trying to do, to contain it in words and in thoughts, to describe the place and to encompass it, not just as it once was, or was believed to be, but as it is, here, now. The book was called, provisionally, *The Valley at the Centre of the World*. She liked that. It made her smile.

Right now, she was finishing up her chapter on mammals. It would be the shortest of the natural-history chapters. There was not much of a list to work with, after all. There were lots of rabbits, and some mountain hares, which she saw most often in winter, in their smart white coats. Hedgehogs were here; as were field mice, known as Shetland mice, and perhaps house mice too. Stoats were probably around, though she'd never actually seen one in the valley, so a question mark still hung over those. There was another question mark over brown rats, which didn't seem to live in this part of the island, though she hadn't made up her mind to exclude them just yet. Ferret-polecats were definitely here – beautiful, horrible creatures – and otters were regular visitors. There were three of them at the moment, a mother and two cubs, that she saw often from the beach, and a fourth, possibly the father of the cubs, she'd seen occasionally. Then, finally, there were the seals, both common and, sometimes, grey, though it was questionable whether these were in fact part of the valley, since they didn't actually breed on the beach, they just hung around in the bay. (The cetaceans – orcas and porpoises, mostly – had been excluded for that very reason.) The livestock were not part of this chapter. They were in the agricultural section of the book, which she'd finished, just about, at the end of last year.

Alice had gathered all the information she could find about these animals: details of their basic biology, diet, population size, rough date of introduction where available (since all, besides the seals, were introduced to Shetland by humans). She had also tried to document sightings of each species to allow her to describe more fully their habits and locations within the valley, which is why the stoats had proved problematic. Everything that seemed relevant would be included, and almost all of it had now been written. The chapter was nearly done.

Lifting her head again from her work, Alice rolled down the sleeves of her dark woollen jumper. She looked younger than her forty-five years but dressed older. She wore glasses when she was writing – wide-rimmed tortoiseshell glasses that were accidentally fashionable. Everything else was merely comfortable. The jumper, the jeans, the T-shirts, the fleece jacket: she liked not having to think about what to wear. It was one of those freedoms she had not even realised was missing until, coming here, she had found it.

Alice often became distracted around this time of the morning.

She would rein in her straying thoughts for as long as she could until she was certain they would not come back into line. Then she would walk. Half an hour was all that was needed usually, unless there was something specific she had to find, observe or figure out. It was enough time for her to get partway up Burganess, then come back, or else to stroll, without hurrying, along the beach. Today, she had nowhere in particular to go, so the beach, probably, was where she'd end up. Putting down her pen, Alice straightened the pages on the desk, picked up a notebook, just in case, then went to get her coat. As she opened the front door, a curtain of cold air folded around her body, and she thrust her thick-gloved hands into her pockets.

★   ★   ★

At the top of the valley, where the road began its stoop towards the sea, David parked his pickup and got out. Sam, the collie, stayed behind in the passenger seat, keeping warm. Along the fence here, on a row of wooden pallets, small blue silage bales were piled, two high and three deep. In the field beyond the gate, the sheep were waiting. The sound of his arrival had brought them running in anticipation.

Though the snow was only shallow, the animals looked hungry and called out to him, impatient. David went to the far end of the row and reached up to a bale on the top. He scraped the snow away, then pulled the bale back towards him and rolled it slowly to the gate. He always took from the far end because he knew, as the winter went on, that his gladness at having done so would increase. The task would get a little easier each day.

He opened the gate and pushed the silage into the park, the sheep already gathered round him, their breath billowing. He split the metal feeding ring and pushed the bale inside, then took a knife from his pocket, slicing first in a circle around the top, then in four vertical lines to the bottom. He lifted the top of the plastic off and pulled the four strips down to reveal the silage. Carefully he peeled the netting away and bundled it into his boilersuit pocket, then began to unravel the bale, loosening and spreading it around the ring.

The sheep pushed their heads through the metal frame and chomped at the damp grass. The smell of it, and the lanolin of the animals, thickened the air like beer half-brewed. David counted them – two dozen – then watched as they forced their heads into the food. They were Shetlands, all of them, small and sturdy. He took a glove off and placed his palm against the cheek of one of the ewes and scratched. She pressed against his hand but kept eating. She'd been a caddy lamb, that one, four years before, abandoned by her mother then bottle-fed by David, so she had none of the jittery edge of the others. She still liked to be scratched sometimes, but she liked her food even more.

David thought back to the other caddies he'd had, generations of sheep hand-reared, some of them mothers and grandmothers of those in front of him now. When the girls were young, they'd looked after them. Emma, in particular. She would get up early to do the first feed, holding the bottles to their little mouths, two at a time, her face glowing in delight as they sucked and slurped and gulped the milk. Then, after school, she would rush home to see them again, carrying them like teddy bears, squirming, around the garden. For those first few months, the lambs were perfect pets. They were cute, they liked company, they played. But it was perhaps their neediness that the children responded to most of all – their utter dependence upon people. No child can resist being needed.

David let himself out of the feeding ring and walked back towards the gate, stopping once to look again at the sheep tearing their way through the grass as though they hadn't eaten for a week. He felt tired, exhausted even, though he had no need to be, and as he sat down in the pickup again he allowed himself a long sigh. From the passenger seat, the dog sighed too, then shifted to rest its head in David's lap. Sam raised his eyes, waiting for something or nothing to happen.

With Maggie gone, David was now the oldest person in the valley. And with Emma now gone, too, he was the only one left who'd grown up here. He wasn't sure what that meant, exactly, but it seemed to mean something. It felt like a responsibility, a weight that couldn't be lifted.

He had never lived anywhere else. Not really. He'd gone away to work after school was done, labouring in Aberdeen, but he'd come home again after only a year. He didn't want the money enough to be away any longer. He came back to his parents' house – now Terry's house – then found a job at the oil terminal in the late seventies. Since then he'd never considered living anywhere else. This valley shaped his thoughts. Often it *was* his thoughts. The slope of it, the tender fold of the land. Somehow it was mirrored inside him. It was part of him, and he could no more leave this place than he could become someone else. That realisation had never once troubled him. Quite the opposite, in fact. It gave him a clarity of purpose, the lack of which he recognised in others. Life would be so much simpler, he thought, if people dreamed only of one place.

He sat in the driver's seat, looking out over *his* place: his present, past and future. From there, at the edge of the upper park, he could see nearly all of the valley. Only the dip, south of this field, where the two little burns melted together, was hidden. Alice's house, Bayview, was the closest, just up the road; then his own house, Kettlester, if you didn't count the Smiths' place up on the hill, which he did not. That was accessed from another track altogether, which came off the main road half a mile away, and neither looked nor felt like part of the valley. It had been built more than ten years ago now – a big, showy house with windows everywhere – but David had not yet fully accepted its presence.

Beyond Kettlester, the road curved southwest as it descended, until it reached the Red House, where Sandy now lived. There had been an old stone cottage there until the 1970s, when it was knocked down and replaced by the wooden one that still stood, which itself was not much more than a chalet. Willie, a cousin to Maggie's father, had lived there all his life and agreed only reluctantly to the rebuilding, which Maggie herself had insisted on. He seemed to take the plan as an affront to his ancestors – to *their* ancestors – who might or might not have constructed the house. But his stubbornness was nothing compared to hers, and so the plan was eventually accepted. His only condition, to which Maggie consented but for which no one ever received a proper explanation, was that the new house should be painted a startling shade of red.

Willie lived another twenty years in that house. When it was first rebuilt, he had seemed old before his time, as though worn out by his own company. But when he died he really *was* old – almost a hundred – and had seemed to enjoy those final years as much as any he ever experienced. David bought the house, then, in part because he had the money and saw it as an investment, and in part because of what had happened to Flugarth, his parents' house. Flugarth lay another few hundred yards down the road. That was where he had grown up and where he had lived until moving to Kettlester with Mary after they married.

His parents died just a few years apart and a few years before Willie. He'd sold their house then because he had no need for it. He'd sold it to Terry, whose brother worked with David at Sullom Voe and who seemed, when he first came to view it, to love the house. The assumption had been that he would move in with his family, but his family never moved in. They came for weekends and summer holidays during the first couple of years, but that was about it. And then Terry began to come alone. Not for holidays, exactly, but to give his family a break. He came to drink or to dry out. Sometimes he'd arrive by himself on a Friday evening and stay until the Monday morning, hardly leaving the front door. Other times, his wife would drive him to the house and let him out at the gate, abandoning him until he was ready to come back home.

More recently, Terry had been staying for longer and longer periods, and for the past six months or so he had lived here full time. David wasn't entirely sure of the story – he'd heard several versions – but it seemed that Terry's wife, Louise, had finally given up and got rid of him. His employers, the council, had presumably done the same. Or at least they'd told him not to come back until he'd got himself sorted. Terry wasn't drunk all the time. There were days when he was fully present – sensible, friendly and good company. But he was unpredictable. He couldn't be relied on. And though David felt sorry for him, he'd always found it hard to see his parents' home used like that. It was a disappointment that didn't go away.

Beyond Flugarth was the house at the end of the road. Officially, it was Nedder Gardie, though no one had ever used its full name in his hearing, except the postman. There was no Upper Gardie from which it had to be distinguished, so the house, like the croft, was known as Gardie. When he was young, his father sometimes referred to it as the Peerie Haa. It was, presumably, a joke, though at whose expense David never knew. Most often, it was just called Maggie's. But Maggie, now, was gone.

A straight line from that house to where he sat took in the greenest part of the valley, though at this time of the year it didn't look very green, even without the snow. The fields on this side of the burn were used either for grazing or for silage, with one narrow strip below Kettlester where David grew potatoes, onions, neeps and carrots. The other vegetable plot was up beside the house. When he was young, there was more growing and less grazing in the valley. There were hay parks and sometimes oats; and Maggie and his father often had a cow and calf down in one of the lower parks, sharing both the work and the benefits between them. He missed seeing those things – that vision, deceptive though it was, of abundance – but he understood it had changed for a reason. Money had become easier to earn than food was to grow; it was as simple as that. And now, though he had retired and so had time, in theory, to do things differently, David found he had neither the energy nor the will, at least not on his own. Each of the fields in front of him belonged either to his croft or to Gardie. And for years now he had worked all of them alone.

David thought again about Maggie. That night when they'd found her, crumpled against a rock on Burganess, he'd been aware of a kind of urgency inside him, a recognition, tinged with panic, of something approaching an end. He had not really understood that feeling at first, had thought it merely grief and nostalgia – and perhaps it was both – but it was bigger than that. The thing he felt ending was not just one person, or even one generation; it was much older and had, in truth, been ending for a long time. It was a thread of memory that stretched back for as long as people had lived in this place. It was a chain of stories clinging to stories, of love clinging to love. It was an inheritance he did not know how to pass on. That recognition brought with it a fearful kind of responsibility, as though he had been handed something he knew he could not help but break.

For several weeks after Maggie's death, David had felt himself to be at an edge, teetering, and his sadness about what was to come was almost as great as his sadness at what had already gone – at the loss of the woman he had known all his life. Three months on, it still rose inside him whenever he stopped to think of her.

He was not entirely surprised when the letter came, a fortnight ago, from the solicitor in Lerwick. Maggie had never said explicitly that the house and croft would be left to him, but he understood why she'd done it. In the end it came almost as a relief – an echo and a partial answer to his own worries. She had entrusted the land to David in death, as she had done in life. But not, he understood, for his own benefit. She had nominated him as a kind of executor, to do what was right, to make a decision about the future.

What was right was for someone to live in the house and to work the croft, as she would have wanted it worked; and three months ago, before Emma left, his decision would have been easy. David would have asked his daughter and Sandy if they would like to move from the Red House to Gardie, and he would have done so joyfully, certain of Maggie's approval. That was, undoubtedly, what she'd had in mind. But with Emma gone, too, everything was more complicated. The sense of continuation he longed for was much harder to see. His connection to both past and future had been weakened at once.

For two weeks, on and off, he and Mary had discussed the options, had woken in the night to talk them through again, and they had dismissed or discounted all but one.

As he turned the key in the ignition, David realised he missed his wife. It had been only a few hours since they'd had breakfast together, but he missed her all the same, and he wanted, then, to be with her. In an hour or so he would be home for lunch, and there was nothing to keep him from being home all afternoon. But he had one more task to complete before then. He had a question that needed to be asked.

Stamping his boots at the doorstep and kicking hard against the wall, David cleared the snow from his feet before he opened the door and went inside. 'Hello! Sandy! Is du aboot?'

There was a shuffling from the kitchen, and Sandy emerged in a thick blue woollen jumper, tattered at the cuffs. 'Come in,' he said. 'I'm just made coffee. Du must be psychic.'

David grinned. 'Well, I wouldna say no,' he said. 'A coffee micht git some life back inta me.'

Sandy nodded and turned back to the kitchen. 'Come and sit doon,' he said.

The two men sat across the table from one another, but both were looking out of the window, over the valley, at the whitened hill and the sea. Their hands clasped around the hot mugs in front of them.

'Looks good fae in here,' Sandy said.

'Aye. Looks pretty good fae oot dere, too,' David replied. 'Juist a peerie bit caalder.' He said nothing for a moment and then turned to Sandy. 'I hae some news fir dee,' he said, then paused a second longer, trying to find the right words. 'It seems Maggie may juist hae decided dy future.'

'What does du mean?' Sandy spoke slowly.

'Well, shu left da hoose an da croft ta me in her will. An since Ah'm quite happy eenoo in me ain bed, someen else'll hae ta live doon dere.'

Sandy waited for more.

'Shu was thinkin at dee an Emma micht want ta move in, I

suppose, if du wanted to wirk da croft, an if du wanted ta hae a family. But, seein as du's chased me dochter awa, I reckon I hae ta offer it ta dee, if du wants it.'

Sandy looked away.

'Ah'd help dee wi da sheep an da idder wark,' said David. 'We can help each idder. Ah'd be happy wi dat.'

'Has du offered it to Emma?' Sandy asked.

'Aye, I telt her da situation, but shu's no thinkin ta come back eenoo.'

'And Kate?'

David shook his head. 'Dey're no wantin to move oota da toon. An I dunna lik ta think o it juist sittin empty. So, if du wants it . . .'

Sandy breathed in deeply, but said nothing.

'Dere's only wan catch, though,' added David.

'Aye?' Sandy raised his eyebrows.

'Well, Maggie was a bit o a hoarder, du sees. And since she didna plan ta be dyin quite sae soon, shu's left aa o it fir wis ta clear up. I could dae wi a haand.' He smiled, then tightened his lips. 'Actually, I could dae wi a lot o haands. It'll tak wis a while.'

'Is her family no wantin some of it?'

'I spak ta Ina, her sister, an shu's asked fir een or twa things. But whit use wid maist o yon shite be ta her in New Zealand? I think shu was juist relieved at Maggie didna leave da hoose fir *her* ta sort oot.'

'Okay, well I'll hae a think aboot it,' said Sandy. 'It's a bit o a surprise. I wasna thinkin to take on a croft. Certainly no by myself.' He paused. 'But I can help dee clear the hoose anyway. When was du plannin to start?'

'Mebbie da moarn, or da day eftir.' David took the last swig of his coffee. 'If du sees da pickup doon dere, juist come alang if du's able, an we'll see whit's needin don. Hit's gonna be a hell o a job, I think. Ah'm ordered a skip, and we'll need ta hae a bonfire or twa as well, I doot.'

Sandy nodded his head but was looking away again, distracted.

'Well, Ah'll laeve dee wi dat thocht,' David said, standing up and setting his mug in the sink. He said goodbye and walked out of the house, leaving Sandy behind at the kitchen table.

SUNDAY,
24TH JANUARY

As she passed the hall mirror, on her way to the kitchen, Mary caught sight of herself and paused. She looked tired, and a shadow lay over the side of her face like a birthmark. She ran a hand through her short grey hair, neatened it, then rubbed her eyes. She turned away from the mirror.

Today was a difficult day. Weekends, always, were the worst. Emma's leaving had been hard for her — harder, it seemed, than the last time her daughter had moved away, as a teenager, to university. Then, the loneliness had been offset by busyness, by pride and by hope. Now, it was offset only by routine. When there was nothing else that needed her focus, Emma's absence would gnaw at her, nagging for attention like a puppy. She had got used to her daughter as a neighbour, got used to her dropping in without warning, and to her presence in the valley, her proximity. She would get used to this distance, too, but not quickly.

This morning she had called Emma, eager to hear her voice, but knowing, also, that it would not be an easy conversation. David had texted her after breakfast to say he'd offered the croft to Sandy. 'Juist ta let her ken,' that's what he'd said, as though it were a minor piece of news. Mary waited until he went out to the shed, then she picked up the phone. Her job was to listen to the things she already knew that Emma would say. She already knew because she understood why her daughter would feel the way she was feeling, why she would flinch at the thought of Sandy moving to Gardie, of him becoming, without her, *permanent*.

David didn't understand these feelings. Or at least he would not admit to understanding them. What he had done was the practical solution in the current circumstances. It was right for him, for the croft, for the valley, and hopefully for Sandy too. And that rightness would last longer than any hurt Emma might feel just now. After all, they had asked her first if she wanted it, and she had not. Mary knew that's what her husband was thinking, and she knew that in essence he was correct. She didn't disagree. She was just less able to weigh that rightness over their daughter's immediate anxieties.

A photograph framed on the hall table showed Emma and Kate aged eight and ten, both wrapped in winter coats, scarves flailing in the wind. The picture used to hang on the living-room wall, until the colours faded in the sunlight, the girls' red jackets paling into ochre. Mary had brought it through to the windowless corridor, fearing the image might disappear altogether. Looking at it now, the day came back to her, as it often did – a day not unlike other days except that it was caught and held by the camera. The two girls were laughing, fooling around down at the beach, on a morning when the waves pawed noisily at the stones.

Back then, the sisters had been as cheerful, as content, as quick to smile as each other. Emma used to follow Kate around, she used to idolise her, and wanted, always, to wear what Kate was wearing, to do what Kate was doing. They were close. They shared friends, even after Kate went to junior high school, leaving Emma behind at the primary school closer to home. Mary never would have guessed, back then, that the two would turn out so differently.

One of the hardest things about being a parent, she thought, was to watch discontent grow in your children. When they were young, their needs and desires could always be met by a mother or a father. There was food when they were hungry; there was a bed when they were tired; there were distractions from boredom. And then, without warning, would come a question for which neither mother nor father could provide an answer. 'Why does Sarah not like me any more?' Mary could still remember when Kate asked her that, aged five or six, after school one day, eyes polished with tears over a friendship temporarily lost. And she could still remember being struck, in those few pained words, by the realisation that her daughters would not always be cheerful and content, that the world would disappoint them, that friends, family, would let them down.

As they both went on to junior high school, the parts of their lives that were beyond Mary's control continued to grow. Then, it was not just other people who caused them consternation, it was their own bodies. They seemed sometimes confused by themselves, by the changes they were going through, by the new pressures under which they found themselves. Mary did her best to reassure, to be open to questions and to offer what advice she could. But her advice wasn't always welcome.

That was the point at which her daughters went in different directions. Whereas Kate, as school went on, seemed to settle into herself, Emma never quite did. Kate, it turned out, took after her father. Her desires were well defined, and never beyond her ability to achieve them. But Emma was different. She seemed always uncertain of exactly what she wanted, uncertain of how to get it, uncertain of who or where she wanted to be. That was hardly unusual these days, but it meant that Emma and David increasingly struggled to understand each other. They were always close, always sought each other's company, but they argued often.

Kate left school, got a job, met a man, got married, had children – one, then another. Mary worried about her, in that unavoidable way. She found reasons to worry even when there were none, and mostly there *was* no reason. Kate's husband was good to her, they seemed happy together, the children were healthy, bright. But Emma . . . always Emma. She went to university, studied history and politics, and they thought perhaps she'd be a teacher in the end. But that wasn't what she wanted. She graduated without a plan or a fixed intention. Mary could see that lack of direction weighing on her daughter, but she could do nothing to lift that weight, except to insist to David that he never ask Emma what she was going to do next. And he never did. He asked his wife instead. He sought reassurance from Mary, and Mary tried, when she could, to offer it.

They had both been delighted when Emma came home three years ago. Not just to have their daughter so close but to see her happy, to imagine her settled. Everything she had done up to that point had felt temporary, as if she were always in the process of deciding her next step. But moving home, that was different. Home was a destination. It was where you ended up. That's what they thought.

When she'd spoken to Emma on the phone earlier, Mary had sat in the hall looking up at that photograph of her young daughters. She saw the face of a girl and heard the voice of a woman. What a distance lay between those two Emmas – the face, still laughing, the voice, holding back tears. Mary was mother to them both.

There was a time when she imagined this feeling might one day recede. That her maternal fretting might no longer fill her thoughts or keep her awake at night. But it didn't work like that. As her children became adults, she simply found herself less able to help them, and therefore, if anything, more inclined to worry.

Mary looked at her watch. It was close to midday. She was meeting a friend in town in the afternoon, but she still had some time to spare. She reached into a drawer in the hall cabinet and took out two seed catalogues, then made herself a cup of tea and sat down at the kitchen table. The catalogues had both arrived in the past week, and Mary pulled the cellophane away and opened the first of them. She skimmed past the vegetables – that was David's department – and began, slowly, to look through the flowers, pausing on every page to read the names and look at the photographs. Some of her favourites were close to the front: the aquilegias, strange and delicate, infinite in their variety; the frothy astilbes, white, pink and scarlet; the bleeding hearts, perhaps her favourite flower of all, so perfect and implausible.

In truth, Mary never ordered more than a few packets each year from the catalogues. She took cuttings and seedlings from friends, she bought plants at the garden centre, she propagated and divided what she already had. But buying was not the point. *Looking* was the point. To read the catalogues was to dream of summer. It was to be reminded that the winter would pass and that warmth would return. It was a ritual she needed more and more.

Flicking to the bulbs, Mary remembered with pleasure that before long the first snowdrops would emerge, unfolding themselves beneath bushes, alongside paving stones and at the edges of the lawn. Later, there would be purple and yellow crocuses too, then daffodils, ablaze about the garden. She had tried other bulbs over the years, though not always with success. Grape hyacinths grew in one of the borders, and *Chionodoxas* too, like tiny blue stars. Twice she had planted snakeshead fritillaries, longing for their purple checkerboard heads to fill the garden, but both times they had disappointed. On the most recent occasion, she'd buried fifty bulbs, but only four of the plants raised themselves above ground the following spring. Last year, just one plant remained.

Gardening in Shetland was an exercise in overcoming disappointment. Each year, Mary tried something new: at least one plant or one packet of seeds she had never grown before. She did her best to be sensible about these, to be modest in her ambitions. She looked for plants that didn't need too much warmth or that were meant to thrive in 'coastal climates'. But sometimes even modest ambitions were thwarted. Even when she took plants from friends' gardens elsewhere on the island, life in this valley sometimes seemed to be too much for them. Facing southwest, as it did, there was little protection from the prevailing winds, little shelter from the gales and the salt that galloped up from the Atlantic, scouring everything in its path.

The worst were not the winter storms, though. Then, most of the plants were tucked up safe beneath the surface. The worst were the storms that hit in May or June, when everything was brimming into life. How many times had she opened the curtains on a spring morning to find her garden withered, burnt and shredded by the salt-filled air? And what else could she do but go out and tidy up the damage, do her best to make it good again, and hope that the summer would be kinder?

Mary needed the garden. Unpredictable and difficult though it was, it had become increasingly important to her over the past ten years or so. David had always seemed content to live within an endlessly turning circle, season following season, year following year. His hope was not for change but for continuation. Mary's hope was different. She longed for growth and progress, a flourishing. That was how she felt able to live in this place, with all its cold and darkness. That hope made it possible. When the girls were young, it was easier – all energy and ambition could be focused on them, on *their* growth. In those years, the garden was hardly more than a place for her daughters to play. But now she needed more from it. She needed it to give something back, which occasionally it did.

Despite all of the disappointments – the seeds that came to nothing, the leaves that recoiled from the harshness of the wind, the flowers that opened then closed again, as though embarrassed by their pathetic display – Mary kept going. She dug and pruned and planted and weeded and waited; and for that work she was, to some degree, rewarded. Each year, in winter, the garden gave her something to hope for, something to look forward to. And each summer, no matter how terrible the weather, it would give her sporadic bursts of pleasure, of joy, even. Coming home on a gloomy afternoon, a bag of shopping in each hand, she would be stopped by the sight of the little red rhododendron, which seemed sometimes almost to glow, or by the thicket of cobalt lupins beneath the kitchen window. Those moments, in which the stubborn beauty of the garden took her by surprise, were worth every disappointment.

Mary closed the catalogue and stood up, draining the last of the tea from her mug. Outside, the sky hung grey above the valley. The temperature was increasing – it was six degrees, according to the thermometer beside the window – and yesterday's snow had almost gone. The forecast was for the wind to swing south and rise to a storm this evening. Everything could change so quickly here, always. She'd often wondered if that was why David looked for stability in the turning of a year, since it couldn't be found day to day, or even moment to moment. Sometimes her husband seemed to her about the most stable thing she had known in her life. He never changed. Or hardly at all. Like the larch tree she'd planted twenty years ago in the corner of the garden, he grew so slowly it was hard to believe he was ever any different from one day to the next. Sometimes Mary felt frustrated and irritated by his inflexibility; other times gratitude welled up inside her until she had to cry just to let it out. She would lean against his shoulder and put her arms around his neck. He would ask, then, 'Whit's wrang?' and she would say 'Nothing', and he would pull her close and tell her he was glad.

★ ★ ★

Since David's visit the previous day, the question had hung in the air like a promise. Sandy wasn't sure, though, if it was a promise of good or ill. The offer of the croft had been so unexpected, so entirely tangential to his thinking, that it had taken some time to establish itself as a question at all.

Where do I want to be? That was what it came down to.

For more than two months, he had stayed on in the Red House, living almost as though Emma were coming back. He'd done nothing to erase her from their home. He hadn't moved furniture around or bought new pictures to hang on the walls. He'd not gone through each room, removing the traces of her that still lingered – the books and clothes she'd forgotten. He'd simply carried on as before, only without her.

It wasn't that he expected Emma to return. He had not left a space for her deliberately, in the hope she might appear on the doorstep one morning, begging to be let back in. He knew that she would not. And though there had been days when he'd longed for her, when he'd checked her Facebook page obsessively, hour after hour, in search of anything – a new friend, a photograph –

that might contort his longing, that might summon the sharp, bitter blow of jealousy, there had been many more days when he had not, when he had simply wished her well.

In truth, he had not felt the need to fill her absence because the space she once occupied in his life had already closed. It had closed before she left – squeezed, slowly, over months, perhaps years, as Sandy prepared himself for a loss he couldn't help but anticipate. It was a loss he did not want, that he dreaded, but which was made inevitable by his very expectation of it.

'Du's shuttin me oot,' Emma would say, as he stepped back in silence from yet another convoluted discussion. And though he denied it, to her and to himself, that was almost exactly what he was doing: shutting out not her but his need for her. He was closing himself down, retreating to a place he knew better than any other. Abandonment, Sandy understood, was more comfortable than the fear of it. Emma had chosen to leave because he had given her no choice.

Since the last time he saw her, a few days after Maggie's funeral, when she'd piled the final boxes into her little Toyota, they'd had only irregular contact. A few businesslike emails, sorting out the practical side of things, and a few phone calls, one of them tearful, sorting out the rest. She was in Edinburgh now, living not far from where they had first shared a home. He was here.

By rights it should have been Sandy who left. This was Emma's place, not his. At least that's how it once had felt. But Sandy didn't want to go. He was happy here. Or as near to happy as he needed to be. He didn't want to lose what Emma had given him – this place, these people – he just couldn't help but lose her.

He understood, without really needing to consider it, that the current situation was temporary. He was living next door to his ex-girlfriend's parents, renting a house from his ex-girlfriend's parents. He was a part of their lives, and they a part of his, to a degree that, sooner or later, might not be okay – for him, for Emma, for them. A couple of his friends had already asked, casually, when he'd be moving. His father, too. But he'd brushed their questions off. It hadn't felt urgent, and for now there was nowhere else he'd rather be. He could wait until a decision was more pressing.

What he had not anticipated before David's intervention was the possibility that he might not have to leave at all, that he might, in fact, remain here in the valley, alone. And what he had certainly never considered, not once, was digging himself in even deeper by taking on the croft and the house at the end of the road. Not without Emma, at least.

Now, though, he had been forced to consider it.

Thinking back to yesterday's conversation at the kitchen table, Sandy had the feeling that David had not just imposed a decision upon him but had already made the decision on his behalf. From the moment it was raised it had felt like a plan to which his consent was expected. Maggie had decided Sandy's fate, David said. But it was not her who had done so, it was him. Walking down the road now towards Gardie, where lights were blazing in almost every window, Sandy felt a kind of vacuum had opened in the space between David's will and his own – a vacuum that had to be filled. What he felt, perhaps, was an obligation, though he wasn't sure why or when such a feeling had emerged. Nor could he tell, yet, if it was a burden or a gift. It was, so far, only a complication.

The afternoon was darkening and straining towards a storm, like an angry dog on a lead. The sharp cold of yesterday had twisted into something wilder. Already the breeze was much more than a breeze. It had come on almost unnoticed, a gust that failed to subside, but now it whipped up the valley, snapping at his cheeks and in the corners of his eyes. Salt hammered his lips. Everything leaned inland.

Sandy had not always felt at home in this valley. It had taken him some time to settle, to feel part of the place. He had resisted that feeling at first, unused to it as he was, but he couldn't do so for long. Now, he moved through it as one might move through the rooms of a familiar house, attuned to its changes, day to day, moment to moment. The light and the weather were always in motion, and these he registered first. The snow that yesterday had covered everything was now almost gone, the sodden ground, the heather and the rock disclosed. The sky was a bruised grey, rushing north.

David's pickup was parked beside the gate at Gardie, with an old chest of drawers lying face-up in the back. Sandy went in the front door of the house and shouted.

'Hi aye, it's just me.'

'Ah'm up da stairs,' came the reply. 'Come du!'

Sandy found him in the spare bedroom, among a dozen or so cardboard boxes piled up and spread out across the floor, most of them open at the top, and each filled with paper and note-books.

'Shu kept aathing,' David said. 'Letters, postcards, diaries, aathing. And I dunna ken whit's worth keepin and whit's no.'

Sandy looked around the room and absorbed the dismay that David must already be feeling. 'Mebbie we should just leave it for noo and start wi the simple things. Just keep it packed up and we can come back tae it later. If we canna decide, we can just put it aa up in the laft.'

'Aye, du's right,' said David. 'Ah'm liable to git bogged doon afore Ah'm even started at dis rate.' He stepped out from amid the pile of boxes and raised his hands in dismissal. 'Okay,' he said, 'let's move on. Ah'm ordered a skip for Tuesday, so we can start heavin bruck doon da stairs for dat. But first Ah'll gie dee da tour.'

The two men crossed the corridor into the larger bedroom. Everything was still as it had been three months before. The bed sheets — white with a string of cornflowers embroidered at the foot end — were neatly folded back. A small selection of creams, powders and bottles sat on the dressing table. In a wastepaper basket beside the door was a pile of tissues, scrunched up and discarded. Neither of them spoke for a moment; they just stood in the doorway, taking it in.

'Fuck's sake,' said David, almost whispering. 'I kinda wish shu'd left da place ta someen else. Hit feels lik we hae ta dismantle her whole life.'

Sandy said nothing but nodded slowly. He'd never been upstairs before in Maggie's house, and he felt, still, as though he were intruding.

'Mebbie it was a bad idea askin dee doon,' said David, still looking around the bedroom.

'Why's that?'

'Well, it's bad enough fir me, an I juist hae ta clear it oot. Du haes ta *live* in it.'

Sandy glared at him. 'I dunna *have* to live in it. I can live wherever I *want* to live.' He backed out of the bedroom, went along the corridor and down the stairs. He wasn't angry, but he didn't want the conversation to continue. He felt cornered.

In the living room, few of the pictures on the walls looked to be worth saving. Besides the family photographs, there were a couple of ugly paintings of boats, a framed postcard from Corsica and two small prints showing fox hunters on horseback, with hounds out in front. Sandy shook his head. He'd never noticed them before, and they seemed entirely out of place on this island without foxes. He wondered where they'd come from.

At what point in Maggie's life had they been bought or gifted? And by whom?

On the opposite wall was a wooden rack, a grid of tiny compartments, each one housing a faded porcelain figure – animals mostly. There were monkeys, cows, dogs, elephants, sheep, fish, a swan, a rabbit and many more. And no matter the true size of the creature, all had been reduced to a few centimetres in height. Sandy looked at each of the figurines in turn. Some were lifelike in their depiction – a cow with its head down, as though eating; a salmon mid-leap – while others were strange and ridiculous. On one shelf was a camel wearing a fez. Beside it, a cat on its hind legs, with a bow tie around its neck. Just as with the hunting pictures, it was hard to square these objects with the old woman Sandy had known for the last few years of her life. He couldn't imagine her standing admiring these figures, let alone going out and buying them.

'I made yon,' said David, from the other side of the room.

Sandy hadn't heard him come down the stairs, and he missed a breath in surprise. He only noticed when he turned around that David was standing in his socks, still following Maggie's rules.

'Made what?'

'Da display case. When I wis at da school. Shu used ta hae dem oot on a shelf, aa cramped lik. So I made dat. I coonted da figures ee day when shu wis in da kitchen, an I built it for her. Shu was delighted.'

'I canna imagine her collecting these. They dunna seem like her, somehow.'

'Shu didna collect dem. Her sister did.'

'Ina?'

'Aye. But when shu giud ta New Zealand, Maggie said shu'd look efter dem. An shu did. For mare as sixty years.'

'An Ina never wanted them back?'

'No, why wid she? Dey're shite. Dey meant mair ta Maggie wi Ina gone as dey ever did ta Ina.' He laughed. 'Fok are certainly peculiar.'

'So, where are we goin to start?' Sandy asked. 'What do you want to keep?'

'Well, most of dis stuff is no fir keepin. Da hoose is needin stripped back and repainted. It's needin a fair bit o wark ta mak it right. The mair we git oot, da easier dat'll be.'

'Aye. Well, let's start in here, then.' Sandy looked around. 'Do you ken aboot these pictures?' he asked, pointing at the two hunting scenes above the television. 'Whit's their story?'

'Well, I asked Maggie aboot dem, years ago. I hidna really thoght aboot dem, ta be honest, until dere was aa yon talk aboot fox-hunting on da news, when dey banned it. So I asked her why shu hid dem dan.'

'And?'

'And shu said shu liked da dugs.' David laughed out loud. Sandy laughed too.

'Right,' David said. 'We can put aa dat's needin dumped in a pile, and dis picters are goin at da hert o it.' He took them from the wall and set them down in the corner of the room, close to the fireplace. 'Next!'

'You can dump the ither pictures, too,' said Sandy. 'Mebbie no the photos, but the rest.'

'I quite lik da boats.'

'They're horrible. Dump them!'

'Okay, if du says so.'

For several hours, the two men wandered about the house, making piles, filling black bags, inspecting and deciding. Sometimes they conferred, asking the other's opinion, but mostly no questions were needed. The house was filled with the belongings of an old woman who was not their relative. What sentimentality they felt had been largely cast aside when they took the first pictures from the wall. Sandy wondered sometimes about his right to make decisions on the contents of this house, but David had brought him here and let him get on with it, and so he did.

In the kitchen he looked through drawers and cupboards, pulling out tins and dry food, leaving behind cutlery, plates, pots and pans. An ugly set of brown bowls was removed; another set, plain white, he left in place. Sandy paused for a second before opening the fridge, fearing what he might find inside. But when he did it was empty. He noticed only then that it was silent. David, hearing the door, looked over.

'We emptied it,' he said. 'Da night shu died.'

Few people would have considered that, thought Sandy. But it didn't surprise him that David and Mary had. He imagined them then, walking through the house, switching off plugs, checking each room, emptying the contents of the fridge and freezer into bags, with Maggie's death surrounding them like a fog.

'Mebbie we've done aa we can do da night,' David said eventually. 'Ah'll come back on Tuesday eftirnoon and git some of dis bruck inta da skip. Will du be at wark?'

'Aye, I'm drivin the taxi all week. I'll be back aboot six, though, I think. So I could join you in the evenin ageen.'

'Is du no stayin in toon fir Up Helly Aa? Hit's Tuesday night, is it no?'

Sandy raised his eyebrows. 'No. Vikings arna really my thing.' In truth, Sandy could hardly think of anything worse than watching nine hundred drunk men in fancy dress march about the town, roaring and singing, waving their torches around. He had never felt the slightest attachment to those parts of Shetland culture that were supposed to make his heart balloon with pride. Particularly that one. And the fact that he had never once been asked to take part only seemed to confirm that Up Helly Aa was a festival for others, not for him. 'Macho, chauvinist bollocks,' he used to call it, when Emma was around. 'I think I'll skip it,' he said now.

David laughed. 'Aye, I dunna blame dee. Hit's years since Ah'm been oot ta see the procession. No since da lasses was teenagers, I think. But, onywye, dunna buther wi Tuesday. We're don a lot da night. Ah'll let dee ken whan I need dee ageen, once dere's bigger things ta lift an so on.'

'Okay, well dunna be fairt to ask for help.'

'Whin am I ivver been fairt o dat?'

Outside, the darkness was as thick as peaty water. Just three scraps of light – from Terry's house, from David's and from Alice's – broke through. The wind was shrieking now into the valley, gathering what it could and dragging it away from the sea. Rain too was squalling sideways, in sputters and bursts, threatening to pour.

'Ah'll gi dee a run,' said David.

Sandy opened the passenger door. 'I'm glad you offered,' he said.

'Is du heard aboot da shop?' David asked, as he set off up the road.

'Which shop? What aboot it?'

'Da wan in Treswick. Billy's shop. He's thinkin o closin up, he telt me.'

'How come?'

'No enough fok buyin no enough food, he said. Simple as dat. Dey come in fir milk an a loaf wance a week, den get da rest in toon.'

'Aye, guilty as charged,' said Sandy.

'Wis too. Hit'll be a shame if he goes, though. Been a shop dere as lang as I can mind.'

'Aye, it's a shame.'

David slowed at the driveway to the Red House, and Sandy got out.

'Okay, I'll see you soon,' he said, then looked down without waiting for a response. He had to give a solid push on the pickup door to get it closed, and then hunched himself against the wind as he walked away. Up here it seemed even stronger, the air walloping his body, threatening to knock him sideways. Once inside, he could hear it groaning and screeching around the building, trying to find a way through the windows and walls.

Sandy picked up his phone from the kitchen table. There was only one message, from Terry, which he ignored. He poured himself a whisky and went through to the living room, then lit a fire and sat in the armchair by the window. He closed his eyes and listened to the storm, as the flames gasped and raged in the grate.

THURSDAY,
11TH FEBRUARY

Alice was on her hands and knees, turning over stones, examining what lay beneath. On the bank, close to the burn, she leaned forward and lifted a flat rock, balancing it on one pointed corner, then peered below. An earthworm concertinaed itself out of sight in the mud; a tiny black beetle scurried into the grass; a cluster of white blobs, eggs of some kind, were tucked into a cranny in the stone. Nothing else looked alive. She laid it down, gently, exactly where she'd found it.

It had been raining for the past twenty minutes or so. It wasn't heavy, but her clothes were now thoroughly wet, and her hands were cold. She felt disheartened. Since setting aside the mammals a fortnight ago – she had a few more observations to gather, but otherwise the chapter was complete – she had started to think about insects and other small creatures, and had begun almost immediately to feel overwhelmed.

She'd known all along that things would get tricky at this stage. The task she'd set herself with this book was a big one: ambitious but achievable, she thought, at least within certain parameters. But it was here, in the realm of the invertebrates, of the beetles, the flies, the worms, spiders, bees and wasps, moths, molluscs, mites, midges, caddisflies, hoverflies and lacewings, that those parameters reared up and threatened to capsize her entire project. For these creatures, these tiny, insignificant creatures, were enormous in number, and Alice didn't yet know what to do about them.

Recently, on her daily walks, she'd been exploring parts of the valley that hadn't previously held her attention: the shadowed nooks, the burn banks, the ground beneath the heather stalks, the dirt and the damp corners. That experience had proved enjoyable in its own way. She liked to see this place from new angles, to look at it from ground level or even deeper. She'd bought a little magnifying glass, a loupe, that she now wore on a string around her neck at all times. She carried tiny plastic boxes to bring specimens home for identification, though she hadn't actually brought anything back yet, as she wasn't sure where to start.

February was not the season for insects. There wasn't much in the air at least, though down on the ground there was still plenty to see. More, in fact, than she knew what to do with. From the window of her front room, this project had always looked achievable. The place, she thought, could be contained satisfactorily in words. There were just a handful of houses, plus the ruins of two more on the southern slope of the valley – abandoned in the nineteenth century. The history could be learned from books and from observation, at least as far as was necessary for her purposes. Most of the *natural* history also seemed within grasp: the mammals, the birds, even the plants. But here in the mud Alice felt the weight of her own ignorance, and the enormity of all she could not put a name to. As she lifted another stone and saw the inhabitants of its shelter shrink away into the darkness, she knew that she could never learn even a fraction of what was here. The closer she looked, the more the valley would expand. Whatever she held a magnifying glass to would grow to fill the lens, whatever was minute would become momentous. Here, she was struck by the vertiginous thought that the world beneath her was in fact infinite, that the more she looked at it, the more there would be to see, and that everything she saw, every atom of it, was its own centre.

Alice was not easily deterred by detail. Research was the part of writing she had always most enjoyed, and getting to know this place as well and as closely as possible had been, in large part, the purpose of this book. Back when she was writing fiction, she would spend months in preparation for each novel, reading up on subjects necessary to bring the books to life. She studied forensics, analysed police procedures, learned about the science of decay – the little details that made the big picture complete. She wanted to write books a detective could read without becoming irritated and frustrated by inaccuracies. Secretly, she wanted to write books a criminal might read and wonder, *Why didn't I think of that?*

Reviewers often assumed that, because she wrote crime fiction, plot was her primary focus. But that had never been the case. For Alice, the detail always came first. She gathered information, gathered facts and photographs. She wrote everything down, then let it brew and meld together. The narrative emerged later. It germinated from the material she collected. It grew almost organically out of that material. She built a world, piece by piece, until, within that world, a story became possible, or even inevitable. It doesn't make sense to ask, *Where am I going?,* she once told an interviewer, until you've first asked, *Where am I now?*

And that was precisely what she had asked herself when she began writing this book. What kind of place is this? Of what does it consist? Those were the questions that had got her writing again, after Jack's death, and those were the questions that had led her, after four years, to be crouching in the mud, with rain soaking her back and cold stiffening her fingers.

She sat down on a rock and tried not to think for a moment. She closed her eyes. It was easy, there, to blank her mind. The fussing of the burn on its way to the sea, the rush and giggle of the water, was all that she could hear. It wasn't loud – the land wasn't steep, and the burn was narrow – but it was enough to cover the usual noises of the valley. She couldn't hear the waves on the beach or the rain hitting the earth. She couldn't hear the sheep in the beach park. Nor could she hear David start his pickup outside Gardie and begin the short drive up the road. Alice only heard him a minute or so later, as the vehicle came parallel with where she sat, then pulled into a passing place and stopped. She opened her eyes as David got out of the pickup and slammed the door.

He waved. She waved back. He shouted something, but she couldn't make it out, so shrugged her shoulders and lifted her palms skyward. Anybody else, thought Alice, would have driven on and phoned her later if they needed to speak. But David wasn't like anybody else. She watched as he pressed his hand on a fence post and stepped over the wire, then began striding down the field in his boilersuit, towards the burn.

'Aye aye,' he shouted from thirty yards away. 'Du's meditatin, I see.'

'Something like that,' Alice called back, smiling.

'Well, dunna git up. I winna buther dee for lang.'

He reached for the peak of his cap and pulled it lower against the rain, turning his head one way then the other, not speaking or looking at Alice again as he walked, though Alice didn't once take her eyes off him. She was fascinated by David, and always had been. He was like an invented person, a character, and yet was somehow more real than anyone else she knew.

'Hit's a fine day for a picnic,' he said, as he stopped a few metres away, on the other side of the burn.

'It might not look like it,' grinned Alice, 'but I'm actually doing research.'

'Aye,' David nodded seriously, 'dat's whit I tell Mary sometimes when I hae a peerie sleep in the efternoon.'

Alice could hardly imagine anyone less likely to sleep in the afternoon than David, but she laughed out loud at the joke.

'So, what can I do you for?' she asked. 'Or is this just a social call?'

'No, I normally do aa me socialisin oota da rain,' David said. 'But I saa dee and I thoght I might just hae somethin at would interest dee. For dy book, lik. An I didna want ta forget.'

Alice wasn't entirely sure what David or her other neighbours thought about her writing, or about the book itself. She'd told them about it, of course, and explained what she was trying to do, but the response had been muted. Nods of heads, a polite question or two, then the subject changed. Either they disapproved or they weren't interested, she thought. Or both. She was aware that it might seem patronising, this project, or presumptuous. She was an incomer here and, to them, a newcomer. She was aware, too, that her neighbours might worry what exactly she was writing about the valley – about *them*, for instance. She had done her best to reassure, in her explanations, but it was hard to tell if she'd done enough. So Alice was pleased and relieved to hear David's offer.

'Well, du kens Ah'm clearin oot Maggie's hoose eenoo, fir Sandy to move intae, hoopfully. Shu's left ahint a few things at micht be o interest ta dee. Things at shu wrote, I mean.'

'Okay. What kind of things?'

'Diaries, journals, dat kind o thing. Dere's letters an so on at shu haed fae idder fok, but dat's probably nae use ta dee. But shu wrote a lot, it seems. Just recordin whit was been happenin. Some o it'll be braaly dull, I reckon, but du micht fin some o it ta be o use. I dunna ken. Unless du can fin oot aa du needs fae dis rock.'

Alice laughed again. 'No, thank you, that sounds great. I'd love to have a look through some time, as long as you don't think it's too personal?'

'Nah, I'm haed a peerie look, an it dusna seem ta be lik dat. Mair aboot da wadder an wark as aboot hersel, I think.'

'Oh right, well that sounds like it might be useful. Do you want me to come and pick them up?'

'Nah nah. Ah'll drap dem aff at da hoose sometime. When I hae a chance.' He turned and looked down the valley, his eyes following the burn towards the wedge of dark sea beyond. 'Well, Ah'll let dee git back ta dee research. Ah'm needin ta research me denner, I think.'

'Thanks, David,' she smiled. 'Thanks for thinking of me.'

'I could hardly no think o dee when du's sitting oot here in da middle o da valley lik dis.' He winked and nodded, then turned his back. 'See dee later,' he shouted, without looking behind him.

'Cheers, thanks again!'

Alice watched him go back up the valley with the same unhesitating stride as he'd come down it. His hands, as always when he wasn't carrying something, were clasped behind his back, as though he were merely out for a stroll. He paused at the fence. It wasn't so easy to cross from this side, but lifting one leg then the other he stepped over without a problem. He started the pickup, then was gone.

Alice was aware of a pain in her backside. The rock she was sitting on was not ideally shaped for the purpose, and one sharp lump in particular was pressed into her right buttock. The other buttock seemed to be numb. She didn't want to get up just yet, but an urgency and insistence had developed in her lower body.

She stood and leaned backward, stretching, with her hands on her hips, then stopped. She felt, suddenly, exposed where she stood. Usually she didn't think for a moment about who might be watching, but the conversation with David had left her aware. At this spot she could be seen from every house in the valley, if anyone was looking. She couldn't see them, but everyone could see her.

Uncomfortable then with that thought, she began to follow the burn back upwards, almost parallel with the road, then cut across through the upper park towards the house. She kept her head down, watching her feet as they squelched into the damp soil, feeling the cling of wet trousers and the grip of wet boots. Back inside she stripped off, then switched on the shower. She stood beneath the hot water, eyes closed, until the chill had left her body, then dried herself, put on clean clothes and went in to the study. She sat down at the desk and looked at the pile of papers, the books and folders, then out of the window.

There were chinks in her thoughts now, after David's intervention. Earlier, she was fretting. The problem of how this next chapter might be constructed, how it might be made to contain all she wanted it to contain, had consumed her. Sometimes, details amassed would take a form of their own, like piled sand. They would direct her and insist on choices without the need for choosing. But this time there was just too much, and it threatened to bury her within a vast, shapeless mound.

What the spiders and the ants and the flies were telling her, in their sheer volume, was that this project was indeed approaching some kind of conclusion. She simply couldn't write about invertebrates in the way she had written about birds and mammals. There was no possibility of what she produced being anything like comprehensive. She could list those creatures she learned to identify, but what would that achieve? A register filled with holes.

She could spend the rest of her life learning the names of insects and make a much longer list, but she still would not eliminate those holes entirely. This was the point, then, when her will for completeness came up against her acknowledgement of the impossible. This was the point when a limit imposed *itself*.

Her fretting had ceased. The recognition of this limit, which had come not as a moment of clarity but, like the dampening of her clothes through the morning, gradually and unignorably, had brought with it a feeling of relief. She knew now what she could not do. And that relief allowed other thoughts to nag.

Alice had always assumed that the final part of her book would focus on the contemporary human story of the valley. It seemed the only proper way to end. But she had not yet given real consideration to how it might be done. When the time came, she figured, she would know what to do. There would be plenty of information available from the past hundred years or so, from the local archives and from David, that would allow her to bring it to life. Photographs, names, dates: the specifics would be important.

She saw the book much as she saw the valley itself: consisting of many layers. The present day could not be understood – it couldn't even be seen properly – without understanding the layers upon which it rested. Like a mountain, with its ribbons of shale and gneiss, and its seams of quartz and iron, each piece was necessary to the whole. If any piece were different, it would be another place altogether. But simply detailing the history, the geology and geography, the flora and fauna, was not enough. Alice wanted her final chapter to show the valley as it *was*, containing and comprising all those things, standing upon them. She wanted readers to see the place, finally, as one might see a clock properly for the first time, having watched it be taken apart and then reassembled.

But David's offer had planted another thought: the thought

of Maggie. Alice hadn't known the older woman well, which had always disappointed her. They would say hello and chat sometimes, but these conversations were never as friendly or as intimate as she'd hoped. Maggie had lost the energy, perhaps, to make much of an effort in welcoming new people. She didn't feel the need to bring them into her life. That was understandable, but Alice would have liked for it to have been different. She would have liked to have known her better.

When Maggie died, Alice tried not to be affected. She went to the funeral, of course – it would have seemed impolite not to – but she avoided talk of what had happened and did her best to push the old woman from her mind. After all, they had not been friends, not even close, so the great welling of grief inside her at the thought of Maggie seemed somehow insincere, somehow dishonest.

This had been the first death she was close to, physically, since she arrived in Shetland. It had been the first since Jack. After more than four years, that loss had loosened its throttling grip on her thoughts, but it was still there, always, like an ache, and to be once again in the presence of death had been difficult.

But grief is an untamed thing, and it rose, still, at unexpected moments. Alice found herself transfixed by it sometimes, not only when the memories came back unbidden or unwelcome but at the very process of memory itself – the gradual disappearance of things that once had been so clear. There were occasions when she'd tried to call her husband's face to mind, for company and for comfort, and had found he was not there, like a book missing from a shelf. She was panicked then, and angered by the realisation that having lost him once she would now have to lose him a second time, piece by piece. In those moments she would close her eyes and shake her head, ransacking her thoughts in desperation, until, again, he would return.

Jack died of bowel cancer when he was thirty-eight, two years younger than Alice had been at the time. He was thirty-five when he was diagnosed, not long after they had started trying for a baby. 'It's now or never,' she remembered saying, her uncertainty at the thought of motherhood finally overcome by his enthusiasm and her age. 'Now or never.'

For almost three years, they lived with the disease between them, first with hope – the statistics and his youth were on their side – and then without. By the time he was diagnosed, the cancer had already spread to his lymph nodes and was on its way to his liver. Once there, the conclusion had been decided. The chemotherapy slowed but did not prevent it. He would end up on the wrong side of the statistics. He was 'one of the unlucky ones', the consultant said, when their fears were finally confirmed.

When someone you love is going to die, when you know they are going to die and there is nothing you can do to stop it, life splits. Half of you continues as if everything were normal. You get up in the morning, eat breakfast, brush your teeth. You do your work, see friends, watch television, go to sleep. You function. The other half, though, is always looking forward. It sees beyond the dying to the dead. It anticipates the absence that is to come. And yet somewhere there, between those two halves, the automaton and the seer, you must continue to love and to care for the one who is not gone yet, who is still there, temporary but real.

Alice lived like that for more than two years, and she did so as well as could be expected by anyone looking in from the outside. She continued to write – with increasing reluctance – and she continued to care for her husband, who remained at home until the last few weeks of his life.

'I'm dying,' he would say sometimes, looking over at her, as though surprised anew by the realisation. He used to tell her he loved her in precisely the same way. The thought came to him, urgently, and needed to be spoken aloud. Her own love for Jack swelled with the imminence of his loss, and continued to swell even afterwards, as if that love might somehow grow and fill the space that he had left. But of course it could not.

On the day he died, in late July 2011, she was called in to the hospital not long after lunch. She'd spent most of the morning with him, then come home to get a little rest. They'd told her a few days earlier that it could be any time, and she'd struggled to sleep since then. When the phone rang, she hardly needed to answer it. She was already reaching for the car keys, she was already on her way.

Alice sat with him for several hours, until he was gone, then longer, until the nurse came and touched her on the shoulder, asking if she needed more time, and she wanted to say *Yes, I need more time, I need another few minutes, another day, another decade with my husband, is that okay, can you do that, can you make that happen?* But she said nothing. She stood and let go of his hand and went through to the waiting room, where a television was switched on in the corner, silent, showing fire engines and ambulances and smoke and wounded people, crying people.

She looked at the screen for a long time, struggling to understand what was happening there, to separate it from what was happening here, in this pale-blue room on the fourth floor of the hospital. She read the ticker-tape of updates as it scrolled, describing the attacks in Norway, in Oslo and Utøya, explaining where the bomb had exploded and the shooting had happened, how many were feared dead, how many were injured. She saw people on stretchers and children wrapped in white blankets, shivering. She had a feeling, then, that she was entirely still, and that the world was galloping around her, fixed in its trajectory and yet spinning with a kind of madness, like a rollercoaster out of control, running faster and faster on its rails, threatening to come loose at any moment and plunge into the empty air. She, Alice, was at its centre, utterly powerless and yet somehow the purpose of it all, as if the spinning, wild, crazy turning of the world were a performance put on for her alone. She was paralysed. To move from where she was would be to step into the madness that surrounded her. The only way to avoid being caught and dragged into that storm was to be at its heart and to let it rage all around her. She stood, then, until she couldn't stand any longer.

For the next two days, Alice stayed at home, watching the aftermath of the attacks on television, the scenes of destruction and death repeated hour after hour. And as she watched, gripped by it all, she saw her own horror and outrage mirrored there on the screen, her own loss broadcast back to her in the loss of others. She felt crippled, disfigured by what had happened, as though she herself were one of the injured. She felt, too, a kind of resentment towards those people, for the sheer *publicness* of their suffering, and the sympathy that it brought. What about her and this *private* suffering? Where were the tributes to Jack? Where was the coverage of his death? Fixed to that screen, hypnotised by it, her grieving fed upon a universal grief. It was everywhere.

For those first couple of days, nobody bothered her much. They put food in front of her, some of which she ate. They didn't ask too many questions. But later it became clear there were responsibilities that were hers. There were choices to be made. She wanted to leave everything for her in-laws to decide. She couldn't find the will to care what coffin Jack would need, what kind of flowers they should buy, or what songs should be played as his worn-out body lay among them for the last time. It didn't matter. None of it mattered. Every question seemed obscene. How could anyone think of such things? Whenever she was able, Alice would slip away to the company of the television, until, eventually, even the news reporters lost interest in the dead children of Norway. Alone in front of the screen, she felt dizzied by the passing of time, straightjacketed by the endless motion of the world.

SATURDAY,
13TH FEBRUARY

'Come on, Jamie. Let's get oot o the hoose for a bit.'

'It's raining!'

'No really. And onyway, du's got dy coat. Let's just get some fresh air. Just for ten minutes or so. Come on!'

Jamie looked up from the sofa and scowled at Terry, then looked back at his phone. 'The wifi here is shit.'

'Aye, du's right, it is. And dat's a good reason no to sit aroond aa day looking at a screen. It's no going to get ony faster.'

Jamie huffed, then raised himself to his feet, as though the effort required were a chore for which he could scarcely muster the energy.

'Where are we going?'

'Just to the beach, okay? Just for a look. We winna be lang, I promise.'

Terry didn't really want to go to the beach any more than Jamie, but he needed to do something. His head was fogged and throbbing, and a few minutes outside might just relieve the pressure. The walls felt too close in the house, too solid. The waves would clear things up, wash away the hangover.

Louise, his wife, had dropped their son off first thing this morning, an hour earlier than he'd expected – though that was his fault rather than hers. He had been awake, but only just. Jamie had hardly said a word so far. He had lain out on the sofa with his phone. Facebook, texting, playing games. Terry wasn't sure exactly what. Going out might do both of them some good. It might improve the day.

Jamie was right, it was raining. Not heavily, but more than enough. It was falling at forty-five degrees and soaked their faces as soon as they turned onto the road. The valley looked shrunken and miserable from here, as if the land itself were hunkered down against the weather. Terry cupped a cigarette in his hand and lit it, drawing the smoke deep into his lungs.

'Dad, let's go back.'

'No, let's keep goin. Ten minutes, dat's aa. And when we get back Ah'll put da fire on.'

Terry had been at this house for seven months now, since Louise finally threw him out. Or at least it seemed final this time. There had been warnings before, plenty of them. But it had never been this serious, never this long. He didn't blame her for doing it. Not when he was sober, anyway. And certainly not when he was hungover. Then, now, he was humbled, shocked that she had put up with him for so long. Her kindness amazed him. He hadn't deserved it. He'd never deserved her.

There were times, though, when he felt differently. Drunk, his self-pity could boil up into rage. Then, it was Louise who had done wrong, Louise who made him miserable, Louise who was ruining his relationship with their son. Then, he imagined all the terrible things he could say to her, ought to say, if only she were there to listen.

But mostly his rage was turned inwards, a roiling current of self-disgust that seemed to be both cause and response to his drinking. He drank because he hated himself because he drank because he hated himself. Occasionally he thought he saw a crack in that chain, some link that might be prised apart and broken. But always the logic of it came back to him: the perfect, inescapable logic.

Louise had been good to him. There was never any question of him not seeing Jamie. It was never even a threat. She let him come by the house, when he was able, and every fortnight, without fail, she would drop the boy off on a Saturday morning and return for him on a Sunday afternoon. She trusted Terry to stay sober on those weekends, and he complied.

He knew, though, that these visits were Louise's choice, not Jamie's. He knew, or at least he guessed, that Jamie protested each time these weekends came around, that he probably begged to be allowed to stay in town, just this once, to see his friends, to go out, anything. Terry wasn't sure which hurt more: the knowledge that those conversations were happening between his wife and his son, or the reality of these visits, during which Jamie would be stubborn and uncommunicative, during which Terry would look at his son as though he were some kind of alien, as though he were entirely incomprehensible and out of reach, as though he were already lost.

Terry didn't look behind him. He knew Jamie would be dragging his trainers along the road, miserable and indignant. He followed the road down to Gardie, then along the track that led out towards the beach. He opened the gate and waited until his son caught up, then closed it behind them. It was still raining, but the damp air was not unpleasant. It felt fresh and right, and Terry was glad he'd come.

'Right, can we go back now?'

'No!'

The pair of them, father and son, scrunched over the pebbles towards the water. The tide was low, and a broad stripe of seaweed lay black along the stones. Tangled in the fronds were scraps of wood and rubbish, mostly plastic. A few old bottles, broken buoys, net floats, a jerry can, a flip flop. Terry had read somewhere that left and right shoes would drift in opposite directions in the ocean, dragged by the currents towards different places entirely. Perhaps most of the footwear that washed up here was, like this flip flop, left-footed. It seemed implausible, but he wanted to believe it. He never remembered to test the theory, though, and so it remained a mere wonder. At this time of year the whole beach was strewn with junk, thrown up by the winter storms. It came from who-knew-where. Tossed from the side of a ship, perhaps, or from some other beach in some other place. In spring, David and Mary would clear it, gathering and dumping what shouldn't be here. But always it came back.

Terry and Jamie were side by side now, trudging the length of the seaweed line with their heads down. Neither was searching more than half-heartedly for items of interest, but looking down was drier than looking up. Ahead, turnstones and ringed plovers jabbed at the vegetation – hungry, hunting – their white breasts blinking in the drab air. The birds scattered as father and son approached.

At the end of the beach both of them paused. Terry's head was still throbbing, but he felt a little better besides that. He turned to the water. A seal bobbed, nose up, ten metres from the shore, then watched them, curious. They watched back. Its dog-like face seemed to be assessing the pair or waiting for them to do something interesting. Terry whistled, and the head twitched, then craned higher.

'Did du ken, folk used to say at selkies could take aff their skins and live as people? As women maistly, I think. Dy great-grandad telt me at his mither was boarn a selkie. She wis aalwis splashin aboot in da water, he said, an naebody swam dan-a-days.'

Jamie looked at his father, a sneer on his lips. 'Folk were stupid in the past, weren't they?'

'Well, du could see it lik dat.'

The boy picked up a stone and threw it towards the seal. It landed close, and the animal disappeared with a splash, then emerged again farther out, still watching. 'Bye, Granny!' Jamie shouted.

Terry shook his head and laughed. 'Aye aye. Du is a one.' He looked down at his feet then, for a flat stone to skim, but they were not easy to find on this beach. He turned like a gull, hunting the tide line, then picked up two that might just work. The first bounced a couple of times, then plunged into a wave. The second didn't even manage that. He flung it, triggering a painful thump in his head, and the stone landed in the water with a plop.

Jamie laughed. 'You're shit at that.'

'Yeah, I am. But Ah'm better as dee.'

'No, you're no.' The boy leaned down and grabbed a slim, awkwardly-shaped rock, then turned his body sideways. He threw it hard, just over the top of the nearest wave, and it bounced, once, twice, three times, four, then shuddered in a series of tiny hops that brought the total, Jamie insisted, to nine.

'Okay, yeah, du's better as me.'

'Don't you want to try again?'

'Aye, okay, best o five, then.' Terry resumed his search for stones, leaning down and grabbing three more likely ones at the edge of the beach, smooth in the hand. He turned himself side-on, drew his arm back with the first stone, then . . . bang. A sloppy smack against his face. A great lump of gritty seaweed slithered from his head to the ground. He looked over at Jamie, who was bent double with laughter, then wiped his hand over his mouth, drew dirt off his lips. He nearly shouted, but didn't. He let the anger slide away until he, too, was creased over.

'Can we go back noo?' Terry said, once he'd stopped spitting and laughing.

The boy nodded and led the way.

At the house, Terry lit the fire then went for a shower. 'Watch that, would du?' he said to Jamie as he left the room. When he returned, the fire was out and Jamie was back in the corner of the sofa, legs tucked in, staring at his phone. He looked up at Terry, then looked at the fire and frowned.

'Oh, sorry, I didn't notice.'

'No, I see dat. Could du try gettin it lit ageen, please?' He did his best not to sound annoyed.

'Mum doesn't let me do that.'

'Well, Ah'm lettin dee. I'm askin dee to reset it, *carefully*, then light it, *carefully*. I can watch if du wants.'

'No, I can do it. Can we have lunch now?'

'Yes, Ah'll mak it. Call me if du needs help.'

Terry went next door to the kitchen, taking four white rolls from the bread bin and a block of cheese from the fridge. He listened, heard the scrunching of paper from the other room, then the muffled clatter of sticks. Jamie was doing his best to be quiet. He was trying to complete this task as well as possible, precisely because it was one that had previously been forbidden.

Terry heard a match strike and felt, suddenly, a weight drop through him, as though the fear of catastrophe, once acknowledged, had fallen directly from his brain into his stomach. He set the knife on the plate and went back to the living room, propelled by panic. There, Jamie was kneeling in front of the fire, holding the match to a corner of newspaper, just as Terry would have done it.

'Nearly lit,' Jamie said, looking up, his eyes eager for approval.

'Well done. Looks good.' Terry tried hard not to show the worry that had grabbed him so unexpectedly. He leaned against the doorframe, watching, until the flames were bouncing in the grate. Sparks crackled in the kindling. 'Throw some coal on now, then put the guard up. We dunna want to burn the hoose doon.'

'You didn't put it up before.'

'No, I forgot. I shoulda been payin mair attention.'

The boy lifted the scuttle. It was full and heavy, but he was trying not to show the strain of it. He tipped it towards the fire, and Terry winced, expecting the whole thing to unload into the flames. Intervene or let him learn: he wasn't sure which was best. Nothing happened.

'Juist shoogle it wi your left hand.'

Jamie did as he was told. A few lumps of coal fell. He did it again. Nothing. Then a few more. And another.

Terry had watched long enough. 'Okay, I think yon's plenty.'

Jamie returned the scuttle and set the guard in place. He looked at his father and smiled. 'Okay?'

'Aye, thank you. Noo, Ah'll just get wis wir lunch. Does du want orange juice?'

'Do you have anything else?'

'Water.'

'Okay, I'll have orange.'

Terry brought the food and drinks, then turned on the television.

'Shall we watch a film?'

'I guess so. Have you got anything decent?'

'Probably no. Hae a look at the DVDs on the shelf.'

'You should get Netflix, Dad.'

'Yeah, mebbie I should. Ah'll bear that in mind.'

Jamie hunted through the discs, pulling out a James Bond film they'd both seen at least twice before. 'This'll do,' he said.

Terry felt a wave of love surge then settle as he watched the boy do his best to be amenable. He made himself a cup of tea, then sat down on the sofa. 'Right, Ah'm ready.' He pressed play on the remote, then turned the volume up loud, drowning out the wind and the rain that now hammered against the window. He felt, for the first time in weeks, something like happiness, and he tried, over and over, to push aside the agonising desire to be alone, for his son to be gone.

★ ★ ★

David grabbed two empty buckets from the back of his pickup and set them down in the shed beside the plastic sacks of sheep's feed that were piled along the side wall. The feeding was done for the day, and he'd managed a few more hours at Maggie's house, putting the last of the rubbish out in the skip, scraping paper from the living-room walls, making plans. There wasn't much left to do now, beyond the decorating, and he was glad of that. He wanted the job to be over with, the house emptied of Maggie and filled with someone else's life – Sandy's, prefer-ably. He wanted the house to be breathing again and unburdened of its loss. He wanted it to be renewed.

The past few weeks had not been enjoyable. Making his way through Maggie's rooms, handling the things that she had once held, deciding their fate, had left him with a deeper sense of loss than he'd had in the weeks immediately after her death. Then, he'd been able to distance himself from it, at least to some degree. She was an old woman, he'd told himself. She wasn't the person she once had been, the person he'd known all of his life. But inside the house, with her gone, she *was* that person again. She was the same woman with whom he'd had the same conversations, year after year, decade after decade, about sheep, about the weather, about their neighbours. She was the same woman who had heckled him on his wedding day, when, overcome by nerves, he'd stuttered and stumbled through his speech at the reception. 'Set dee doon an gie soomeen else a shot,' she'd called, to uproarious laughter. She was the same woman who had looked after Emma and Kate when they were young, when he and Mary had been at work; and she was the same woman, too, who had looked after him when he was a child, letting him help her in the garden, or else walking around the croft and through the valley with him, David always trailing, struggling to keep up. She was a young woman herself, then, perhaps dreaming about children of her own, children that never arrived. That was the Maggie whose memory still inhabited the house, and he missed her.

He had reached that time in his life – a time he had not anticipated in advance but which now seemed strangely significant – when the last of the adults he'd known as a child were gone. A few of his teachers would still be on the go, he imagined, but he hadn't seen or heard of them in many years. There would be other folk, too, contemporaries and friends of his parents, perhaps frail and forgetful. But there was no one whose absence he might now notice. In truth, the fault was largely his own. He had kept to himself too much, or kept to the valley at least. He lost touch with people easily and did little to try to change that. Sometimes, in Billy's shop or in the aisles of the Co-op in Lerwick, he would see some familiar face – a schoolmate of his or a former colleague of Mary's – and he would turn away, trying not to be noticed. When he failed, he was always jovial, always friendly, but often he succeeded.

It wasn't that he disliked speaking to people. He took pleasure in chatting to friends of Emma's and Kate's when he bumped into them, or with folk who lived nearby, but he struggled sometimes to know what to say, once the pleasantries were done with. So much of his thinking was centred here in the valley that, dragged on to other topics, he could find himself floundering or, very often, entirely uninterested.

With the exception now of his daughters and grandchildren, David had all he needed here. And Maggie had always been part of that *here*. From the moment he was born until the moment she died. Longer than that, in fact. She had been a link not just to his own past but to a time before he existed, a time he knew from stories, and which lived even now inside him. Now that she was gone, he felt a peculiar kind of responsibility towards that past, though he didn't understand precisely what that responsibility entailed.

David had never been resistant to change. He'd never feared it, the way that some who were older than him had done. The life in which he'd been brought up was hard, infinitely harder than the life he lived today, and he'd never glamourised or idealised that hardship. He was glad it was gone. The comfort he enjoyed, the freedom from hunger and from poverty, were luxuries his grandparents had not experienced until late in their lives. Those changes couldn't be wished away. It wasn't easy to say, then, what exactly he longed for that had been lost. He couldn't put into words quite what was missing that once had been present. Perhaps it was that sense of permanence and continuation that he'd felt in his youth, which had been replaced, now, by something more like precariousness and transience. Perhaps it was only that.

Growing up here, David had felt he was inheriting something. His parents had not merely given him a start in life then let him find his own way. He had inherited the way along with the start, and he had accepted it. Never once had he thought of that inheritance as an impediment. Never once did he look at his life and wish it had been spent elsewhere, doing something other than what he had done. He didn't feel regret in that way. The valley had been both a gift and a choice for him. The giving of the gift and his acceptance of it were somehow inseparable.

He knew, of course, that things were different now. Choice was everything, and the options seemed limitless. How could anyone now do as he had done, as young as he was, and accept the place in which they were born, as though it were the greatest gift they could imagine? How could anyone settle for *this*? Today, each choice made was a thousand other chances missed, so *this*, always, would be outweighed by *what if*.

Perhaps that was a good thing, that freedom. David wasn't sure. He thought of Emma. She had gone away, then returned, now gone away again, unable to be quite satisfied or quite content. She saw choices everywhere, and she took them. She was tangled up and bound by her own will, unable to escape it. He looked at her and he knew that the choices he'd been faced with in his life were very different from the ones she faced. They were simpler choices. When he moved back here, and then when he married Mary, he stopped choosing and started living. He gave himself up to something like fate. He gave himself up to life. Emma, perhaps, had never given herself up to anything. He missed her now, more than he thought possible.

At the back of the shed, behind the tractor, were a few pieces of furniture that he'd rescued from Gardie: the kitchen table, a wardrobe and chest of drawers, a writing desk and a rocking chair. He wanted to keep these and to put them back once the decorating was done. He liked the idea of some continuation. But they needed a bit of work first. Nothing major. Two of the drawers in the chest were coming apart; the table needed sanding, and the desk too. The rocking chair had been painted cream at some point, but the paint was now flaking away. He lifted it out to the front beside the work bench. He could use the electric sander on the others, but this would have to be done by hand.

He began at the top, with the roughest grade of paper he could find, pressing his fingers into the wood, rubbing hard. The paint came away easily – a dull, dead skin, ready to be sloughed – but it clogged the sandpaper, and David had to tap the sheet every few minutes to clear it. When the headboard was stripped, he moved on to the upright dowels, wrapping his hand around each one in turn, sliding the paper up and down until the dark wood emerged. From there he went on to the armrests, the seat, and downward, piece by piece, to where the perfect curve of the rockers met the concrete floor of the shed.

As he worked, David hardly thought of anything beyond what he was doing. Only now and again did his mind drift, wander, then correct itself and return. The job required no particular skill or concentration, but it held his focus. It was the kind of work he loved, work in which he could become lost and yet be more fully present than he felt at any other time. Sometimes he wished he had done something more practical in his life, become a joiner or a boat builder, as his mother's father had been. The completeness of it appealed to him. It contrasted with the never-ending cycle of the croft. You worked on a project, you finished it, you moved on. You took pride in the things you created, and others took pleasure in them. You turned your labour into useful, sometimes beautiful, objects, like the rocking chair in his hands, its solid curves like bone and muscle. But David had never been a natural carpenter. He learned how things were done, how they worked. He had some of the skills but not the aptitude. When he helped his grandfather, as a boy, he always had to be told what to do. He was always one step behind. He would watch the old man moving, his skin against the boards, rough on the fingers, smooth on the palm, as though his own hands were made of timber. He watched the boats take shape, and it seemed to him like a magic trick. David could never quite understand how the trick was done.

These days, he avoided any difficult jobs. He didn't have the ambition or the patience for it. His cousin Andy was a joiner and would help with anything he needed done. But jobs like this, basic repairs, he liked to do himself. They had an innate satisfaction guaranteed. He knew his limitations, but within those limitations he could find pleasure.

The paint was all gone, and David had begun going over the chair with finer grade paper when he remembered that he was hungry. A deep, rumbling complaint in his stomach wakened him from the work. He had come home from Gardie to eat lunch but had become distracted. It was now the middle of the afternoon. Beneath the stripped chair was a puddle of paint and wood dust and discarded sheets of sandpaper, creased and worn right through. He would finish the job and tidy up later in the day.

He stood. His fingers were stiff from the cold, and his toes were numb inside the leather boots. He was tired. The rain that had blustered through earlier had now stopped, but the air outside still felt damp, and the breeze was as sharp as cats' claws on his cheeks and ears.

David stood at the door of the shed for a moment, looking out. He felt old. His hair was thin and mostly grey, with a bald patch the size of a beer mat on the top of his head. Since it first appeared, he'd developed a habit of resting his palm up there, on his scalp, as though to check the gap in his hair was still present and that it hadn't grown any larger since he last checked, which usually wasn't very long ago. He knew that he did this, and he knew it was ridiculous, but he couldn't seem to stop. His mind would wander and his hand would drift upwards, as though drawn by a lodestone at the peak of his skull.

He walked around the side of the house, from where he could see the upper park. Several of the ewes were gathered around the feeding circle, stripping silage from the bale. Others were grazing close to the wall at the north end of the park, where there was a bit of shelter from the wind. He wasn't looking for anything in particular, just checking in. Still sometimes he felt pangs of guilt when the weather was bad. This past fortnight it had been cold, unrelentingly, with sleet some days, then rain, then hail. But the sheep endured it; they didn't complain. They just ate and slept, mostly in silence, while inside them little lives were growing.

In the porch he untied his laces, then pulled off his boots, using the toe of each foot on the other heel. Sam got up from his bed in the corner, wagged his tail a few times, then lay down again, curled up and closed his eyes. David shook his head and laughed. 'Du is a lazy bugger, Sam.' He could hear Mary in the kitchen – plates being moved, cupboards closing – and he went through, smiling, to meet her.

'I wondered what'd happened to you,' she said. 'I thought I saw you get back hours ago.'

'I did, but I lost track o time. Ah'm been wirkin in da shed, until me gut reminded me o whit me head forgot.'

'You're not going to eat now, are you? I'll be making dinner in a couple of hours.' Mary stopped emptying the dishwasher and looked at him, eyebrows raised.

'Well, if I dunna eat noo I winna be livin in a couple o oors. Dunna worry, Ah'll leave space enough fir later.'

David opened the fridge, grabbed a thin block of cheese, then a box of oatcakes from the cupboard above the microwave. He cut six slices from the block, laid them on a side plate and sat down at the table.

'Are you wanting tea?' Mary asked, when she'd finished with the dishes.

'Aye, go on. I wis dat fantin I forgot I was needin a drink an aa.'

Mary filled the kettle and switched it on, then set two mugs down, a bag in each, and a pint of milk alongside.

'How's your day been?' she asked, looking over at her husband, engrossed in his food.

'I dunna really ken, ta be honest,' David replied. 'I feel lik Ah'm somehoo missed half o it. I got up, giud oot and dan it was noo. I got a bit don at Maggie's, I ken dat. An I wis sandin doon a chair. Dat's aboot it, I think.'

As the kettle came to a boil, a ringing noise made David lift his head from the food. He looked at Mary and then at the phone on the wall, his mouth too full to ask.

'It's *your* phone,' Mary laughed, reaching into the pocket of his fleece, which he'd hung around the back of a chair. She looked at the screen and handed it across the table to him.

'Sandy,' she said, smiling.

David shook his head and swallowed, taking hold of the phone in front of him, looking for the right button.

'Aha!' He pressed it and lifted the handset to his ear.

'Hello, boy, how's du?'

'I'm okay, thanks, aye.'

The line was bad, and David closed his eyes, concentrating on Sandy's voice.

'I just wanted to tell you that I'm made a decision,' Sandy said.

'Okay,' David nodded. 'Aboot whit?'

'Aboot the hoose.'

'Aha! Well, believe it or no, Ah'm had twa folk on at me askin ta buy it. Mak a fine holiday hame, een o dem telt me.'

'Oh.' Sandy sounded surprised. 'Well, are you *wantin* to sell it?'

'No, I dunna. Ah'm telt dee whit Ah'm wantin. Dat's no changed.'

'Okay, that's good.'

David paused for a second. 'Does dat mean at du wants it?'

'Aye, I'll give it a try.'

'Well, dat *is* good news, Sandy boy. Ah'm aafil glad ta hear it.'

'Yeah, I'm glad too. At least I think so. Anyway, I'll speak to you later, an we can work oot a plan. I'd lik to move in as soon as it's ready, if that's possible, afore I can change me mind.'

'Dat suits me fine. Hit'll be ready fir dee as shoon as I can finish up wi pentin an so on. A couple o weeks, or mebbie less if du's helpin.'

'I'll help,' Sandy said. 'I'll be alang later. We can speak aboot it then.'

'Cheers ta dee,' said David, and took the phone away from his ear, grinning. He looked up at Mary, who was standing by the table, watching.

'He's wantin ta move ta Maggie's,' David said.

'Aye, I got that.' Mary nodded, slowly. 'Well, I hope it works out for him,' she said. 'I do hope it works out.'

TUESDAY,
22ND MARCH

Sandy moved on the first day of March, a morning studded with hail. He had already shifted a dozen boxes or more, one at a time, from the Red House to Gardie, so on the day itself the job didn't take long. David came down with the pickup and a trailer, they filled both, and that was it. He had fewer belongings than he'd feared, and most of the furniture was staying where it was. David had bought new things for Gardie, or else left and repaired those things of Maggie's that were worth saving.

The house felt strange. For days, Sandy struggled to shake off the feeling that it was still someone else's home, that he was a squatter or a lodger. It had been redecorated – new paint, new carpets – and he'd even been given his choice of colours. But still, Sandy wondered if he'd made the wrong decision.

By the time the new tenants arrived at the Red House, three weeks later, he was more settled. His things were back out of their boxes and spread around the house, and that helped. So too did the numerous discussions he'd had with David about the croft, the older man's enthusiasm offered like a gift to him. He laughed sometimes at David's excitement, and the efforts he made to keep it in check.

'Dunna be too ambitious,' David would caution. 'No till du's feelin mair confident wi it aa. Tak a year or twa an see how du gits on.'

Then, five minutes later: 'Mebbie we could git pigs. Share

twa ir tree atween wis. An a coo. Juist a peerie Shetlan een. I can pictur dat. Hit's been a lang time since Ah'm haed a coo.'

Sandy could picture it, too. He was not immune to the vision David had of what could be done here, and he was flattered that David saw him as part of that vision. There were times, sitting together at the kitchen table in Gardie, or else up at Kettlester, that Sandy was reminded of the excitement he and Emma had shared when they first moved to the Red House. It was odd, now, to be sharing that excitement with Emma's father, to be feeling it without her. He felt almost unfaithful.

From the kitchen window, where he stood washing dishes, Sandy could see up the road towards the Red House. Outside, a white van was parked, from which two people were lugging boxes. They were a Shetland couple, David said, from Lerwick. A few years younger than Sandy. He'd heard their names before but knew neither of them by sight.

Sandy was pleased. Some younger people in the valley felt like a relief. He wouldn't be quite such an odd one out any more. He was glad, then, to see the van arrive first thing this morning, and he stood at the sink now watching the two figures go back and forth to the house. He'd have liked to go and help, if only out of nosiness. But he had to work for a few hours today, driving taxis in town. And anyway, this was their time. He'd be intruding now. Better to wait until they were fed up carrying and unpacking. He could go later and say hello, make them feel welcome.

Sandy remembered the day he and Emma had arrived, with three suitcases between them. Their boxes came a few days later, shipped up on a lorry from Edinburgh. His father, Jim, had arrived afterwards with the contents of Sandy's bedroom – the detritus of his teenage years – most of which he neither needed nor wanted any more and would happily have never seen again.

That was the limit of his family's assistance on that occasion. His father came, unloaded, looked around and then left. He wished them luck in their new home, but without much enthusiasm. That was his way. Keeping his distance was tantamount to a pat on the back. Outward displays of love or affection were as alien to him as ballroom dancing. If Jim experienced such emotions, Sandy sometimes thought, it was as others experienced shame: as something to be suppressed and pushed aside, as something that made him weak.

The help they had, in those first few days and afterwards, came from David and from Mary. It came in the form of physical assistance — shifting boxes, decorating, cleaning — and it came, later, in the form of space. David in particular had spent a lot of time at the house at first, until Emma told him, quietly, to go away and give them a bit of time on their own. He went then and didn't come back until they asked, three days later, to borrow some tools. Afterwards, they rarely had any problem with her parents. Or at least Sandy didn't. It was different for Emma, of course. Fond though she was of them, living a few hundred yards down the road meant she would feel crowded, sometimes, by their love. She would complain of the physical proximity of her father and the emotional proximity of her mother. She longed, she said, for a bit more distance.

But though at times Emma found it claustrophobic, she didn't lose sight of the fact that her claustrophobia was a luxury. Sandy's parents would not allow her to forget, she told him. His father, though only half an hour away, might as well have been in Peru. He came to visit just a few times a year, and then only when he was specifically invited, which happened rarely.

Sandy's mother, Liz, had left when he was seven. A Saturday afternoon in July. He remembered standing by her bedroom door as she packed things into bags, then took them out to the car. She didn't explain what was happening, just carried on, ignoring him; but he knew that whatever it was must be important. His father was out, with no idea of what was going on back home. When she'd finished packing, she drove Sandy to a friend's house, left him there, then drove away, catching the ferry south that night. He didn't see her again for almost a year.

Nor did he see his father for several days. What exactly happened in that time Sandy never found out. Perhaps Jim had gone after Liz, begging her to return, or perhaps he just couldn't face his son again so soon after their shared abandonment. Nothing was explained to Sandy at the time. He just remained at his friend's house, eating there, sleeping there, until he was allowed to go back home – a home that was never the same again.

In the first few weeks after the disappearance, Sandy might as well have been entirely alone. His mother was gone, somewhere, but his father too had retreated, still visible but absent nonetheless. Several times, Sandy went in search of him, hungry and uncertain, after meals had failed to materialise. He would find him curled up on the bed he had previously shared. There were never any tears that he saw, just a gaping silence that spread through the room and the house like a disease.

Neither his mother nor his father ever fully returned. She did not come back to Shetland. She sent birthday cards most years, and Christmas presents sometimes, but he saw her only rarely. Jim, in turn, seemed to loosen his grip on everything that had once been important to him. For the young boy observing, it was as though his father had evaluated the world, found it wanting, and then turned his back on it, preferring instead to concentrate on things that demanded little or nothing of him emotionally – his work and the television. That was how it felt to Sandy growing up, as he saw this once cheerful, sociable man withdraw into a world so utterly limited that it barely had space for the boy still in his care. Sandy saw judgement. He felt judged. He could no longer engage his father's attention as he once had, and so he came to feel himself to be a disappointment – a disappointment so great he had caused his mother to abandon him, and his father to shrink, like a hermit crab, into the hard shell of his own loneliness.

As he grew older, though, Sandy came to understand it differently. Emma, ultimately, forced him to do so. It wasn't disappointment his father felt, she told him. It was fear. He was terrified of losing everything he had, so he'd convinced himself he had nothing to lose. The result was the same, but it was easier for Sandy to swallow. Bitterness melted into pity. His father was not a judgemental man – except perhaps of himself – he was just pathetic and distorted by grief. He wondered, now, why Emma had failed to see that he was suffering from the same affliction.

In the twenty-two years she'd been gone, Sandy had seen his mother only a dozen times or so, for a total of a month or even less. He went to stay with her once, when he was sixteen. She was living in London at the time and had decided they should start again. She wanted to be a part of his life, now that he was an adult. He remembered her from that trip as someone baffling, someone simultaneously clingy and remote. She tried to be his friend, asked him questions about girls, about ambitions, but she didn't want to know anything about home or about his father. She introduced Sandy to her friends, some of whom seemed to be learning for the first time that she was a mother. She showed him off like a handbag or a puppy, then ignored him. The trip was supposed to last a fortnight, but he asked to go home after just a week. Liz offered no opposition. She seemed as relieved as he was at the thought of his departure.

Sandy finished the dishes and glanced up at the clock. He was late. Too busy staring out the window to notice the time. He looked around the room, as though something needed doing, but he couldn't work out what it was. Everything was switched off. Everything was fine. He grabbed his coat.

Spring had not yet arrived on the island. One morning the previous week, there had been something almost like warmth in the air, but the rumour of a new season proved untrue. A bitter wind came galloping from the north that same afternoon and didn't cease blowing for days. The land was still saturated around the croft, and everything was still winter pale and washed with brown. As Sandy went out to the car, a dozen oystercatchers came piping above the house, frantic, as though escaping some unseen disaster. One after another they cascaded into the beach park and began, at once, to interrogate the soft ground with their beaks, jabbing and prodding, orange into brown.

Sandy started the car and eased away from the front of the house, onto the road. He took it slow, hoping for another glimpse of his new neighbours, but there was no sign of them. The doors of the van and the house were closed.

There was a pang, then, of something unexpected. It was the house and it was Emma and it was time and it was the valley. And it was all wrapped up in a tight, sharp-edged bundle that struck him in the gut as he looked into the windows of the Red House.

What was he doing here?

When he first met Emma, Sandy was selling mobile phones in a tatty little shop near the university. It wasn't minimum wage, but it wasn't far off. He kept that job for eighteen months or so, then moved on to another, doing much the same thing. Previously he'd worked as a barman and, briefly, in a call centre. None of these jobs he liked very much, but none of them he hated. His main criterion when choosing work was always its forgettability. He'd ask himself, will I ever need to think about it outside office hours? Will it cause me stress? If the answer was yes, he wasn't interested.

He thought, then, that he knew who he was, knew the kind of life he wanted to lead. Freedom was the absence of drama, of anxiety. He'd had enough of that in his childhood, wanted no more of it. So he made himself impervious to the fractured world. He made himself solid and whole. Or at least he thought so.

Emma challenged that thought. She was the first person with whom he'd ever felt a desire – a *need* – to peel away some of the protective layers around himself. How or why that happened had never been entirely clear. Perhaps because she kept a phys- ical distance at first. They didn't kiss until the fifth time they met. They just talked and kept talking. She forced him – by holding that distance – to step towards her. And by the time he realised what was happening he was nearer to her than to where he'd come from. He had no real choice but to go on.

He had, in those early months with Emma, felt deeply vulner- able. In allowing her to know him, he had made himself weaker. It was as though he'd handed over the manufacturing diagrams and instruction booklet for his own self, as though he had imparted dangerous knowledge to someone without being entirely certain of what they might do with that knowledge.

The strength that had come from his former independence was always a kind of power. But it was an impotent power. He couldn't do anything with it, other than survive. He saw himself sometimes like a castle on a small island: his strength entirely defensive. He was safe, and he was lonely.

The fear subsided in time, as it had to, and the relationship with Emma drifted towards a kind of comfort. His wholeness was subsumed within a larger whole, and his safety was replaced by a different kind of security, of which loneliness was not a part. When he thought of the future, he no longer thought of himself alone.

Coming north again, after two years together, was a risk for them both. Some of their friends had already returned to the islands, to settle and start families, and Emma had felt that pull. More so than he ever did. Had she wanted to live in Lerwick, or anywhere else in Shetland, for that matter, he might have resisted. He might have said no. But the valley was different. The valley made a kind of sense. Here, he'd felt insulated from the fractured world that once had seemed so threatening. Here, he'd felt absorbed by the place, without being destroyed by it.

For most of his life, Sandy had fought to avoid becoming his father. He'd fought against that diminishment of self that comes when one loses what one cannot afford to lose. In pushing Emma away, he realised, he might already have lost that battle. He might already be diminished.

Sandy finished work early that afternoon, then went out to the far side of the beach park to mend a fence that hadn't survived the last storm. Two of the posts had fallen, rotten, and another was about ready to go. He'd done similar jobs with David on several occasions, but this was the first time he'd done it himself, on his own croft. Though he managed the repair, it had taken longer than it should have done, and he returned in the dark, tired and hungry. There was macaroni cheese left over from the night before, and he stabbed the cling film with a fork and set it in the microwave to heat. The bottle of white wine in the fridge reminded him he'd intended to go up the road to intro-duce himself.

He looked at the clock. It wasn't too late, and he wouldn't

need to stay for long. He could just hand over the wine and card on the doorstep if necessary. They might not be ready for guests just yet anyway. That would probably be for the best.

After eating, Sandy scribbled a quick message in the card he'd found in the hall bureau – Emma used to buy them in anticipation of moments like this and must have left a few behind. He picked up the wine from the fridge, then stepped outside in his boots and jacket. There was no rain for the moment, so he decided to walk. The half-hour he'd been inside had brought warmth back into his muscles and bones, and he felt ready for the air again, or just about. A strict breeze from the northeast bumbled down the hill, flooding the valley, and Sandy winced as it pawed his face. The night was dark, but the sparse necklace of house lights on the road ahead showed the way. Behind, his own outside light was on, declaring, as was the tradition here, that he wasn't home.

Sandy paused at the door of the Red House a moment before knocking. The curtains were closed in the living room, but the lights were on, and he could hear footsteps coming from there towards the hallway. He stepped back and smiled.

'Hello?' the man in the doorway said. Sandy saw his eyes flick towards the road, perhaps noticing there was no car.

'Hi aye, I'm Sandy. Fae doon the road. I just wanted to say hello really, and welcome, and to bring you this. A hoose–warmin present.' He handed the card and bottle over, then stepped back again, ready to leave if necessary.

'Oh aye, Sandy!' said Ryan. 'I thought I recognised dee. Ah'm sure we've met afore. At a party or the pub or somewye.'

Sandy laughed. 'Nae doot,' he said, though he felt quite sure they hadn't. The man's face was only vaguely familiar. The football shirt draped over his jeans marked him out as someone Sandy would ordinarily try to avoid. A grin too close to a sneer.

Short hair, needlessly lubricated. Probably goes for pints with 'da boys' on a Friday after work. Probably thinks he's a fucking Viking, too.

And he's probably perfectly nice. Sandy tried to push the negative thoughts away and continued to smile.

'Will du come in fir a drink? Since you've so kindly provided some.' Ryan lifted the bottle and smiled. 'We havna got that far yet.'

Sandy hesitated. The thought of his own bed was pulling him away. But he couldn't say no. 'Aye, of course. If you're no too busy unpackin.'

'We're needin a break,' said Ryan. 'Du's come at exactly the right moment.' He stood aside and turned back into the house. In the hallway several small cardboard boxes were stacked against the wall. A shoebox was lying open with postcards inside. The one on top showed a picture of a white-sand beach and a turquoise sea. In large capital letters it said 'GREECE'. Ryan walked ahead of Sandy, leading him into the living room that, until a few weeks earlier, had been his own. 'Come in and sit doon,' he said, stopping just inside the room and motioning vaguely towards the sofa. 'I'll go and get some glasses.'

Sandy sat in a scarlet armchair that matched the scarlet sofa. He looked around the room, so familiar and yet entirely changed. It was still mostly empty. There were, as yet, no pictures on the wall, no books on the shelves, no ornaments or personal touches of any kind; only a blue glass vase that stood on the coffee table, with a clutch of daffodils splaying from the top. Sandy recognised the vase. He knew where the flowers had come from.

The stairs creaked – the top two had always been noisy – and the pad pad of socked feet descended to the hall. The door opened. 'Hello, I'm Jo,' the young woman said. And she smiled, a wide curve that lifted the corners of her hazel grey eyes and circled her cheeks with creases.

He stood up and walked towards her, hand outstretched. 'I'm Sandy,' he said. She stepped forward and shook his hand. A clutch of dark hair fell forward from behind her ear as she nodded a greeting.

'I've been sorting things out upstairs,' she said. 'Starting in the bedroom, so we have somewhere peaceful to escape to when all this gets a bit overwhelming. I'm not good with chaos.' She smiled. 'Ryan texted me from the kitchen to say you were here,' she added, then tightened her lips into a smirk and raised her eyebrows. The gesture left Sandy somehow helpless. He laughed and turned his head away.

Ryan arrived with a tray, interrupting Sandy's awkwardness. He was carrying the bottle of wine, three mugs and a wide carrot cake, together with plates and forks. 'Whit mair could we ask for?' he said.

Sandy laughed again. 'I see you've haed a visitor today,' he said, nodding at the cake and then at the vase on the table.

'Aye,' said Ryan. 'We have indeed.'

'Mary came down with them this morning,' added Jo. 'It was very kind of her.'

'Everything Mary ever does is kind,' Sandy replied.

'Weel, it's certainly the first time a landlord has brought me presents,' Ryan said approvingly.

All three of them sat down then – Sandy back in the armchair, Ryan and Jo on the sofa. Jo poured the wine and handed a mug to Sandy. 'I'm sorry about these. We haven't emptied the box of glasses just yet.'

'That's no problem at all. These are ideal.' He lifted his mug. 'Cheers! And welcome to the valley.' They did the same, then each sipped in silence.

Ryan cut the cake. 'I'm fantin. We've no had a chance to get much food in yet, so this is a godsend.' He passed the plates out and began to eat, shovelling forkfuls to his mouth.

'So, how long have you lived here then?' Jo turned and looked at Sandy. 'You were in this house before the other one, weren't you?'

'Yes, I moved here just over three years ago, with Emma, David and Mary's daughter. But she left last year. I moved a few weeks back.'

Ryan looked up, one eyebrow raised. 'Is that why du moved oot then? A bit weird, renting from dy ex's parents?'

'I'm still renting from them, actually,' Sandy smiled. 'David owns the hoose at the end of the road as well.'

'Aha! Quite the property tycoon he is, then.'

'I'm no sure he would look at it that way,' Sandy laughed. 'He's certainly no making a fortune off me.'

'So that must be strange, living here with them, is it not?' Jo asked. Her concern sounded genuine.

'Well, it's okay actually. We get on well, we just dunna speak much aboot Emma now, obviously. I guess it is odd, but . . .' He shrugged. 'It's working oot for the moment. I like bein here, I think, and they seem happy for me to stay.'

Jo looked at him, nodding as he spoke. 'They do seem like lovely people,' she said. 'We're lucky to have found this place.'

'You certainly are,' said Sandy. 'Folk were queueing halfway fae Lerwick to get this hoose, according to David. You two must be special.'

'Why did he turn them doon?' asked Ryan, scraping the last crumbs of cake from his plate, then washing it down with another swig of wine.

'He wanted young folk,' said Sandy. 'He's hoopin you'll stay for a while, become part of the community, that kind of thing.

I guess he was just wantin to help folk that's startin oot. He's sentimental like that.'

Ryan snorted quietly. 'Well, dat's ironic,' he said, looking furtively at Jo. She turned her eyes away.

'How do you mean?' asked Sandy.

Ryan took another gulp of wine, then poured more from the bottle into his glass. 'Well, he's certainly helping wis oot, but mebbie no in the way he thinks he is.'

'Oh?'

'I hae a flat in toon,' Ryan went on. 'Three bedrooms, like. I inherited it fae me nan, and we lived there for a year or so, but we figured we could rent it oot and get somewhere cheaper. Make some money. When we heard we'd got this place, we advertised wirs online and haed the paperwork signed the next day. We're gettin three times as much for it as we're paying in rent here every month. An we could of asked for mair, I reckon. So if we stick it oot here fir a couple of years . . .' He shrugged. 'We'll be doin pretty well.'

Sandy didn't smile, but tried not to look shocked. It was a perfectly logical situation, after all. Certainly from their side.

'Well, that soonds like a good deal,' he said. 'But I wouldna tell David aboot it, if I were you.'

'Why? Does he no like young fok gettin on for themselves? Is he wantin wis to stay dependent on his charity? I mean, we're very grateful he wants wis ta be here, but . . . du kens, fok have to get on in life.'

'Aye, that's true. But David doesna see things like other folk. If he did, he'd be chargin you a lot mair in rent.'

Jo winced. 'Well, we are very grateful,' she said. 'It's a big help for us, and it *is* such a beautiful place.'

Sandy nodded, allowing her to defuse the tension that Ryan seemed not to have noticed. It was clear from her expression that she felt uncomfortable with what had been revealed – uncomfortable, perhaps, with appearing to take advantage of someone else's generosity. Or perhaps she simply recognised Sandy's loyalty more clearly than Ryan did and understood better why discretion might be necessary.

Sandy sat back and smiled. 'It's certainly a bonnie place,' he said. 'Once the summer comes, you'll be glad you're oot here and no stuck in toon.'

'I know,' said Jo. 'I lived up north until I was sixteen, so I get nostalgic for the country, especially when the weather's good. Which is not that often.' She laughed.

'You lived up north till you were *sixteen*?' Ryan smirked. 'Aye, but only from when you were ten.' He turned to Sandy. 'She maks oot she's a Shetlander, but she's fae Cambridge really, as du can hear.'

Jo pursed her lips and continued. 'Ryan is a toonie, through and through. But he'll get used to it. He'll be out caain sheep before the summer's over.'

'Well, David would certainly be glad of the help,' Sandy said, grinning. 'As would I. But be careful, he'll have you hooked. I'd never even looked at a yowe afore I moved into this hoose. And now look at me: a crofter!' Sandy shook his head in mock dismay.

'Are you enjoying the croft?' Jo asked.

'It's a bit early to say. I always liked helping David oot wi the work. It always seemed more fulfillin than anything else I could be doin. But I suppose anything can be enjoyable when you have no responsibility. Now I have to think aboot it and worry aboot it and pay for it. An I dunna hae a clue yet what I'm supposed to be doin or when. I'm just relyin on David to tell me. I think he likes to be a teacher. I just hope that I can learn fast enough.'

'Do you no get bored oot here?' Ryan asked. 'You're kinda far away fae everythin.'

'Well, so are you guys noo,' said Sandy. 'And it depends what you need. If you're wantin to be in the pub or the cinema every night, you'll maybe no be happy. Otherwise, what's ta miss?' He stood up, smiling. 'If I was bored, I woulda left by noo. Instead, I'm moved deeper into the valley. Which is where I'm goin to return noo, as, frankly, I'm knackered, and you're likely needin to do a bit more unpackin tonight, afore you go to bed.'

Jo let out a long sigh, as though she were slowly deflating, her arms slack at her sides. 'I suppose we should,' she said. 'It feels never-ending at the moment, but we'll get there eventually.'

'No, you probably won't. There's always one box that doesna get emptied. You'll look inside and have no clue what to do wi it, so you'll shove it in a cupboard or in the loft, and you'll leave it there until you hae to move all over again. And you'll take it wi you, or if you're lucky you'll forget aboot it.'

'That sounds like the voice of experience,' Jo said.

'Aye, except in my case it's not one box, it's half a dozen, shoved in the spare bedroom where I dunna have to think aboot them again. I'm hoping that one day I'll open the door and they'll all have disappeared, magically.'

'I'm sure we can organise a bonfire for you,' said Ryan. 'I'm no very practical, but I can do a fire.'

'Ah, but I dunna want them destroyed,' Sandy said. 'I want them disappeared. It's very different.'

He walked towards the door, and Jo and Ryan stood up and followed him. Outside, he turned around and smiled. 'Well, thank you for the cake. It's very nice to hae some new folk here, liven the place up a little.'

'Thank you,' said Jo. 'Thanks for coming along, and for the wine, and for your kind words. It's very nice to meet you.'

'Aye, good to meet you, and I'm sure we'll see dee again soon,' said Ryan, though Sandy barely heard those words, for

Jo's were still shimmering inside him, like a deep vibration that ran through his nerves and into his guts. He took a slow, cold breath and stepped away, raising his hand in a farewell gesture.

'Cheers!' he shouted, turning his back on the house. He heard the door close but felt the presence of Jo still behind him. Stepping out onto the road and down towards his house, the thought of her seemed to him like a kind of intrusion, unwelcome and yet irresistible. He reached the end of the road exhausted and went upstairs to bed, pausing only once to look from the window towards the lights that shone in the Red House, where Ryan and Jo now lived.

FRIDAY,
25TH MARCH

When she thought about it, really thought, it just didn't seem possible that she could have lived so long. To be teetering now near the edge of old age, with work behind her and children gone away, was inconceivable somehow. Her youth did not seem long enough ago. The years did not seem full enough to be entirely gone. It was as though a trickle of water had run past her until a loch was almost empty. As though she'd nodded off during a film and now found herself in the final quarter, trying desperately to remember what had gone before.

When she first came to the valley, Mary dreamed often of the home she'd left behind. She dreamed of the street in Edinburgh where she'd grown up and where her parents still, then, lived – where they would continue to live for another twenty years, until her father died and her mother decanted to the suburbs. On that street Mary had played and laughed and cried. She had held hands, first with her mother, then, later, with Andy Buchan and James Brodie, puff-chested boys with greasy hair and clammy palms. Lying asleep, hundreds of miles to the north, she dreamed of the grey-faced buildings and the stripe of sky that hung like a sad banner between them. She dreamed of the green square at one end of the street and the church at the other – a church her father insisted she attend each Sunday, though he no more believed in God than he did in fairies. 'It'll do you good,' he told her. 'It'll do you good.' And perhaps he was right.

She dreamed of the tenement in which she'd lived: her parents, her two brothers, her sister and herself. They'd been comfortable, really. More comfortable than some of her friends. Her father, Robert, was a barber – his little shop a ten-minute walk away – and, as he was fond of saying, 'Sae lang as hair grows, I'll ae hae a job.' Which was true, up to a point.

He'd begun his business in 1946, nine years before Mary was born, and one year after he returned from Stalag XX-B, the prison camp near Marienburg, Germany, in which he had spent most of the war. That was a silent part of him, that time. He rarely spoke of it, never mentioned it unprompted. And if others brought up the war, as they sometimes did, he would loosen his focus or change the subject. But what he did say was that the camp had given him a career. When he signed up, he was sixteen, working in the North British Rubber Company at Fountainbridge, making hot water bottles. But when he returned, he was a barber. How he came to that position in the camp he never explained precisely, but that's what he became. He would cut the hair of British soldiers, and some of the Germans too. They would give him cigarettes as payment, and sometimes even chocolate. It gave him a purpose, that work, gave some meaning to his time. Within a few months of returning home he had rented a little shop, which he later bought, and hung a sign above the window, the letters painted white on red. Soon, a steady flow of customers, many of them ex-soldiers like himself, came through the door.

By the time Mary was ten, Robert had taught her to cut his hair, which she did every weekend. 'A barber cannae afford to look scruffy,' he'd say. Her first attempts were rough, but her father was patient, and Sandra, her mother, was always on hand to avert any disasters. Later, Mary looked forward to the time she and her father spent together, as close, then, as they ever would be. As she moved around him, scissors clasped in her hand, he would sit, eyes closed, as attentive to her as she was to him. He asked questions about her week: what had she learned in school, what was she reading, what was she planning to see at the cinema. And she told him. She spoke freely and without fear of judgement. For her father was a man who was easy to like. She rarely saw him angry, and never once was his anger directed at her. He was a quiet man who'd seen things he wanted to forget, and who covered the memories that must have roiled inside him with a calm cheerfulness that, to those who did not know him well, might have seemed impenetrable.

Mary remembered his shop, where she'd sit sometimes after school, listening to the customers talk. (She was, he said, the only woman allowed in during the week. Only on Saturdays was the rule relaxed further, when mothers brought their sons to be sheared.) She remembered the sound of the place – the chatter and snip – and she remembered, too, the smell: the sharp tang of the tonics and the barbicide, the warm leather of the chair from which the men looked back on themselves in the mirror. It was, for her, a place of unending fascination.

Returning home from work each evening at half past six, Robert would sit at the kitchen table while Sandra cooked. At those times he wouldn't speak a word. He sat, contained in himself, gazing at the walls or floor. It was as though he was sifting through all he'd heard during the day, choosing what to absorb and what to discard. 'A barber hears many secrets, and keeps them aa,' he used to say. Confidentiality was as important to him as it was to a doctor or a priest. He stored away those stories like a miser. A wealth that could never be spent.

It was during Mary's early years that Robert first began to be challenged by change. His younger clients no longer seemed satisfied with the cuts he gave. To begin with, they came less often. Boys who had previously visited every few weeks would not be seen for two months or more. And when they did return, their hair would be oiled and shaped and combed back, slick as an otter. The boys didn't dare, at first, to ask for anything different, so Robert would return their heads to the states in which he'd last left them. But increasingly he heard requests for styles he didn't know how to cut, for ducks' tails and pompadours. Or else the boys brought photographs torn from magazines, showing film stars and singers: Tony Curtis, James Dean, Elvis Presley. Robert felt himself overtaken by change, and he could no more stop it than he could have stopped the war, fifteen years earlier.

At first he resisted in the only way he knew how, by refusing to cut hair in anything but the traditional styles. But he recognised, quickly, that such resistance was worse than futile. Not only could he not stop these changes but by trying to do so he risked harming his business. And that would make him a fool. So he learned. He did what was asked of him. It didn't make him happy, but it made him a living.

Mary was too young to notice how her father was affected. The changes began not long after she was born, and by the time she was ten years old he had long since ceased resisting. But as she reached her teenage years, in the late 1960s, she came to see that her father was part of a very different time. Though he was not an old man, he had still somehow been left behind, clinging to something that had once seemed like certainty but which was now entirely out of his grasp. The world he had returned to after the war had slipped away from him, and he seemed lost and uneasy, not carried by the current but trying only to keep his head above water. He never quite succeeded.

Perhaps, when she first met David, that was what she recognised: a man out of time. Even back then, in the late 1970s, after oil arrived and Shetland was hurtling in a new direction, David had seemed to have an odd relationship with time. He didn't look towards the future, the way others did, but nor was he stuck in the past. David seemed to live in a kind of eternal present, looking neither forward nor backward but always, somehow, towards the land. So focused was he, indeed, on that present, that to begin with Mary wasn't even sure he had noticed her at all.

She was a young teacher at the primary school in Treswick, just a few miles from the valley, and David was the person she called to fix anything that needed doing in the school. He replaced the tiles that fell during the winter storms. He fixed the boiler when it stopped working, as it often did. In the summer holidays, he repainted the classroom.

When they first met, David had been courteous rather than friendly. He kept their conversations to a minimum. 'I didna think du'd be interested in whit I haed ta say,' he told her later. But she *was* interested, and she was also lonely. Though she loved her job, loved the handful of children who attended, she also missed home. She missed her family and the friends she'd made at school and at college. Her neighbours in Treswick were welcoming, but she sensed a nervousness among them, as though a single woman without local connections was a kind of risk. Nobody said it, but she sensed it.

Whenever she and David did talk, she would try, increasingly, to push him, asking questions about what he was doing, his other work, about other people in the village. David didn't gossip, not like some of those she spoke to, but he did eventually learn to speak to her without always seeming like he needed to be elsewhere. He learned not to fidget. He told her that he still lived at home with his parents, though he was five years older than she was, and he told her quite a lot about sheep. That, presumably, was the part in which he expected her not to be interested. But instead she found herself drawn to him. She found herself caring.

David then had been, if not exactly handsome, an attractive man in his own way. He was tall and stood straight-backed in a way that many of the older crofters couldn't manage, and which he himself would struggle to maintain in later years. He was clean-shaven and solid-jawed, and his hair, far from the neat, short cuts of which her father approved, always looked like he had just rubbed his hands through it, which often he had. He wasn't scruffy, exactly, but he was always heading in that direction. Even in clean clothes and newly showered, he looked like he'd been at work in the shed. But there was a kind of quiet dignity with David. He was confident in what he knew and in where he found pleasure. Confident, it seemed, about everything except Mary. And that, ultimately, was how she guessed that her own interest in him might well be reciprocated. For this solid, certain man would increasingly seem nervous and awkward around her. He avoided her eyes whenever possible, and when they did look at each other he would blink and wring a shy smile that flickered like an apology at the corners of his mouth.

That smile, Mary thought, years later, was one of the most beautiful things she had ever seen. It was the sight of a man upended by his own emotions, dazzled by the possibility of something he had never dared to anticipate. When she reached out to him, finally, it was like reaching over the gunwales of a boat to a man flailing in the ocean.

These days, Mary hardly thought back at all to the time before she moved to the valley. Or at least, when she did think back, it was not with the wistfulness that people of her age were supposed to feel. She still missed certain things. She missed, now and then, the busyness and anonymity of a city, though she went south a couple of times a year to visit her siblings, which was often enough to get her fix of that. But the landscape of her dreams had long since ceased to be the landscape of her childhood. Like her husband, she felt herself now fully enclosed within this valley that had, for over thirty years, been her home. The time that came before this time felt as though it belonged to another life, or to another person. Even her parents, both now dead, seemed distant to her. In a sense they always had done. Growing up, she had felt her home to be something from which she would, once old enough, escape. It was a feeling she knew that David had never had. It was a feeling, she hoped, that her daughters had never experienced either. At least not in the same way. Emma lacked her father's certainty, but she was drawn to this place as much as she was pulled away. She loved it, even as she left it. Kate, on the other hand, seemed not to feel strongly either way. She lived in town, visited often, but had never seemed unsettled wherever she was. Whether Kate and Emma saw their parents as belonging to another time, as Mary had felt about her own father, it was difficult to say. Perhaps they did.

Turning onto her side, looking at the man asleep beside her, Mary saw someone who certainly did not and never had belonged to the future. The future, when it arrived, would always take him by surprise. But he wasn't, as her father had been, stuck in the past. The time in which he was stuck was still here, now, and it would be here, now, again tomorrow. The present always had plenty of room for David.

The clock beside the bed said 7.23. The alarm was set for half past, but Mary knew that her husband's eyes would open in the next few minutes. Though they set the alarm every night, it rarely had a chance to ring. David would wake just before the allotted time and turn it off. Mary, sometimes, would lie in bed a little longer while he showered or made their breakfast, but this morning she had been awake for more than an hour already and was ready to move. She leaned forward and kissed David's forehead, his skin warm against her lips. She stood up, dressed and went to the window. The valley was drab, almost sepia, and bathed in a thin, softening fog. In the park, the sheep were quiet and alert, looking at each other as if unnerved by the morning.

Mary went downstairs to the kitchen. She filled the kettle and set two mugs on the counter. She put a pot on the stove, poured oatmeal and covered it with milk. She turned the hob to low, then stood and listened. The kettle, bubbling. The rumbling of the oats as the heat coursed through them. The quiet complaint of the floorboards upstairs.

'Morning, love,' Mary said, looking up from the porridge.

David crossed the kitchen towards her, placing his hand on the back of her neck. He leaned forward and kissed her hair. 'Good morning. How's du?'

'I'm okay. I didn't sleep too well. Woke up lots of times. But I'm all right.'

'Ony reason, particularly?'

'No, I don't think so. My brain was just turning things over.'

'Turnin whit over?'

'Oh, you know. Sandy, Emma. Everything that's happened. I miss her being near, that's all.'

'Aye, me too,' David nodded. 'Me too.'

'I'm fine though, really. I've got nothing to worry about, I suppose, so I'm worrying about nothing.'

'Aye, dat's dee,' said David, pulling out a seat at the table. Mary set a bowl of porridge and a mug of tea in front of him, then another of each at her own place and sat down. He unfolded a newspaper and began to read.

'They seem lovely,' said Mary, changing the subject, as her thoughts drifted down the road.

'Wha does?' he asked, looking up from the paper.

'Jo and . . . oh, what's her man's name again? Ian?'

'Ryan! Oh aye, dey seem fine. Were dey here?'

'No, no. I went down a few days ago, just to say hello, and I bumped into them again yesterday evening, on the road. I said to them to come up here if they're needing anything.'

'Aye, dey ken dat. Are dey needin onything?'

'No, they seem to be just fine. But I wanted to make sure.'

'Dat's good. Ah'm glad ta hear it.' David turned a page, then let out a long breath between pursed lips. He shook his head, muttering 'Idiots!', then closed the paper and folded it once. He looked at his wife. 'Ah'm pleased dey're here. They seem lik fine fok. I think we're been lucky.'

'Yes, I think you're right. You chose well,' she smiled, then stood to gather their dishes.

'It'll aa wark oot, I reckon,' David said. 'Dunna du worry.'

★ ★ ★

Since David brought Maggie's boxes round to the house more than a month ago, they had lain unopened in the spare room. Alice was busy with other things. She was busy editing her earlier chapters, carving them into shape, and with writing what she could about insects, which wasn't much but was probably enough. An introduction to the invertebrates of the area: that's all she needed, and that's all she could do. With the help of her books, and an amateur entomologist, Colin, whom she'd met in Lerwick, she'd made a start. A good start. It was coming together.

The boxes had not crossed her mind often since they'd arrived. The door to that room was closed most of the time, and she had little reason to go in. There was a double bed in there, for when her brother Simon and his family came to visit; there was a chest of drawers, mostly empty; and there was a shelf of books she'd read and didn't want to read again. That was about it.

But last night, lying awake, Alice had thought of them. She'd remembered first the look on David's face as he dropped them off, the evening after they'd spoken by the burn. There was a smile on him that night, not quite the same as the smile he usually wore. It was the look of someone who knows something you don't, and who knows how you'll feel when you find out.

'When do you want them back?' she'd asked him, as he carried the last box in from the pickup.

'Nivver,' he said. 'Wi ony luck.' Then he laughed. 'If du thinks ony o it wid be o interest ta me or ta her family, juist let me ken. An if du's needin rid o it aa den Ah'll tak dem back. But it'll likly end up i da laft if du's no wantin it, so Ah'm in nae hurry fir dat.'

There were ten boxes in total, though none of them large, and judging by those that had been opened, each was packed full of notebooks, letters and assorted sheets of paper. When they arrived, Alice had hidden them away deliberately. It had not been the right time to start exploring what was there. The very thought was overwhelming. She had a sense, somehow, that the contents could be important, but the sheer quantity of it made her nervous. It was hard to imagine how she might weed out what was useful from what was not, without reading every word. There had been no stress though, no hurry. She had not felt the need to get started or to get them out of the way. She had plenty of other things to do, and the spare room would not be needed again until at least September, when her brother was due to visit with his wife and children.

So it wasn't obvious, then, why exactly she had sat up last night, unable to think of anything but these boxes. There seemed no reason for it, no trigger she could identify. They just came to mind, unheeded, then refused to leave her alone. She lay for hours, in fact, imagining what might be inside, pressed by an urgency that was neither logical nor ignorable. Twice, she almost leapt out of bed to come through to the spare room, and twice she talked herself out of it. Wait, she thought. They'll still be there in the morning.

Now, the morning was here, and Alice had not slept nearly as much as she would have liked. She ate breakfast in the kitchen, made a cup of coffee, then another. She read the first few pages of last Friday's *Shetland Times*. She postponed what she'd spent hours thinking about, the way, as a child, she used to postpone opening her Christmas presents until everyone else in the family had opened theirs. That clench of anticipation was somehow more comfortable to her than its release.

Breakfast done, coffee drunk, she cleaned her teeth then went through and sat beside the boxes on the bed, looking them over. She stood up and went to her office, then returned with a tall, blank notebook, sticky labels and a marker pen, ready to impose some order. She began at random, with a view to systematising along the way. That was how she did her research: dive in and start gathering whatever came to hand. Then, as she went along, she would think about how it might all be divided, labelled and understood.

She picked one of the boxes and peeled back the lid. Inside were stacks of letters in envelopes, some of them strapped together with elastic bands. They all looked to be handwritten – personal, not bills – and there must have been well over a hundred, or perhaps even double that. Alice took one out. It had been opened with a knife, the envelope sliced neatly along the top. She put her fingers inside and removed the letter, taking care not to crease it. The signature was Ina's, Maggie's sister, dated March 1985. She drew out another, also from Ina. Then more. She checked the signatures, then slotted them back in the box. Flicking through the envelopes, she saw the handwriting on all of them was the same, the stamps all from New Zealand. Alice closed the box and peeled a sticky label from the roll. She pressed it on to the cardboard, wrote 'LETTERS: INA' on it and moved on.

The next box also contained letters. Most of them, too, were from Maggie's sister, though a few envelopes had different handwriting. Lynette, the signature said, again with New Zealand stamps. The niece, she guessed. She would have to check with David. She made another label.

The next two boxes held notebooks: journals by the look of them. Shiny black and red hardbacks mostly. On some, a year had been etched into the spine with blue pen, but others had no indication of what they held. The pages themselves were covered with a broad scrawl, not easy to decipher. Alice merely glanced over a few pages without reading properly, then closed them again and moved on. The journals would probably contain more of interest than the letters, but she wanted to get through all the boxes before looking in more detail. She wanted to get it right.

Over the next couple of hours, Alice opened three more boxes of journals, two more boxes of letters – mostly from Ina, though there were other, unfamiliar names there, too – and one box of random papers and official-looking letters in folders. To each of the boxes, she affixed a label.

By the time she'd finished looking through all of the boxes, it was close to twelve, and, though the day was wet and bound thick with fog, she decided to take a walk. There was something voyeuristic about what she was doing, she thought. It seemed odd for her, who had hardly known Maggie at all, to have access to all this personal information. Really it ought to have been David who went through them, if only to take out anything he wanted. But he didn't seem to want anything and, as he'd said, Maggie's family would not thank him for posting ten boxes of paper across the world for them to sort out, especially when half of it had come from New Zealand in the first place. Better to do it here, close to home.

Striding through the drizzle, Alice looked down towards the house at the end of the road. She couldn't see it yet — the fog hid most of the valley — but that was where she was aiming. She thought about Maggie, the woman she had hardly known, the woman she would see sometimes on walks like these, out feeding the hens or pottering in the garden, sometimes just leaning on her walking stick looking out at the fields or towards the beach. Alice wished that she'd made more effort to speak to her, to get to know her. That old hopeless wish.

She reached the turning circle and leaned against the gate there for a moment. A memory came back to her. A day quite unlike this one, warm and bright, the summer after she first arrived in the valley. She had been leaning just here, against the metal gate, when Maggie had shouted over from the garden, 'Is du lost?' The old woman was standing beside the fence with her hands cupped above her eyes, shading them from the sun. She was wearing a long dress, a deep green with white flowers patterned over it, and what looked to be a dressing gown hanging over her shoulders.

'No, I'm not lost, Maggie, I'm just enjoying a bit of sun on my face.' She'd smiled wide.

'Aha, it's you,' said Maggie, 'fae up the road. Sorry, my eyes aren't that'n good any more.' She spoke in a strange, stilted way, Anglifying her voice so that Alice would understand. It was as though she'd taken elocution lessons but only turned up for the first week.

'That's okay. I don't have a very memorable face either,' Alice joked.

'No, I suppose you don't,' Maggie said, looking down towards her feet. She seemed to be poking at something with her stick, engrossed suddenly in whatever it was that she could see and Alice could not. Nothing was said for a moment or two, then Maggie looked up again and seemed almost surprised to find that Alice was still there.

'Well, it's no a bad day anyway,' she said. 'That's a mercy.'

'No, it's lovely. A few more days like this would be great. Then we can say we've had a summer.'

'Aye, but we can't be greedy, lass,' Maggie replied. 'We take what we're given and be thankful. That's what the Auld Fellow said, was it no?' She waved her walking stick heavenward, her mouth now cocked into a grin. 'Typical man,' she added, then laughed and turned away. 'Well, we'll see you again, no doubt.'

'Yes, have a good day,' Alice called. 'See you soon.'

She laughed again, remembering, as she walked back up the road towards Bayview, her waterproofs swishing in the quiet, wet air.

It's funny, Alice thought, a few hours later, as she lay belly down on the sheepskin rug in her study, a sheaf of letters open in front of her. It's funny what people decide to record, the information they choose to share with each other. The very fact that Ina's letters had been kept – hundreds of them altogether, going back decades – brought to them a weight, a significance, that the contents seemed firmly to contradict.

Most of them began with a bland note of gratitude – *Thank you for your letter, Thanks for the card, Thanks for your kind words* – a greeting that seemed entirely unnecessary given how regularly they wrote to each other. These openings were oddly formal, too, and would be followed, invariably, by an account of recent weather conditions, often in considerable detail. *This month has been hot*, Ina wrote in one, *too hot mostly, you would have hated it. It rains in the evenings sometimes, which is a relief, so the garden is thriving. You wouldn't believe the colours at this time of year. It's nothing like home at all.*

'Home,' Alice thought. Home is still the place Ina left behind.

This morning there's a few more clouds about, so a change is maybe coming. It's funny how quickly you tire of sunshine. You long for it all winter and then complain about the heat when it comes. I'm sorry, I know you'll be sitting there with the fire on all day at the moment. It's hard to imagine now how it must be there. I wish our seasons were the same.

Alice picked up the next letter, written two weeks later. More of the same. More rain, a bit less heat.

From the weather the letters mostly moved on to answering questions – often the same ones month after month. Ina would say how Lynette was doing in school, then at university. Alice guessed that grandchildren might appear at some point, but she hadn't reached them yet. Ina's health was sometimes mentioned, and her husband Graham's too. Occasionally Ina would write of something she remembered from childhood, or ask Maggie to remind her of something, to expand on some detail she'd thought of, to clarify her memories. She would ask how the garden was doing, or enquire about the house, the croft, the neighbours. These, for Alice, were the most interesting parts.

Reading through the letters it seemed that, beyond the odd formality with which most of them began, the two women wrote to each other as they might once have talked to each other. The banal details were the kind of thing that occupies a mind in the course of a day, particularly here: the weather, the state of the ground and the garden, the everyday activities that are the unexceptional bulk of a life. The two women's thoughts, their memories, were so entwined that the geographic separation felt false. They were half the world apart and yet, in these letters, they were hardly apart at all. They were chatting across the fence to each other, sister to sister. Perhaps, had they tried to imbue their correspondence with more significance, the distance would have been amplified. Banality brought them closer together.

For the rest of the afternoon, Alice read letters. She read scores from Ina, then a few from Lynette, which were even less engaging: the polite words of a niece who had never really known her aunt but who, presumably, felt a sense of responsibility to keep in touch. There were other correspondents, too. There was a William, in Aberdeenshire, and several women from elsewhere in Shetland. Some of those letters were written in dialect, which slowed Alice down.

She sorted the envelopes as she went, though most were already in date order. She kept Ina's separate, putting the other writers in a box of their own, creating a new label. She wrote their names in the notebook, making a list on which to consult David later.

By late afternoon, she was bored of the letters. It seemed there was little in these correspondences that would be of any interest to anyone except their recipient. And there was little to make her feel she was getting to know the person to whom they were addressed – which is what, after all, she had wanted to do. She put aside the letters, then, and took out a box of journals. She opened one at random.

SUNDAY,
1ST MAY

S andy stood beside the fence, just watching for now. The ewe was turning in circles, as though trying to investigate her back end, to understand where the pain was coming from and why. She was uncomfortable, that was obvious, but she wasn't yet in trouble. Sandy had learned not to call for help too early. Twice already he'd rung David in a panic, worried that a sheep was needing help, and both times he'd been wrong.

'Nothin needs doin here,' David had said. 'Shu'll sort hersel oot. Laeve her tae it.'

So far, the only one that *had* needed help Sandy hadn't seen at all. He'd been at work, and David had spotted it lying against a fence, unable to deliver. He'd gone to her and assisted, pressing his hand inside the mother and manoeuvring the first lamb until he could drag it, front legs first, out onto the grass. The second had followed without any trouble. Sandy had come home to a note on his kitchen table: *Gave a yowe a hand. All fine now.*

Part of him was hoping for problems. Not because he wished harm on the animals, of course, but because, for the time being, he felt useless. And without experiencing difficulties himself, without watching and learning, he would remain useless. That wasn't any good for him, and in the long run it wasn't any good for David either. Or for the sheep.

He was watching this ewe, then, with a mixture of feelings. The past couple of weeks had been tiring and exciting, and filled with a strange, almost inappropriate sense of pride. 'It's da best time o year,' David had told him, in mid-April, as the date of the first lambs approached. 'Dis is when du gits ta be a faither mony times ower.' Sandy had laughed at the suggestion then. But when they did start to arrive he immediately understood. Controlling your emotions, suppressing sentimentality, were essential for running a croft. Life and death were all part of the job, and you couldn't be carried away by it, lifted and sunk by each day in turn. It wasn't possible to live like that. But for now, for these few weeks of lambing, getting involved was excusable. It was inevitable.

'If yon sight doesna mak dee happy, quit noo,' said David one morning, just after four, as they stood together in his shed, watching a new mother lick the afterbirth from her twins, the rough comfort of her tongue triggering life in the pair of them. The lambs lifted themselves to their feet, wobbling, trembling, their knees stiff and unsteady, limbs splayed. Slowly, as though drawn by a weak magnet, a force they could neither understand nor resist, they moved towards their mother's teats, seeking them out for the first time. She looked up then, still licking her lips, moved, no less than her twins were, by something mysterious, something that was bigger than all of them, bigger than everything.

The colostrum that filled the lambs' bellies then seemed to make them grow almost before the men's eyes. The animals straightened and strengthened with that first meal inside them. Sandy and David stood watching for a long time. Both were tired, after days of broken sleep, but they couldn't turn away from what was happening in front of them, a ritual that was utterly normal and yet utterly extraordinary.

'Well,' said David, finally, pushing himself back from the metal gate of the pen, 'I suppose Ah'll try and get anidder coupla oors horizontal. Du should probably do the sam.'

Sandy nodded. 'Aye, that's likely a sensible plan.'

The pair of them had stepped out into a morning that was itself only just coming to life, but which already was overflowing with it.

Sandy's thoughts drifted from the animal in front of him back to those of the past few weeks. His mind turned and rolled, concentrating, relaxing. He watched the ewe, now lying awkwardly on her side, and waited to see how the birth would progress. Above him, a lapwing lolloped through the grey sky, chasing itself from one side of the valley to the other. A bird, a black shape, an absence.

'Is she okay?'

He hadn't noticed Jo come up alongside him, so he jumped when she spoke. Then, as he turned to her, he felt a crick in the centre of himself. It was a strange sensation, like when you turn your back the wrong way, feel something give, something amiss.

'She's okay,' he said, turning back to the field and the expectant mother. 'I'm just makin sure she stays okay. I worry too much. I'm a first-time parent,' he said. 'Unlike her.'

Jo smiled. 'I can understand that. I don't think I could do it, you know. I'd never be able to sleep for worrying about them.'

'Who says I can sleep?'

Both of them were silent for a moment, standing, watching.

'Do you have many left to go?' Jo asked.

'I'm aboot halfway. They should be done in a couple of weeks, unless there's a few stragglers, which there might be. It was David's Cheviot ram, and I think he was gettin braaly tired by the time he was doon here. He's gettin old too.'

They both laughed, then fell silent again.

For the past month, Sandy had been fighting and failing to keep Jo from his mind, fighting and failing to suppress the awkwardness of his attraction. It was circumstantial, after all. He knew that, or thought he knew. It was a manifestation of his loneliness. Jo was a surrogate for Emma, or something like that. He had worked it out, explained it to himself. But that didn't make it go away. In fact, his feelings seemed somehow more imperative once he'd established they were false. And the more he tried to quash them, the harder it was to think of anything else.

He had hardly seen Jo for the fortnight after that first meeting at the Red House, and he hadn't spoken to her at all. Once, as he drove up the road, she had been outside and they'd waved; and once, when he was at David's, she had appeared, looking for Mary. Sandy had turned and walked towards the shed, trying to keep his distance. He knew that distance was his best hope. Sitting in his living room in the evenings, he could see the lights from the old house glowing. They were a beacon, a warning to steer clear, and he followed that advice. But when David and Mary invited him for dinner one night in early April, he found, to his horror and delight, that Jo and Ryan had been invited too.

The evening was good. Everyone enjoyed it. Ryan had irritated Sandy a little, but mostly his attention had been elsewhere. He wondered on several occasions whether Ryan was deliberately trying to goad David, talking about money and about crofting in a way that seemed too close to teasing. But when Sandy quizzed him about it later, David had seemed oblivious. He liked Ryan. 'He's a toonie,' he said, 'but he's fine. Means well.' Sandy was far from certain that Ryan did mean well, but just as he found his loneliness tangled up with his desire for Jo, he found that desire equally entangled with his dislike for Ryan. He couldn't prise the two things apart, and so he tried, as best he could, to keep that dislike to himself, just as he had, of course, to hold on tight to the desire.

The first time they were alone together, two days after that meal at Kettlester, Jo and Sandy hardly spoke at all. His fear kept him close to silent, and she – shy perhaps, or discomfited by his quietness – had said little more. He had been stepping out of Billy's shop, in Treswick, a bag in each hand, just as she arrived. He paused, waiting. 'Hello, Sandy!' she called, walking towards him as he stood, unmoving, in the car park. He felt paralysed. So intense and convoluted were his feelings then, it seemed impossible that she wouldn't notice. It was as though his desire glowed just beneath his skin. Once, two years ago, Mary had walked in to the Red House as Sandy and Emma were having sex in the bedroom. They heard the door and jumped into their clothes, then slinked down the stairs into the hallway, Emma first, then Sandy. If Mary understood what had happened she didn't let on, but that feeling – that crimson brimming, that surfacing of shame – was how Sandy felt, then, in Jo's company, as though he were utterly transparent to everyone, and most of all to her.

Sitting down in his car, outside the shop, he leaned forward and rested his forehead against the steering wheel, his heart gasping. He closed his eyes and dragged air to his lungs. He tried to untether himself from the mess inside. He breathed, quietly, until a tap against the window brought him back, upright and awake. He wound down the glass.

'Are you okay?' Jo asked. 'Is your car not working?'

He smiled, weakly, trying not to seem shocked or deranged. 'No, I'm fine,' he said. 'I'm just tired, and I had to make a phone call. Don't worry.'

'Oh, you can get a signal here, can you? I get nothing.' Jo shrugged. 'Okay, I thought something was wrong. I'm glad it's not.' She turned to leave. 'Well, I'll see you soon I hope.' She walked back towards her own car. He waited until she'd pulled away before he started the engine and drove in the wrong direction for a mile, to give her time to get to the house, then turned back and drove towards home.

That evening, he gave in and added Jo as a friend on Facebook. He added Ryan, too, but didn't even glance at his profile page. He scrolled through all of Jo's photographs, when she accepted his request an hour or so later, cursing himself as he did so. There was a kind of self-torture to the act, and a sting of voyeuristic guilt. He turned, then, to Emma's page, reading all of her posts from the last six months. He'd read them all before, several times, but he was searching for something now, he wasn't sure what. He found only a glimmer of regret, and considered for a moment calling her on the phone. But he didn't. Distance, again, was the solution. They'd both agreed.

'What are you thinking about?' Jo asked, after a long silence.

He turned to look at her and tried to explain it with a smile.

'I'm thinking aboot that yowe, I suppose.'

'No, you're not. You're looking at the sheep, you're not thinking about it. What's to think about? You can see how she is.'

'Well, maybe I wasn't thinkin then. Maybe I was just lookin. Sometimes it's no easy to tell the difference. My eyes and my brain are quite close together, you know.'

'Yes,' Jo said. 'You just seemed like you were thinking about something important. You were frowning.'

'Sorry, that's just my face. It's a frowny one.'

'Do you always joke to try and avoid talking?'

'Do you always ask difficult questions?'

'Sometimes. Not always. I ask difficult questions when I want to know the answers. If I don't ask, I'll never know.'

'And why do you want to ken?' The question seemed more unfriendly than Sandy had intended. He was trying to avoid sounding flirtatious, but he couldn't find the right tone.

'Well, we're neighbours. You seem interesting, but I know very little about you. Maybe I'm being nosy, but I'm just trying to be direct. I'm asking you instead of asking someone else. I hoped you'd be okay with that. I'm sorry.'

'No, it's okay. You dunna need to be sorry. But I'm no sure I'm all that interesting. I do think aboot sheep quite a lot. At least this year I do.'

'Well, that's all right. If you find them interesting, then they're interesting.'

'I don't know if "interesting" is the right word. I find them *necessary*. At the moment, anyway. I have to think about them. I'm responsible for them.'

'But you chose that, didn't you? It's not like you're here against your will. You must have *wanted* to think about them.'

'I'm no sure if *wanting* had anything to do with it. I'm no sure what I want, exactly. I used to ken, but now I don't.'

'What do you mean by that?' Jo asked. Sandy wondered what he did mean by that.

'I guess some days I feel like I've just found myself here, like I've been dragged here on some kind of current. Other people have made the choices; I've just gone along wi them.'

'So you're not happy then?'

'No, I wouldn't say that. I am happy. Most of the time, anyway. It's no ideal takin on the croft on my own, when there's so much I hae to learn and do. But it's aaright. I'd still be on my own whatever I was doing. This is as good a place to be alone as any.'

'But you don't want to be alone, do you?'

'Ha! Not forever, no. But I'm better company as some folk.' He smiled. 'I'm not desperate. Yet.' Part of him flinched, though he wasn't sure if he flinched at the lie itself or at the fear of being disbelieved. Part of him wanted to be disbelieved. 'So are *you* happy here?' he asked, reversing the focus of the interrogation.

'Yes, I think so.' She offered a hesitant smile. 'It suits me. More than the town, I reckon. Ryan is not so sure about it, but that's to be expected, I suppose. He's never lived in the country before. It'll take some getting used to.'

'Are you secretly hoping you won't have to move back to toon?'

'Well, we'll see. If we save up some money and sell the flat, we can buy a house anywhere, really. If we decide we like it out here, we can look for somewhere nearby, or a piece of land to build on. And if we don't, there'll be somewhere in town.'

'And what if one of you wants to stay and one of you wants to go?' It was a stupid question, a crude attempt to force a thought between her and Ryan. He regretted it as soon as the words left his mouth.

'I guess we'll just have to cross that bridge when we come to it. I'm probably less fussy than he is. I can manage wherever I am, near enough. At least I think so. I hope so.'

Neither of them said anything for a moment, and they continued to say nothing as a car came down the road towards them. Mary was driving. She stopped alongside Sandy and Jo and rolled down the window. Sandy leaned over.

'David's been trying to call you,' said Mary.

'Oh, sorry, I left my phone inside. What's up?'

'He's got a yowe that's needing a hand, and he thought you'd want to come and help out. I thought you'd have better things to do, but he insisted I come down and check. It's entirely up to you.'

'No, of course, I'll come and help. I was just watching one of my own,' he said, 'but she seems to be doin okay.'

'Right,' said Mary. 'You can come back up the road with me then. If you wait, he'll likely have it all sorted.'

'Okay, yeah, I'll come wi you.' Sandy turned to Jo. 'I'm sorry to rush off and abandon you,' he said. 'I need to go and help. Well, I need to go and learn.'

'That's okay,' Jo answered. 'You go on. Nice to see you, Mary,' she added.

'Yes, you too,' said Mary, as Sandy jumped into the passenger seat. He closed the door and held up his hand to Jo in a wave. She waved back as Mary turned the car at the end of the road, then drove back towards Kettlester, Sandy's heart pitching like a lifeboat in a storm.

★   ★   ★

It was not the quantity alone that made reading Maggie's journals and letters difficult. The contents too slowed Alice down. For several weeks, she had read and sorted and made notes for hours each day. She continued with her other work – writing and editing through the evenings, mostly – but once she had started on the pile of boxes she couldn't bring herself to stop. There was little in any of them, though, to help her along, to make the effort feel worthwhile.

The first diary entry she read had set the tone.

May 23rd 1989. Dry, mostly. Best day there's been aa week. Wind light fae soothwast. 53°F. Morning in the garden, weeding, planting oot kale. Soup for lunch – tattie and carrot. A bannock. Back oot this afternoon checking on lambs. A few limping. Beach Park braaly weet, especially the wast corner. Picked rhubarb. Made stew – lamb, tattie, neeps. Took some up to Willie this evening. Sat for an hour with him, watched the news, then hame. Cold evening, but clear. Tomorrow will likely be fine again.

And that was it: a day in the life. The handwriting was large, sprawling, so it filled most of a page. But with what? The details she recorded were even more banal than those in Ina's letters.

Weather, work, food. That was all. Short sentences. English studded with a few Shetland words. Amounting, it seemed, almost to nothing. Some days Maggie wrote about what she'd watched on television; occasionally she recorded snippets of conversation she'd had with others – with Willie, with David, with Mary – and sometimes she described her work in more detail. But mostly that was all she allowed herself: a hundred words or so describing each day, without so much of a hint of what she was thinking, how she was feeling.

There were more than twenty notebooks in the first box she opened, and five boxes of them in total. Most, in fact, were not diaries at all. Dozens of them contained nothing but shopping lists. *Milk, bread, dog food, oats, honey, WD40.* Page after page of domestic trivia. Others related to the croft, with notes on sheep, lambs, feed and planting times. There were several that held only numbers – weights, measures, prices, calculations – but with little to indicate to what those figures might refer.

There were other books too, with drafts of letters – most of them, naturally, to Ina. Alice was able to match some of these with their replies, and to start, then, to get more of a feel for the conversation. That was satisfying, certainly, and she would admit to some small excitement as she pulled these pieces together. But the conversations themselves were hardly more illuminating than the contents of the diaries. Maggie's letters were, if anything, even less personal, less revealing, than Ina's had been. So far as Alice could tell, the two sisters had carried on a conversation for more than six decades that hardly ventured any deeper than chit-chat.

Yesterday, she had finally reached the end of the last box. She hadn't read every word of every page, far from it, but she'd opened every letter and every notebook. She'd written down the names of each of Maggie's correspondents; she'd divided the journals up by their contents, labelled them.

Only once in all of this had Alice felt she was intruding in a stranger's private life. Indeed, reading these thousands of words, it had been hard to think of Maggie's life as private at all, so bereft did her writing seem of anything like intimacy.

It had been intentional, that one intrusion, a conscious effort to seek out something hidden. Upon finding the diary for the second half of 1980, when Walter had died, Alice went in search of grief. She wanted to locate the human being behind all these words. But what she found was nothing. Literally nothing. There was no entry on the day of Walter's death, in late November. There were no more entries for the rest of that month, in fact, or that year. The remaining pages all were blank.

Alice scoured through the journals, then, looking for the next one. But the silence continued. There was no diary for 1981, it seemed. She put the notebooks in date order, double-checked them. But there was nothing. Not until January 1982 did the words continue. And when they did, everything was back to normal. The entries resumed, in regularity and in subject matter, exactly as they had been while Walter was still alive. It was as though Maggie had made a New Year's resolution to write again and had stuck to it, banishing the blanks that were the only evidence of her loss.

Alice had been struck by this, had thought about it for a long time. At first she was horrified. There was something cold in Maggie's refusal to open up, even to her diary. There was something strange about it – perverse, even. But in recent days she had reconsidered. She had never kept a journal, not since she was thirteen, and even that had lasted only a few months. She had burned it two years later, had torn the used pages out, crumpled them and thrown them in the fire, embarrassed already by her juvenile ramblings.

She had always written, from that time till now, just never

about herself. Or at least not directly, not in the first person. It was hard, of course, to avoid yourself when writing fiction, even when your characters were murderers and policemen. She was there in each of her books, in each of her characters: a thought here, a turn of phrase there, a fantasy lived out in fiction. But never more than that. Never had she tried to recreate herself on the page, to share herself in words.

As she reread some of Maggie's journal entries again, she remembered that – her own reluctance – and felt sorry for having been so judgemental. She felt sorry for wanting what she herself had never given. But still, sitting amid those detailed records of Maggie's existence, she couldn't help but wonder if this could really be all that was left of a life. Was this all it amounted to: a pile of paper where once there had been a woman?

Even with all these hundreds of thousands of words around her, she couldn't get a sense of who this woman had actually been. Maggie was ghostlike, as if she'd hardly lived at all. Only there, on those missing days in 1980 and that absent year of 1981, was there a hint. Only there, in those silences, was there something recognisable, something familiar.

Alice wrote nothing after Jack died. When she'd finished her last book, in the final weeks of his illness, she put down her pen and closed her computer. With that obligation fulfilled, there seemed, then, nothing worth writing for. The whole act, indeed, of manufacturing sentences, of filling pages, seemed not creative but wasteful. How much time, in the years she shared with Jack, had she lost to her writing? How long had she been looking away from the world when she ought to have been living in it?

Until then, Alice had never needed a reason to write. Even before it earned her any money, she wrote every day. Not for pleasure, exactly – there wasn't always enough of that – but simply because *not writing* didn't feel like an option. It was just a thing she did, like getting up in the morning, cleaning her teeth, or calling her mother on a Sunday evening to chat. But with Jack gone, with the future and the family they had talked of gone, her lack of a reason to write became a reason not to. Cauterised by grief, she became silent. She wrote nothing more until a few months after she'd arrived in Shetland.

This morning, Alice read from those diaries again. She read slowly, with care, the days leading up to Walter's death, and those first entries of 1982 – as though searching for something she knew was not there, some way to understand this woman, about whom she seemed to know so much and yet, simultaneously, so little. In those pages, it seemed – in the words left unwritten – Maggie might still be found.

* * *

The knock came just after eight in the evening. Sandy paused. Most visitors would come in without waiting for an answer, but the door didn't open. He stood from his seat in the living room and went towards the porch. He recognised Jo through the frosted glass, and his head, again, flooded. He had not washed or changed or looked in a mirror since he'd come back from David's shed in the afternoon. He had a large hole in the sleeve of his jumper and a long, unidentified stain on the front of his jeans, probably mud, but possibly worse. He had eaten garlic in his dinner, and lots of it. He felt, and almost certainly looked, exhausted.

'Hello again,' he said. 'Come in. How's du?'

Jo stepped past him into the narrow hallway, and he held his breath. She was closer to him than she had ever been. He could have turned around and his shoulder would have brushed hers.

'Go on through,' he said, closing the door behind her. 'Are you wantin tea or anything?'

'No, I'm fine,' Jo said. ' I won't keep you long.' She looked left and right at the end of the hallway, where the kitchen and living room opened out. She turned right and took a seat in the far corner of the room, beside the window. She looked up at Sandy and grinned, or at least it was something like a grin. Sandy tried to read it, tried to untangle the motives that drove that tightening of the muscles. But nothing he was thinking could be detached from what he was feeling. His interpretation of Jo's actions was translated and distorted through a lens of his own desires.

'Well,' he said. 'Where did we get to before Mary cut wis off?'

Jo laughed. 'Hmm, I think I was telling you how happy we are here. Which was almost true.' She sat back. 'We *are* doing okay, you know. Pretty settled for the most part. Or at least I am. Ryan does plenty of complaining. But that's just Ryan. He's not happy unless he has something to complain about.' She lifted her eyebrows in a look of exasperation.

'Does that mean he's never happy then?'

'Well, maybe not,' said Jo, awkwardly. 'It can be difficult to tell sometimes.' She was quiet then.

'Are you aaright?' Sandy asked, looking at her directly while she looked away.

'I'm okay, yes, I'm fine. Sorry, I didn't come here to complain.'

'You can complain aa you like,' said Sandy.

'Sucker for punishment, are you? Well, I couldn't do it to you. Once I started I might not be able to stop.'

Sandy longed for her to start, but he knew that she wouldn't.

'Well, if you've no come here to complain, what did you come for?' The question could have been put better.

'I came to invite you over. We've decided to have a house-warming. That's what I meant to tell you earlier, but I didn't get the chance. Anyway, now everything feels fairly settled it seemed a good time to get everyone around. Even you.' She winked. A strange gesture. Or perhaps it wasn't. Sandy couldn't tell what was strange and what was not.

'That sounds excellent,' he replied. 'When were you thinkin?'

'Next Saturday. Would that suit you?'

Sandy nodded. 'Aye, don't see why no. Any particular time?'

'Maybe half-seven, eight? You can eat beforehand, but I'll have some snacks out too.'

'Can I bring anything?'

'Just yourself and whatever you're wanting to drink.'

'Okay, I'll do that.'

Both of them were silent then, for long enough that Sandy started to feel uncomfortable. He sighed, louder than expected, his tiredness rising in the heavy breath.

'Ha!' Jo laughed. 'I'll take that as a hint.' She stood up, lifting her jacket from the arm of the chair.

'No, sorry, I didna mean to chase you off,' Sandy said. 'It's been a long day, that's aa.'

'That's okay, I'm needing to head anyway. I'm trying to get round all the houses this evening.'

'Who've you signed up so far?'

'I'm still to speak to Terry, next door. We haven't really met him properly yet.'

'I canna think he'll hae plans. He hardly leaves the hoose at the moment. You'd mebbie better ask him tomorrow though. If he's been drinking tonight, he'll likely forget. He's a fine enough guy most o the time. Just a bit lonely.'

'Like you, then?' Jo laughed again.

'Aye, just like me.'

'Well, we can keep both of you lonely old men company for a night in that case.'

'That's very charitable of you.'

'It's not charitable, Sandy,' Jo smiled. 'It's something different from that.'

'Aye, you're right. It's something different.'

SATURDAY,
7TH MAY

'Come on, love, let's get moving. We don't want to be late.' Mary stood beside the front door with her shoes and coat already on. Her husband was still in the bedroom.

'We winna be late. We're nivver late. We'll be da first eens dere, as aalwis. Do I hae time to iron a shirt?' Mary heard the wardrobe open and the clatter of hangers.

'No, you've no need to iron a shirt. Just put a jumper over it and no one will see if it's creased.'

'Aye aye. Du's juist no wantin me to look too smart, in case I attract da ladies' attention.'

Mary laughed out loud. 'The *ladies*? What ladies is this I need to worry about? Jo? Or Alice? Or are you expecting anyone else to be there tonight?'

'Well, du nivver kens *wha* micht be dere. An du nivver kens whit micht happen. Ah'm quite a catch, I can assure dee.'

David was standing now at the bedroom door with a grin on his face. He had a dark blue and white Fair Isle jumper on, with the collar of a grey shirt escaping unevenly from the top. His thin salt-and-pepper hair was still damp from the shower and lay flat against his head, aside from a tuft above his right ear that protruded, stubbornly, like a tussock of thick grass in a mown field.

'Well, I quite agree. You're looking fine, my dear,' said Mary. 'Now, have you got everything you need?'

'I dunna ken. Whit do I need?'

'Nothing. I have everything here. A bottle of wine, beer, salad, chocolate cake.'

'Jo said no ta tak ony food, didn' shu?'

'Aye, she did. But we're not going empty-handed.'

'No, I should think no.' He grinned again at his wife. 'Okay, so we're ready den. If du juist gits oota me wye so I can git me jecket on.'

Mary stepped towards the front door and opened it. 'I've got the wine and salad,' she said. 'You pick up the beer and cake from the floor. And try not to drop it.'

Sam, the dog, looked up from his bed in the porch, as if to ask what was happening. 'Du can go back to sleep, boy,' said David. 'Du wasna invited, Ah'm afraid. It's no fair, I ken. Mebbie next time.' Sam's ears drooped, and he laid his head down against his paws. He watched David and Mary as they went out and closed the porch door behind them.

The evening was cool, but dry and calm. The light was curdling on the flank of the hill, yellowing, sweetening.

'Shall we tak da car?' asked David. 'Save carryin aa dis doon da road?'

She looked back at him. 'If you can't walk a few hundred yards with a six pack of beer in your hands, then you're not the man I thought you were, David.'

'It was dee I wis thinkin o,' he smiled. 'I dunna want dee ta git sore airms.'

'My arms will be quite all right, thank you very much.'

Once upon a time, neither of them would have dreamed of driving such a short distance. Today, had the weather been worse, Mary would have happily taken the car. The world had become so much smaller than it once had been – everything was more accessible now. But sometimes it seemed that what was nearby had become further away. What ought to have been close had grown distant.

They turned right at the end of the drive and walked down the hill, beneath the swooping, bubbling call of a curlew. The bird seared through the other sounds of the valley: the fissing of the burn, the steady wash of the waves down at the beach, the clap of their feet on the road, the excited lambs and their anxious mothers.

Mary sighed. She was struck sometimes by a sense, not of déjà vu exactly, but of time piling up, now upon now upon now. These sounds, this place, the journey from their front door to another door in the valley: they were so deeply layered within her that it was hard to prise the present moment away from those that had gone before. A palimpsest of evenings, of footsteps, of bird calls. If she tried to separate one out from the rest it seemed too flimsy, too transparent to be true. A few months back, she and David had watched a programme on television about three-dimensional printing. They could make almost anything that way now, it seemed. There were hearing aids, tools, even body parts, each constructed slice by slice. Perhaps memory is something like that, she thought then, a shape of shadow-thin layers. Except its final form is not predetermined or designed. It is random, haphazard and always incomplete.

The first time Mary made this walk was the day after she and David had moved in to Kettlester, when Maggie and Walter invited them down for dinner. They had walked hand in hand, then. They'd had no gift, nothing to offer, since the kitchen was still almost empty. That was why they'd been invited, and they knew it would be okay. They knew all that was expected was their presence, there in the house, here in the valley. Mary remembered the uncertainty she'd felt about everything then – everything other than that welcome. She had not really known how to talk to Maggie and Walter, for one thing. The couple were the same age as her parents, near enough, but they didn't treat her like her parents' friends treated her. They didn't treat her like a half-formed person, in the process of becoming someone else. Arriving in the valley, it seemed, Mary had ceased becoming and had instead become. Maggie and Walter accepted her as she was, and in doing so they offered her their trust. It was, at first, an extension of the trust they had in David, but it would become, in time, her own. That trust was one of the few things that would ever belong only to Mary. But she had no way, then, of knowing that.

'Hit's a boanny night,' said David, as they passed the gate into the lower park. The Red House was just ahead of them now, and the pair slowed, allowing the walk to consume more time. That change of pace was the only response needed to her husband's remark, and the two of them continued in silence to the door of the house.

Mary smiled at David and transferred the wine and salad into one hand. She opened the front door, looking back for a second, then stepped into the hall.

'Hello, hello, come in,' said Jo, emerging from the living room. She leaned forward and hugged Mary, then David, then led them through to the kitchen. 'You shouldn't have brought anything,' she said. 'I told you that, didn't I?'

'Yes, you did,' said Mary, setting the bowl of salad down beside the sink, then taking the cake from David's hands. 'Yes, you said that.'

'Well, thank you, anyway. They look delicious. What would you like to drink? And do you need any food now? You're the first here, but I'm sure others will be along soon. Ryan is just upstairs getting changed. He'll be down in a moment. We can go and sit through in the living room.'

She was talking too fast. Mary could see the anxiety coursing through Jo, could recognise her own younger self in Jo's fluster. She leaned forward and placed a hand on the girl's shoulder.

'Don't worry,' she said. 'A glass of wine will be perfect. David will have himself a beer. Come and let's sit down.'

Jo smiled, her lips squeezed in gratitude. David was already trying to find a space in the fridge for his beer, amid the food and drink packed onto every shelf.

'Okay, let's sit down,' Jo said. 'I'll have some wine, too, I think.'

By the time everyone had arrived, Jo already seemed a little drunk, as much on adrenalin and anxiety perhaps as on white wine, but drunk nonetheless. David too was drinking faster than usual, and Terry had obviously had plenty before he even left his house. Alcohol made Mary nervous. It always had, so she rarely consumed enough to feel more than a faint hum of relaxation. She trusted her husband when he drank. He became merely an exaggerated version of himself – funnier, more talkative, a little more annoying, but still the same David. Others she didn't trust, only tolerated, and Terry was one of those.

Terry's drunkenness seemed to exaggerate parts of himself he otherwise suppressed. Alcohol allowed those characteristics to rise to the surface. It lifted them, like a flood lifts debris from the ground. A kind of bitterness, a niggling sneer that he never showed at other times, was the first thing Mary noticed. He would throw snide remarks into conversations the way a child might hurl themselves at a flock of pigeons. The motivation was not anger, she thought; it was more a desire to exert some influence over a situation, no matter how destructive. And just as the child is disappointed when the pigeons lift off and flee, Terry would sometimes seem horrified and ashamed at his own interventions.

Tonight, he appeared more himself, gentler, when he arrived. But still he made Mary uneasy. She smelled the drink from him as he greeted her, the warm bite of it surrounding him like a fetid halo. She felt the smudge of his intoxication rubbing off onto her.

'Lovely to see you, Terry,' she said. 'How have you been?'

'Oh, du kens. Trying my best not to think aboot the misery of my existence,' he smirked.

'Life can't be that bad, can it?' she asked.

'No, no every day,' he replied. 'Sometimes it's worse. But I try to forgit those days.'

Mary had no interest in pandering to Terry's self-pity, even when it was wrapped up in a grin. 'How's Jamie?' she asked. 'I've not seen him recently.'

'Oh, he's here every fortnight. I juist struggle to git him to leave the hoose. I'm hoping he'll come for langer in the summer holidays. We're still negotiating, though. He's no as keen on the idea as I am.'

'He must be going in to third year in the autumn, is he?' She shook her head. 'Time rushes by, doesn't it? You see it move so much faster when there's children around.'

'Though for dem it feels much slower.'

'Yes, that's true. A summer seemed a lifetime at that age. Now it's like a heartbeat.'

'An I thought *I* was the depressin een,' Terry said. 'Right, I'm goin to git a drink. Does du want anythin?'

'No, I'm fine, thank you,' said Mary, cradling the same glass of wine she'd held for the past hour, sipping it, letting the sharp liquid touch her lips then fall back into the glass, barely a drop passing onto her tongue.

She sat down on the sofa, then, beside her husband, who was talking to Jo about sheep. It was difficult to tell if Jo was interested in what he was saying. If not, she was a good actress. In David's lap was a plate with a few lumps of potato salad. Jo was holding a piece of Mary's chocolate cake but wasn't lifting it to her mouth. Mary hadn't eaten anything.

'Da price wis better last year as it's been fir a while,' David said. 'But you nivver really ken whit it'll be until da day dey sell. Dat's da problem. Dis must be da only industry where du buys whit du needs at retail price – feed, machinery and so on – and den sells dee product at wholesale price. We're got it aa backwards really. Nae winder dere's nae money in it.'

'But that's not why you do it, though, is it?' asked Jo, smiling.

'No. If it wis, Ah'd be a fool. I do it because I couldna think of givin it up. If I mak ony money, it's a bonus.'

'And you get your own food out of it.'

'Aye, we do.'

'How many lambs do you kill each year?'

'At hame? As mony as we need wirsels. Dat's aa.'

'Can you sell your own home-killed lamb? Can we buy it from you?'

'No. Dat wid be illegal.'

'To sell to a neighbour?'

'In theory, aye.'

'And in practice?'

'In practice it would still be illegal.' David smirked.

'Okay, well, I wouldn't want you to break the law.'

'It breaks my heart to break the law, as du can imagine. But unfortunately law-makkers dunna aalwis ken whit's right fae whit's wrang.'

'So you might sell lamb to a neighbour, then?' Jo was laughing now.

'In theory, no.'

'Okay, I understand. Well, in theory we wouldn't buy any

from you anyway because it's illegal. In practice, we'll see how hungry we are by the end of the year.'

'You do dat,' said David, forking potato salad into his mouth, followed by a swig of lager. 'You do dat.'

'Well, my love, how's du?' He turned to Mary.

'I'm splendid, David, I'm splendid. Just needing a seat for a moment.'

'Well, du kens Ah'm aalwis blyde ta share a seat wi dee.'

'Thank you, that's very kind of you. And it's very kind of you, Jo, to invite us round.'

'That's quite all right. We meant to have everyone over earlier, but you know how it is. One week passes, then another, and you still haven't done what you meant to do.'

'I know that feeling all right.'

'But it's lovely to have you all here. Or at least it's lovely now that the panic is fading.'

'Nothing whatsoever to panic about. It's a lovely party.'

'Thank you,' Jo said, then looked up. 'Hi, Alice, have a seat, join us.'

Alice was standing beside the sofa but pulled in another chair and sat down. She wore a smile that looked, to Mary, too much for the occasion. Like ornamentation, or protection. But perhaps she was nervous, too. She wore a long patterned dress, and her hair was down. Mary had rarely seen it like that. It was usually pulled back in a tight ponytail. She looked younger like this. It suited her.

'How are you, Alice? How's things?'

'Oh, I'm grand, thanks, yes. Busy busy, as always. But that's my own fault.'

'That's the problem with being your own boss,' Mary said. 'If you're a hard taskmaster, then there's no escaping yourself.'

'Exactly,' Alice said. 'Exactly. Well, I'm certainly that. Mostly it's okay. I like what I do. But occasionally I could do with a break.'

'I think we could all do with a break from ourselves sometimes.'

'Yes, that's true.'

'An how's du gettin on wi Maggie's things? Ony use ta dee? Ah'm guessin no.' David leaned forward to speak.

'Most of it is probably not much use, I suppose. She wrote about the weather a lot, which is only interesting up to a point. But there's some of it that I might be able to do something with. I'm just not sure what exactly.'

'Du's no been through it aa yet, has du?'

'Pretty much, yes.'

'Christ! Dat's dedication. I read a few pages an dat was enough fir me.'

Alice laughed. 'Yeah, some of it was a bit dull.'

'Du can say dat ageen.'

'Was she like that in person, though?' Alice asked. 'Not dull, I mean, but, you know . . . I'm interested to find out what she was like.'

David hesitated. 'Well, I dunna ken whit ta say, really. Shu wisna dull, no. At least, I didna think so. Shu wis fine company, most o da time. Shu wis funny. Shu telt a lot o stories.'

'What kind of stories?'

'Well, du kens, juist stories aboot fok. Aboot da valley. My parents, her parents, idder fok at used to bide aroond here.'

'What else can you tell me about her?'

'I dunna ken, really. Shu wis juist . . . normal.'

Mary intervened then, patting her husband on the arm. 'Maggie was much like David, in some ways. Her interests more or less ended at the top of the road.'

'Aye, dat's aboot right.' David nodded, raising his eyebrows.

'It must have been strange for her, then, having her family at the other side of the world.'

'I can't even imagine what she thought about it,' said Mary. 'She used to speak about Ina and Graham as though they were just in Lerwick. She'd tell you what they were up to, how they were doing. But she hardly ever saw them. They came over maybe once every five years or so, when Lynette was young, and Maggie even went over there a couple of times, though I can't remember what she thought of it.'

'Fine enough,' David said. 'Dat's aa shu ivver telt me aboot New Zealand. Hit was fine enough!' He laughed, shaking his head.

'Livin here,' said Ryan, leaning in close, 'do you no find it kinda . . . *restrictive* or somethin?'

Sandy could smell the beer on his breath, could feel the clammy warmth of it on his face. He shifted his feet to make some distance.

'In what way?'

'Ach, du kens. It's lik du has to live by stricter rules to fit in. Lik du has to conform.'

Sandy shrugged. 'I dunna feel like I'm conformin. I'm just . . .' He shrugged again. 'It's no as simple as that.'

'So does du feel as free here as du did afore, then? In the city?'

'What does du mean?'

'Well . . . free to be dysel. And to do what du wants.'

Sandy shrugged again. He wasn't deliberately trying to annoy Ryan, but the questions seemed pointless somehow. He sighed and made more effort to answer.

'I dunna think I felt free like that in the city,' he said. 'No really. And onyway, I feel like a different person noo. I couldna be *this* person then because I wasna *here*. And I prefer this person to that one, if you see what I mean. At least at the moment.'

'Yon soonds lik bollocks.'

'Mebbie,' Sandy went on. 'But I guess what I mean is that I was pretty comfortable bein that person, there. And noo I'm pretty comfortable being this person, here. Most o the time. That's aa.'

'And is du ever mair as comfortable? Lik happy, for instance?'

'Same thing, is it no?'

'I dunna think so.'

Ryan turned to Terry then, who'd said nothing throughout the exchange. 'Well, what aboot dee?'

'What aboot me?'

'Is du . . . happy?'

'Look at me. Whit does du think?' He took a swig from his can. 'But Ah'm no sure at I rate happiness as highly as dee.'

'Du's a weird bastard, Terry.'

'I try me best.'

They all laughed then, relieved that Terry had allowed them that.

'And what aboot *free*?' Ryan went on. 'Does du feel free here?'

Terry looked away and drank again. He seemed to wince as he considered his answer. 'Well, my parents were married when dey were eighteen. That's braaly young, I think. Dey grew up togither, then lived togither. Dey were hardly ever apart. I dunna think dey were ever *free*. No in the way du means. But I dunna think either o dem woulda ivver felt *unfree*. I think dey foond freedom athin the boondaries they chose. Some people can do that. Dey need to see the limits o their freedom in order to feel free. But . . .' Terry paused, as if he'd lost his train of thought. 'Mebbie it's aboot choices. Du chooses dy boondaries and du lives wi'in them. Du chooses dy cage and du lives in it. Efter a while, du dusna see the bars.'

'That soonds great,' said Ryan. 'But it's definitely bollocks.'

'Aye, it might be,' Terry agreed. 'An I certainly dunna feel free, so . . . what the fuck wid I ken?'

'No, I think you could be right,' Sandy said, as much to rebalance the conversation against Ryan as to prolong it. 'Look at David.' He lowered his voice, nodding across the room. 'He hardly ever even leaves the valley, but he dusna seem restricted to me. And I dunna think I ken a happier person as David.'

'I didna say onything aboot happiness,' Terry interjected. 'The twa things aren't the same. Du can be free and miserable or du can be a happy slave.'

'So why would you want to be free if it didna make you happy?'

'Du's got to aim for somethin.'

Sandy shook his head. The conversation was going nowhere in particular. Terry didn't have the will to keep it from sinking into nonsense, and Sandy was too distracted by his dislike for Ryan. He wanted to walk away and speak to someone else. Yet somehow that dislike also attracted him, drew him closer, the way one is drawn to disgust, to an operating table, or to someone tearing off a dead toenail.

'Sandy, du went to uni, did du no?' Ryan was talking again.

'Aye, to Edinburgh. I didna finish, though. Only managed three years.'

'What did du study?'

'Geography.'

'And du's a taxi driver?'

'Aye.'

'Ony particular reason?'

'No really. I've done a few different jobs afore, but I like driving. It stops me feeling restless. So it works for me.'

'Does du plan to carry on, or does du want to do somethin else in the future?'

'I dunna plan, I just *do*, and at the moment I'm still doing. Next week, wha kens? Next year . . .' Sandy shrugged again. He hated this question, but he hardly ever had to face it any more. His father had long since given up asking. He'd only ever done so in the first place, Sandy assumed, because he thought that's what fathers were supposed to do.

Terry was swaying now, shifting his weight from one foot to the other. He still looked as though he were trying to concentrate on what was being said around him, but his focus had retreated, drawn inwards, as the effort of keeping himself upright increased. Sandy felt protective, then, wishing to save Terry the embarrassment into which he seemed determined to dive.

'Fancy somethin to eat, Terry?' Sandy asked. 'I'm hungry again.' A bit of cake, he figured, might be just enough to keep Terry conscious.

'Aye,' Terry said. 'Mebbie some of yon cocktail sausages.'

'I'm no sure there's ony o those left,' Ryan chipped in. 'Du's aaready finished them aff.'

'Well, I'll see what I can find. Gie me a minute,' said Sandy.

He stepped away from the two men and into the hallway, then carried on towards the kitchen. The door was slightly ajar, and as he pushed it open he saw Jo standing in the corner of the room, beside the oven. She pulled her sleeve over her fist as he came in, wiping her eyes and sniffing. He paused, then pushed the door closed behind him.

'Sorry,' Jo said.

'For what?' Sandy replied.

'For being a pathetic host who comes to cry in the kitchen.' She tried to gather a smile together.

'Well, you've been an excellent host so far. Plus, it's your party, so you can cry if you want to.' Sandy gave a grin, offering Jo a route out from the situation. But she didn't respond.

'Are you okay?' he asked. 'Well, obviously I can see you're no okay. But is there anythin I can do, other than stand here askin questions?'

'No, not really. I'm not exactly sure why I'm crying, to be honest. That sounds ridiculous, but it's true. I'm having a good time. I feel happy, really, with everyone around. I feel very happy. It's amazing. I think maybe that's just reminding me that I'm not always this happy. It's reminding me what's left once you lot go.' She looked up at him, tightening her lips.

'Ryan, you mean?' Sandy lowered his voice.

'Yes, Ryan. Or else, no, I shouldn't say that. I don't mean . . . Oh, I don't know. Life is complicated, that's all. People are complicated.'

'Well, that's certainly true.' Sandy longed to be having this conversation anywhere else but *here*, any other time than *now*. Somewhere that wasn't a few yards away from Ryan and all of their neighbours, sometime she wasn't drunk and liable to forget or regret everything she said.

'We're just very different, you know? Well, it's always been like that, of course. That was part of the attraction to begin with. The things I felt were inadequate about me were things that were not in him.'

'There's nothin inadequate aboot you,' Sandy said.

Jo looked at him with a half-sneer. She was even more drunk than he'd thought, and her reply sounded both cruel and slurred. 'You don't even know me, Sandy,' she said. 'You might imagine you do, but that's just wishful thinking. I'm probably nothing like you think I am.'

He didn't respond, just waited for her to continue, as he flinched inside.

'Anyway, he's not exactly . . . he's not what I . . . oh, I don't know. I shouldn't be telling you any of this.'

'Well, dunna worry, you havna told me *anythin* so far.'

Jo sighed, then shook her head. 'I'm sorry, Sandy.'

'What for?'

'For what I just said about you.'

'You dunna have to apologise. You were right. I don't know you. I just want to.'

'You're kind.'

'Why? For wantin to know you? That's an entirely selfish desire. It has nothin to do wi kindness.'

'Well, it seems like it from here. You're nice. Thank you, Sandy.'

'No need to thank me. I just wanted a piece of cake, and you got in the way.'

Jo laughed then. 'No, really. Thank you.' She looked up at him, her mouth cocked as though she might laugh again. But she didn't laugh.

Sandy felt a tightness in his chest, as if all his organs had grown suddenly too large for the space in which they were held. He felt a pressure in his lungs that reached up almost to his throat, and his heart thumped like an axe striking a log, over and over. He moved towards Jo, hoping she would speak again, fill the silence her words had opened up between them.

'We should go back through, Jo,' he said, almost against his will. 'Terry will be gettin impatient. I promised to get him some food. He's no in the best state.'

'No? Well, nor am I. We can go through in a minute. I'm just wanting a quick cuddle if that's okay. I'll feel a lot better after that. If you can manage.'

Sandy nodded. 'Yes, I can manage that,' he said, and leaned forward.

Jo's arms around his shoulders made his skin clench and shiver all the way down to his stomach. She pulled him closer, then turned her head and rested it on his shoulder. He held her body against his and tipped his own head just a little so it leaned on hers. He sighed. His fingers shifted over her dress, rubbing her back.

They stood together like that, barely moving, for several minutes. Neither of them spoke. Sandy wondered if Jo might be asleep – her breath whispering against his neck, gentle as cotton grass. He felt, beyond the welling of relief and desire inside him, a clench of terror, too. Neither of them was going to move, he realised. Neither of them would release the other until something made them do so. He waited for that something to happen, fear and elation colliding inside him in a toxic, intoxicating brew.

When the door finally opened, it was Jo who jumped first, pulling her head up off Sandy's shoulder and releasing her hands from behind his back. But not quickly enough. Sandy moved more slowly, resigned as he already was to being caught doing something that was little more than nothing but which looked much worse.

He didn't see Mary at all. He didn't turn around. He only heard her voice: 'Oh, sorry!' she said, flustered. Then the door closed again, and he heard her walk away. Jo and Sandy stood apart now, looking at each other.

'Well, it coulda been worse,' he said.

'Yes, fuck, yes, it could have been. But it's still bad. Fuck, I'm sorry. You need to go back through. She won't tell anyone, will she?'

'Well, she winna tell Ryan. Dunna worry aboot that.'

Jo seemed almost to shrink. Her arms drew inward around her chest, her head lowered. 'Fuck. Fuck! That was *so* stupid. I'm *so* drunk. Sorry. Go back through now, *please*.'

Sandy reached a hand out to touch Jo's shoulder, but she pulled herself away.

'Go!' she hissed.

He turned, picked up two plates and set two large pieces of cake on them. He found a single remaining cocktail sausage and set it on one of the plates, then went out into the hallway, closing the kitchen door behind him. His breath was racing.

SUNDAY,
8TH MAY

'I'm still not sure if it's a good thing us keeping both of those houses,' Mary said, over breakfast. 'It seems wrong, somehow. It makes me a bit uncomfortable, owning half the valley.'

'I ken. Me too. Ah'm no cut oot ta be a landlord, I dunna think.' David swigged his tea. 'Sandy'll mebbie want ta buy yon hoose affa wis eventually, if he's happy doon dere. I think dat wid be fir da best. But we'll see hoo he gits on.'

'Aye, well, it's early days for that. And to be honest I'm not sure it's very good for him being here anyway.'

'How no?'

'Oh, I just don't think he's as settled here as he's making out. He hasn't really got anyone for company except us and Terry. And Terry's a miserable so-and-so at the best of times.'

'He haes idder pals. An Jo and Ryan's here noo as well. Dey aa seem ta git on.'

'Aye, well. Oh, I don't know. I'm just worried about him.'

'Ach, he's fine, darlin. He's juist got a lot ta tak in at da moment. Hit's a big change, wi da croft. Once he settles in tae it, he'll be oot an aboot ageen. Dere's plenty a time fir him ta start lookin fir a girlfreend.'

'I'm not talking about *girlfriends*. I'm not even sure I want to think about that just at the moment. Emma's hardly out the door.' Mary shuffled uncomfortably. 'I just worry about him, that's all. He needs a life beyond the valley.'

'Why? I dunna.'

Mary laughed. 'No, that's true, but Sandy is not you, and I think we should try and help him stay that way.'

'And whit's dat supposed ta mean?' David asked, in mock outrage. 'Dere's worse role models as me, widn' du say?'

'There certainly are. But not everyone can be happy the way you've been happy.'

'Hmm, mebbie. Fok need ta learn hoo ta be happy, I think. Dey mak dere aen unhappiness half da time.'

'I'm not sure everything is that simple, love. Folk can't help how they feel, once they feel it. You're lucky. You shouldn't take that for granted.'

'I ken. But du's happy as well, is du no?'

Mary paused longer than she needed to, allowing David to consider the possibility that she might not be. His straight-mindedness frustrated her sometimes.

'Yes, I am. Most of the time. But not always. Sometimes I'm unhappy.'

'Why?' asked David, responding just the way she knew he would.

'I don't know. Sometimes I just wake up in the morning and I feel sad. You know that. I think about sad things. I think about things I wish were different, people I wish were alive, people I wish were closer than they are. I think about things I might have done with my life that I didn't do and now I never will.'

'Lik whit things?'

'I don't *know*. All kinds of things. I could have done anything. I could have had a totally different life from the one I've had, and sometimes I think about that. I wonder about it.'

'But du dusna regret bein here, does du? Du dusna regret the choices du's made?'

'No, of course not. It's not about regret. It's about only having one life and only being able to fit so much into it. Now I'm getting older I know there's less and less that I can fit in. That's not regret, exactly, it's just . . . I don't know, *imagination*?' Mary knew David would struggle with that. 'Most people just can't be as *certain* about everything as you are,' she said.

'How does du ken Ah'm aalwis certain?'

'I've known you almost forty years, love, and the only thing you're ever uncertain about is when to plant the tatties each spring.'

She leaned forward and cupped her palm over his cheek, feeling the stiff bristles of his face against her hand. Then she kissed him gently on the forehead.

He didn't look up but bit at his lip, staring through her.

'It's not a criticism,' she said. 'It is one of the many things I love about you. Doubt can be poisonous for some folk, but you never let it take hold. You're the same man you were when I first met you all those years ago. You think the same way and you feel the same way. You're like that burn out there,' she said, gesturing towards the window. 'Always moving but always the same. That makes me very grateful and very lucky. But it doesn't stop me thinking my own thoughts.'

David was silent. He looked hurt, and Mary understood why. She knew that, by reminding him of their differences, she was reminding him of the parts of her he didn't fully understand, that he couldn't reach. She also knew that, in conversations like this, David could be confronted by a sense of his own failure. He was not someone who ever judged himself against other people – that was something she deeply admired in him – but he did judge himself against standards that he himself had set. And high among those standards was a rather old-fashioned sense of responsibility towards the happiness of his family. The recognition that he did not have control over Mary's happiness, or the happiness of his daughters, was not news to him, of course, but he didn't like to be reminded of it. Mary knew that her own occasional doubts and sadnesses were a personal blow to him. In someone else, such an attitude might seem pathetic. In David, it was something quite different.

She smiled at him. 'I've never regretted for a moment the life I chose,' she said. 'I would choose it again if I had to live life over. Now drink your tea before it gets cold.'

She stood up and tipped the dregs of her tea into the sink, then rinsed the mug. She left David where he was and went out through the corridor and into the living room. It was just after nine, and neither of them had plans for the day. It wouldn't be very long before David was back to normal, as though they'd never had this conversation, as though nothing whatsoever had been said. He could be funny like that, switching suddenly into the most intense of sulks. But they were always short-lived. If she walked away, leaving him with a kind word or two, he would sit, as though absorbing those words fully, until he was ready to accept them. Whatever it was that had been troubling him would fade away, and then there he was, just as he'd always been.

It had taken Mary years to understand how to deal with her husband when he was like that, when he disappeared into himself in that way, like a mussel closing shut, excluding the world. It was so unlike the openness that she loved in him, so unlike the David everyone else knew. It had made her panic when she first experienced it, a few months before they were married. Until then, she had only known him as he usually was − solid and unshakeable − but then, without warning, he changed. They were talking about the wedding, making plans, and she noticed him wincing, as though he had stomach pains. His hands were clenched, and he rubbed his right forefinger repeatedly over the knuckles of his left hand. Then he stopped talking. She asked him a question, and he just didn't answer. Nothing. It wasn't a difficult question; there was no sharpness in her voice, no accusation. But he was gone. She called his name, but he said nothing. It was almost as if some kind of trance had fallen upon him, except his eyes were not glazed or dull; they burned urgently with life. He seemed engulfed by whatever it was his mind was doing, turning things over, an engine with nowhere to go.

On that first occasion, and for several years afterwards, whenever it happened Mary would try hard to bring him back, to prise open the shell he closed around himself. She would plead with him, stroke his face, tell him how much she loved him. She took responsibility for his disappearance. But when he did return – as he always did, usually before even an hour had passed – it seemed entirely unrelated to her efforts. It just happened. He was absent one moment, and then he was present again. The shadow passed without changing a thing.

David never apologised for these spells of silence. Nor did Mary ever ask him to apologise. But she did expect some kind of acknowledgement. It was so out of character, so seemingly unrelated to the person he otherwise was. But there was nothing. Most often, after a time he'd simply sigh, stand up and wander off. When he returned, it was as though nothing had happened. He'd be smiling, or humming under his breath, and though he'd sometimes rest a hand on Mary's shoulder, or lean over to kiss her hair, she never mistook those acts for apologies. Those were things he did anyway. They didn't mean sorry.

Mary learned that her best course of action was to do nothing, to walk away and try not to be affected. Soon enough he'd be back, and they could carry on as before. It went against her instincts, leaving him like that, when he seemed at his most vulnerable, but it was the right thing to do. That, it turned out, was when he needed her least.

So Mary waited in the living room. She was too distracted to read, but she closed her eyes and tried to think of something else. She drifted back, reluctantly, to the night before. To the Red House. To Jo and Sandy.

Mary hadn't told David what she'd seen in the kitchen at the party. She wasn't even sure what it was that she *had* seen. It might, conceivably, have been nothing. But it didn't look like nothing. She hadn't told David because she wasn't exactly sure how she felt about it, and a conversation with her husband was unlikely to clarify those feelings. *Och, it's juist young folk bein young folk*, he would say. *Hit wis juist a drunken cuddle.* Or words to that effect. But she wasn't sure if he would mean them, and she wasn't sure if she disagreed. She wasn't sure of anything much about it, really. Part of her had almost hoped, at the time, that she would simply forget, that the encounter would slip from her mind, so she didn't have to think about it again. She didn't want to think about it. It was none of her business, after all. But it worried her, for the moment, just a little.

From the kitchen, there was a stirring. A chair moved back from the table. Mary opened her eyes and waited. She heard David make his way down the corridor to the bathroom, heard him pee then flush then wash his hands, then go into their bedroom, leaving the door ajar. She got up and went back to the kitchen to put the kettle on. Any minute now David would be back, with a smile on his face and a thirst in his gut.

★ ★ ★

It wasn't clear if he was already awake before the banging started or if it was the banging that woke him. At first it was hard to distinguish whether the noise was in fact separable from the pounding in his skull, so closely entwined were sound and pain.

The night had ended late. Sandy's drinking hastened after the encounter with Jo in the kitchen – an encounter that replayed itself as he woke, as though it were an event long forgotten, then suddenly brought back to mind. What happened afterwards was not nearly so clear. It was muddled and patchy. But the kitchen, the conversation, the . . . what the fuck was that banging?

Sandy sat up in bed and expelled air from his lungs, a grimace fixed on his face. The noise stopped. He took a T-shirt from the wash basket and a pair of boxer shorts and his slippers. He shuffled out into the hall, then looked down the stairs. The banging began again. Fuck. Fuck!

The banging was knocking. A door. His front door. And at the moment of that connection – the image of a fist upon the glass – last night replayed again. The hug. Jo. Mary. Ryan. Fuck!

Each step down thundered through his body like the blast of a kick drum. He felt his bones jar and shudder, his brain tremble in its cave. Sandy went expecting Ryan. He went with the jagged anticipation of a guilty man striding to the dock. He tried to reassure himself that a hug wasn't much to get worked up about. And that was true. But preceded and embellished by those weeks of longing it seemed to him enough. Enough to be shouted at, certainly, and pushed, maybe. Or, if he was very unlucky, punched. It occurred to Sandy that the latter possibility might be less likely right now, dressed as he was. The dirty underwear might be enough to put Ryan off touching him.

Still, as he reached the bottom step and opened the door into the living room, he prepared himself for the worst. And frankly, the pain in his head was then so great that the thought of being punched was not nearly so worrying as it might otherwise have been. He looked up along the hall towards the glass door of the porch and saw the figure standing on the other side.

He was expecting Ryan. He was not expecting his mother.

'Well, you certainly know how to make a woman wait.'

Sandy looked at her, the door held open in his hand. It had been almost four years since he'd last seen her, and she'd aged. Her hair was cut short and dyed dark brown, and her jeans seemed looser, more comfortable, than she used to wear them. Her forehead was lined. Her cheeks, too.

'Are you not going to let me in?'

'I'm no sure yet. How did you find me?'

'You gave me your address, a few years back, when you moved, remember? Well, actually you gave me the address of that red house up the road. I went there first, and a girl sent me here. She didn't look well either, actually. Is there something going about?'

Sandy shook his head. He looked at his mother as though she might be a mirage – a hangover hallucination that could disappear at any moment, back to whatever corner of his mind she'd sprung from. But she didn't disappear. She stood looking at him, waiting, eyebrows raised expectantly.

He opened the door fully and turned around, walking back into the house, then into the kitchen. He didn't invite her, but she followed.

'Well, it's lovely to see you, Mam,' Sandy said, taking a seat on the high stool in the kitchen. His voice was expressionless. No trace of sarcasm, no trace of sincerity.

She looked at him. 'It's lovely to see *you*,' she said. 'Really, it is. I'm sorry it's been such a long time.'

'Yes, it *has* been a long time. And yes, an apology is necessary. But I don't accept it.'

'Well, my apology is meant. I *am* sorry. I could try to explain, but I—'

'Now is not the time, Mam. My head is fucking splitting. Do you want coffee?'

176

'Yes, please.'

Sandy filled the kettle, then clicked it on to boil. He fetched two mugs down from the cupboard and took a carton of milk from the fridge. He shovelled coffee into the cafetière.

'Oh, fancy coffee!' his mother said.

'You can have instant, if you prefer.'

'No, it wasn't a complaint. Definitely not a complaint.'

As the kettle boiled, Sandy tried to think if he had ever made his mother a cup of coffee before. Perhaps not. And if he had, it was so long ago that he had no idea now how she might take it.

'Milk, one sugar,' she said, anticipating the question. Sandy poured the boiling water into the cafetière, then reached into the cupboard again for the bag of sugar, showering grains over the work surface as he lifted it down from the shelf. He waited in silence for the coffee to steep, then pressed the plunger and poured it out, one mug then the other.

Sandy led the way to the living room and took a seat in the armchair. He made no attempt to speak, just sat clutching his mug, waiting for it to cool.

'This is a lovely house,' she said after a few minutes. 'And a beautiful place. Do you own it?'

'No, I rent the croft fae Emma's father.'

'The croft!' his mother spluttered. 'You're a crofter now? Seriously?'

Sandy didn't rise to the question, just nodded. 'Aye. I have a croft.'

'And Emma. How is she?' His mother had met Emma only once, when the three of them got together in a cafe near Trafalgar Square. Emma had suggested the meeting; Sandy had gone along with it.

'I've no idea, really. I think she's okay, but she moved south at the end of last year, and I've no seen her since then. We dunna hae much contact.'

'Oh, I'm sorry.'

'It's fine. It was mutual. Pretty much.'

'Well, I'm sorry anyway.'

They drank their coffee, then, slowly and in silence. Sandy closed his eyes, pressing his fingers to his lidded eyeballs now and then, trying to release some of the pressure from inside his head.

As the silence stretched out beyond five minutes, beyond ten, towards fifteen, and their empty mugs lay cold and stained beside them, Sandy finally gave in.

'Mam, why are you here?'

His mother looked at him. 'Does there have to be a reason?'

'We've no seen each other in four years. I've no even heard from you in the past *two* years, aside fae a Christmas card. So, yeah, there has to be a reason.'

'Well,' she paused. 'Trevor threw me out last month.'

'Trevor? Who is Trevor?'

'He was my boyfriend.'

'Your *boyfriend*?' Sandy laughed.

'Stop repeating what I say. Yes, he was my boyfriend. And I don't think it's very funny, what I just said.'

'Well, I do.' Sandy closed his eyes again. He felt a little better after the coffee, but the laughing hurt.

'So why did Trevor leave you?'

'He didn't leave. He chucked me out.'

'And why did he do that?'

'I don't really want to go into it.'

'Why no?'

'I just don't.'

'Did you cheat on him or something?'

'Sandy! I said I don't want to go into it.'

'Well, you musta done something wrong for him to chuck you oot.'

'Well, thank you for your support, son.'

'Is that why you came here? For support?' Sandy sneered.

'No, of course not.'

'Well, why then?'

'I'm not sure. I just felt I needed to come north for a bit. I felt a bit lost. I want to sort my life out, decide what I want from it.'

'You soond like a nineteen year old. You're fifty.'

'Forty-nine actually. And people don't change that much, Sandy, you know? It doesn't matter how old you get, you can still be confused.'

She was angry now, on the edge of tears. Sandy looked indifferent, though he wasn't.

'So what are you going to do,' he asked, 'noo that you're back?'

'I don't know yet. I'm going to figure it out as I go. I might get some part-time work for a while. I'm going to see what happens. But I wondered if I could stay with you for a bit. Until I figure things out.'

'Are you serious?'

'Yes, I'm serious. It won't be for long. If I decide to go south again, I'll be gone soon, and if I decide to stay, then I'll find my own place.'

Sandy stared at his mother, the woman who had walked out on his father and him twenty-two years earlier, the woman whose absence had shaped him, shaped every edge of him, whose indifference had cut him time and time again, and whose love he still craved, unwillingly. Sandy looked at her, and he wanted more than anything to shout: *No, just leave and don't ever come back.*

But that wasn't what he said.

Sandy stood up. 'Sure,' he said. 'Just make yourself right at home. I'm going back to bed.'

FRIDAY,
13TH MAY

Alice had spent the past week working in the archives in Lerwick, eating lunch in the cafe up the stairs, looking out on the little dock and on Bressay Sound beyond. It was hard to find a still point there, some place on which she could focus. Everything was moving. Not just the boats in the harbour but the herring gulls that muddled the air, and the waves, and the people below, and the bumbling clouds above. Everything. Sometimes, looking out through the glass, she found herself caught within all that movement and carried, her mind drifting like a bottle tossed overboard, on incalculable currents. When she returned, washed up again in the present, the food in front of her would be cold, her fish chowder congealed. Once, a waitress had tapped her on the shoulder, concerned, and asked if everything was okay.

And everything really *was* okay. Alice's mind drifted over her food because, for hours, she did not allow it to drift. She anchored it to the pages on her desk. In the hush of the archives, Alice read and cross-checked and followed footnotes back onto the shelves. She scrawled in pencil on an A4 notepad. She scanned through microfiche copies of the *Shetland Times*, peering through her glasses at the tiny print, checking dates, pulling things together.

None of the staff had asked her what she was doing. When she needed help to find something, they would look it out for her, occasionally making polite, whispered suggestions – 'If you want to know about *that*, you might also want to look at *this*' – but they never enquired as to *why* she might want to look. Even if they had asked, there wasn't a great deal she could have told them. She was trying to piece together the life of a woman who, so far as Alice knew, had hardly ever left Shetland – a woman who, in fact, had hardly left the valley in which she was born, and in which, eighty-eight years later, she had died.

Maggie was, most people would think, an entirely unpromising subject for a writer. If her diaries were to be believed, her life had been one of repetition and of drab concerns, with little drama, little in the way of *plot*. But Alice thought, or sensed, that Maggie was important. Something about her life, her story, made her part of the story Alice wanted to tell. She just hadn't figured out yet what that something was.

Perhaps, having trawled through those thousands of pages of letters and notebooks, it was Maggie's very elusiveness that appealed most. Despite having left behind this trove of words, the old woman herself had managed to remain almost invisible. It was curiosity that was drawing Alice in deeper. All those words had somehow conjured more blanks than they had erased, and the more Alice thought about it, the more she convinced herself that the blandness of the journals must be hiding some extraordinary truth.

There in the archives, she tried to build a framework in which the woman could be found, a shell that might contain her. Just as with her novels, she began with the details, with the basic facts of Maggie's life: her dates of birth and death and marriage, her family, her work. Then, around each of these facts, she began to sketch a picture, gathering information that might later be useful. She had historical notes, social notes, cultural notes. She wanted to know what life in the valley would have been like in the 1930s, Maggie's first full decade. What kind of place was it then? She checked the newspapers from key dates in Maggie's life. What was happening in Shetland on those days? Then she looked further. What was happening elsewhere in Britain, in the world? Somewhere in all of this, she hoped, was the woman she was looking for, hidden amid the details. Somewhere, a narrative would emerge.

Today, back at her own desk, she was trying to make sense of those notes, trying to figure out what to do with them all.

Alice thought of Maggie as she'd met her first, in the living room of the house at the end of the road. Alice had gone to introduce herself, at Mary's suggestion, soon after she arrived in the valley. Maggie had opened the door and invited her in. They'd spoken for twenty minutes, maybe a little more, and as they did so Maggie had continued to knit, glancing back and forth between her hands and her guest, the patter of the needles marking out a rhythm to the conversation. She was knitting a glove, in a Fair Isle pattern of navy blue, white and black.

'Ah'm sending them oot to my niece in New Zealand,' Maggie said. 'It's heading towards winter there.'

'Yes, I suppose it is,' Alice replied.

Neither of them said anything for a moment. Alice just watched the needles dancing, watched as the wool was coaxed into Maggie's hands, then transformed by them into something wonderful.

'Your niece is very lucky,' Alice said.

'Why's that?'

'To get such beautiful gloves.'

Maggie smiled. 'Well, Ah'll make you a pair sometime if you like them. It's nae bother.'

'I'd love that. Thank you!' Alice smiled, delighted. 'I could pay you for them, of course.'

Maggie didn't say anything to that, she just shook her head as if such a thing were unthinkable. Alice regretted mentioning money, but she hadn't wanted to assume the gloves would be a gift. That didn't seem right, so soon after meeting.

Either way, the gloves never arrived, and when the two women met again the subject didn't ever come up. Alice didn't want to impose or to be a pest by asking about them, but she wondered now, thinking back on it, whether Maggie had just been waiting for confirmation of her interest. Perhaps she had thought Alice's compliment to be merely politeness. Or perhaps she had been so offended by the mention of payment that she had chosen not to repeat her offer. It seemed strange that two people could say so little and yet still misunderstand each other.

That thought worried Alice a great deal. She fretted over it. Having failed to understand Maggie in life, having failed even to communicate with her in any meaningful way, how could she hope to understand her now that she was gone?

Alice sat back in her chair and looked up at the ceiling. She tried to picture the old woman again, to animate her, but the memory had stalled. She could dredge up Maggie's face, see the shape of it, the creases and the lines, but it wasn't right. It was blurred and lifeless now, like an unfocused polaroid. She felt herself squinting, as though her eyes might bring clarity to what she could not see. But it was hopeless.

She stood up, lifted a CD from the shelf beside the door, then opened the machine and settled the disk in place. The drawer clunked shut, and the player began to whirr.

The music arrived loud. Double bass and acoustic guitar tumbled into the room, as though escaping the silence that lay behind them. A shaker punched out a rhythm, simple and insistent. And then the voice, the wild, bellowing voice. Alice closed her eyes, leaning her head back against the music, resting on it as the strings shivered into life.

When they were at university, Jack used to play this album, *Astral Weeks*, on repeat. Alice had never heard it before – she was born a few years after it was released – but she soon became as hooked as he was. Sometimes the pair of them would get stoned and listen to it in his bedroom, but the drugs were not required. The music seemed to lift them and hold them all on its own, entranced, without letting go. There was something about it, something that insisted on their attention, their involvement. The band seemed to be feeling their way through the music, like they weren't sure what was coming next or what was expected of them. Even after hearing it a hundred times, there seemed the possibility that, next listen, everything might fall to pieces, might crumble into imperfect parts. And then there was Van Morrison's voice, bounding above it all. It seemed to soar, that voice, not constrained by the melody, not fixed to the music, but levitating, somehow, in a space entirely its own. The voice sounded untrained and unrestrained, and yet, as well, utterly precise.

Sometimes, when the pair of them were lying in bed, unsleeping, Jack would tap his fingers on the covers. She would see his lips trembling, and she knew he was listening to one of these songs in his head. So ingrained were they inside him that he hardly needed to play the music any more – he just closed his eyes and it was there.

Putting the CD on now did not bring Alice closer to her younger self. It did not make her forget, even for a second, all that had happened. She had not put it on for that reason. She played the CD because now, as then, it reminded her there was more beauty in the world than there needed to be, and that, sometimes, what was beautiful was also achingly sad. Listening to this album, she could cry and be grateful for the tears as they fell.

These days, Alice didn't cry often. Her grief had lost its urgency. Still sometimes it surprised her, caught her when she didn't expect it, like an old injury, forgotten then reignited. But mostly she felt numb to it, so conditioned to the absence of Jack that she did not, any more, feel that anything was missing. What she felt, instead, was old. Since Jack died, in fact, she had thought of herself that way. Some of her friends back home said the opposite: since turning forty they'd never felt younger. Alice wondered if that was self-delusion. Could they really feel that way? After all, the point at which one becomes old is surely the point at which anticipation is overwhelmed by hindsight. What was it her friends were still looking forward to, she wondered. Children getting older, leaving home? Promotions? Retirement? Maybe that was enough. Maybe that was all they needed.

Jack's death had crushed the anticipation Alice had once felt, the excitement she had about her – *their* – future. It wasn't just that all the plans they'd made were destroyed, that the children they might have had went unborn. There was also the strange, simple fact that her life was no longer a shared event. Anticipation, it turned out, was more difficult to sustain alone. A sense of purpose, of direction, was more difficult to sustain alone. She had lost, almost entirely, that sense of moving forward, of progress. She had lost her own sense of narrative.

Leaning back, listening, she danced. Not the way she and Jack used to dance around the room together, drunk and giddy. She just swayed, eyes closed, her steps not following the rhythm but feeling the beat inside her, feeling the words, the instruments, and the way they held together.

Since coming to the valley, Alice had felt herself changed. For decades, she'd thought she understood who she was. She knew what she liked, and what she wanted; she knew how she reacted under stress, and how she responded to pleasure. She was rarely surprised by herself. But after Jack died, the surprises began. After Jack died, it was as though she had to reshape herself. The basic material was the same, but the mould no longer fit the world in which she existed. She was forced to alter, to re-form. That was why she'd felt the need to move, to relocate to somewhere nobody knew her, to find a space where she could become herself again.

It had occurred to Alice more than once that her current work, this book filled with stillness, had been part of that process, part of that effort to remake herself. It was, after all, a kind of accounting: a log of all that was here, insured against loss. It was about seeing the island, seeing the valley, as clearly as she could, and understanding from that picture who it was she needed to be. Because she could be anyone now. She didn't need to be the Alice that her friends had known, or her family. That Alice was another person. This one was her.

The book was as much about herself as it was about her place, and somehow, in Maggie, she had found a subject that spoke to her in a new way. This woman – this old, dead, childless woman – had got a hold of her. She wished, often, that she'd made more effort to know her when she was alive. She could easily have visited, spoken to her. Maggie surely had been lonely, just as Alice had been. If she'd been a better neighbour, she would have gone to visit. But it was too late for that now, and it was no use regretting what she hadn't done. The book would be her penance. It would be her tribute to the friend she hadn't known.

Still swaying, Alice made her way to the cupboard in the corner of the office and took the bottle of whisky out. She poured a couple of fingers in a tumbler, then returned to the music, sipping then throwing back her head and closing her eyes.

★ ★ ★

Since the day Sandy's mother arrived, the two of them, mother and son, had barely communicated, other than at meal times. He went to work in the morning, then came home in the evening. He did chores around the croft, called David to ask his advice about a lamb that kept escaping onto the road – 'Fix da fence or fix da lamb,' David said. Sandy cooked for the first couple of days, then Liz took over. They didn't discuss it; she just made it her business to have something already on the stove by the time he came home, and that was fine by him. He never asked what she'd done with her days. He wasn't interested. At least he didn't *want* to be interested. He assumed that his mother's presence would be short-lived, that she would disappear as suddenly as she had appeared, and he refused to get used to her being there. Each day as he returned home and opened the door he expected to be met with silence, with an empty house, but each day the sound of another person greeted him as he entered.

'Is that you, Sandy?' Liz shouted as he hung his jacket in the hall and took off his shoes.

'Are you expecting anyone other?'

'No, but you never tell me when you're getting home, so I'm never sure exactly when to expect you.'

'Well, I dunna always ken when I'll be back.'

'Also, there was someone here earlier. He just walked in, too, so I thought it was you. We gave each other a bit of a shock.'

'Okay. Do you want to tell me wha it was?'

'I'm just trying to remember. He was older than me. Sixty.

Maybe more. Your height. Grey hair. John, maybe. Or Dennis. Said he was your neighbour.'

'David?'

'Aye, David, that's it. He said he thought this was your day off.'

'Okay. That's Emma's dad. My landlord. Did he want anything in particular?'

'He didn't say. I told him who I was, and he just said he'd give you a call.'

'Right, okay. Thanks.'

Sandy went upstairs to change his clothes. A pair of jeans and a tatty grey jumper replaced the trousers and shirt he'd worn all day. Taking them off, he felt he was shedding something more than fabric. The world outside the valley seemed to fall away too. He tossed them into the laundry basket and went back downstairs.

'When do you want to eat?' Liz asked. 'There's curry in the pot, and we can have it any time. I just need to put on the rice.'

'Mebbie half an hour. I'll just go up the road and see what David's wantin. I winna be long.'

'Okay, that's fine. Half an hour is perfect.'

Sandy knew he'd be longer. Not because the visit would take any time – he might, in fact, just phone David from outside – but because the thought of inconveniencing his mother was irresistible. He would be late to spite her.

Liz's arrival had forced son and mother into a cage whose bars were built of hurt and obligations. They faced each other off across this space, performing a silent balancing act, a convoluted manoeuvre, directed by disappointment and by the urge towards love. Sandy jabbed at her when he could, reminding Liz of her failures, and feeling guilty each time he did so. But not guilty enough to stop.

Liz, in turn, was doing her best to ignore these digs. Or at least it seemed so. She flinched sometimes, when he spoke curtly to her, but she didn't defend herself. He guessed she must have been truly desperate to have come running to him for help, but since that first, brief conversation on the morning she arrived, he had never asked for more details. He wanted her to think it didn't matter to him whether she stayed or went. He wanted to punish her with indifference, either genuine or manufactured. Most of all, though, he wanted to hide from his mother the insuppressible sense of relief he felt each evening to find she had not yet gone away.

Sandy crossed the drive to the shed and went inside. It was a small building, not much more than a garage, and it used to house Maggie and Walter's tractor. Now, it held a pile of scrap wood waiting to be sawed up, as well as the few crofting tools and accoutrements Sandy had so far bought or borrowed. There were several pairs of shears for clipping, each flecked with scabs of corrosion; there were paint markers and antiseptic spray; there were rubber docking rings, some strewn like orange sweets over the workbench; there were shovels and hoes and hay rakes; there were fencing pliers and a heavy maul.

At the back of the byre, beneath the window, there were four open boxes, torn and rust-stained, each holding a jumble of tools in various states of disrepair. These had once been Maggie's. Most had been rescued from the wooden lean-to out back, which leaked. Others had been brought from the house. Since he moved in, Sandy had intended to sort them, figure out what could be dumped, what could be saved and kept. He wanted to fix them neatly to a board on the wall, the way David had done, so they were always to hand when he needed them, if he needed them. But he wasn't really sure what he might need.

He tipped the first of the boxes out on the concrete floor,

then laid the cardboard aside. These had come from the house, it seemed, as they were mostly clean and free from corrosion. The usual assortment of screwdrivers and Allen keys were there, together with some hammers, wrenches and pliers. There were also several glass jars filled with nails and screws and washers and nuts, in no kind of order. Sandy laid the tools out neatly, then continued.

The next box was more of a mess. There were several more spanners here, though all but one were caked in a muddy canker. A pair of wire cutters were in a worse state, the blades a crusty orange, impossible to prise apart. Sandy knelt on the floor, inspecting each item, throwing them into three piles: those to be kept, those to be discarded, and those on which he couldn't yet decide. The third pile grew quickest. There were tools he couldn't identify, and others that were rusted or damaged but which might just be salvageable. Throwing things out was difficult. He wasn't a hoarder by nature, but he wasn't quite ruthless enough for this task.

By the time the fourth and final box had been emptied out on the floor, then sorted, roughly, into piles, the shed looked considerably more messy than it had done previously. Sandy put the tools he wanted to keep back into one box and set that up on the workbench, which stretched most of the way along the northwest wall, then put the ones for dumping in another box by the door. The rest he left where they were, ready to be inspected by David at some other time. He wiped the rust and grease from his hands on a rag that had once, by the looks of it, been a pair of pyjamas, then he went outside and closed the door.

The byre faced northeast, up the valley, and Sandy paused for a moment to look at the sheep in the nearest field. He was trying to develop the habit of noticing the animals, but he wasn't always sure what to notice. David would comment often on his own sheep, usually spotting a problem without even seeming to look for it. He'd nod and say, 'Yon yowe's limpin ageen, Ah'll need to fix her feet.' Or else, 'Yon lamb's no thrivin. His mither is fit fir naethin.' Sandy, meanwhile, would be struggling to work out which one David was even looking at.

This evening, all seemed normal. Mist was creeping up the valley – not thick, but enough to conceal the top of the hill. Everything, including the animals, was subdued, as if made heavy by the weather. Sandy stood, watching, and was struck in that moment by how beautiful it looked, and how still. He felt entirely at the centre of something, as though the rest of the world, and the rest of his own life, were a satellite of this place and this moment. Nothing was expectant. All was now. It was a peculiar sensation, not quite overwhelming but somehow disorientating. Sandy leaned against the corner of the byre, not thinking, just watching, listening, leaning, feeling the weight of his body supported by the frame of that building and by the ground beneath it. He sighed, bunched his fists into his pockets, waiting for nothing to happen, until it did.

'Sandy!'

He'd heard the door open but hadn't moved. He still didn't move, just lowered his eyelids a little and breathed deep.

'Sandy! Dinner's ready.' A pause. 'Are you okay? You've been standing there for quite a while. I could see you through the window.'

'Yeah, I'm fine. I'm good. I'll be wi you in a moment.'

He lifted his eyes again, scanned this way and that, taking in the valley, then turned towards the house. Inside, the table was set, and a pot of curry was steaming in the centre.

'Sorry, the rice is overcooked,' Liz said, without a hint of irritation – almost as though it were, in fact, her fault. 'But it'll be fine. Tuck in! I hope you're hungry.'

Sandy sat, served himself and took a swig of water.

'So, what did he want then?' his mother asked.

'Who?'

'David.'

'Oh, I don't know. I didn't get that far. I'll call him later.'

SATURDAY,
14TH MAY

David stood with his hands in his boilersuit pockets, looking at the pool of muddy water in the beach park behind Gardie. He didn't turn around when he heard the gate open, then close again, he just kept looking until Sandy was standing beside him. The two men were dressed almost identically, in navy-blue boilersuits, PVC gloves, and yellow wellies streaked with dirt. Neither of them wore a hat, though the morning was chilly.

'Aye aye, boy.' David gave a sideways nod and a grimace. 'Is du ready ta get clerty da day?'

Sandy laughed. 'Aye, I'm lookin forward to it. Drivin taxis is too clean for my likin.'

'Aye, nae doot,' said David, nodding in agreement.

'So, what's the plan?'

David had explained the problem on the phone the night before. The water that had lain in this park for the past six months was not, as he'd thought, a simple drainage problem. It had been a wet winter all right – it had rained almost every day for the whole month of February – and early spring hadn't been much better. But it had been mostly dry for three weeks now, and the pool hadn't got any smaller. If anything, it was still growing. 'Hit's fillin up fae somewye, an we need ta figure oot whar,' David had said. 'If we dunna sort it noo, du'll be floatin awa afore lang.'

That, then, was the problem. But the plan had yet to be decided. David rarely came to a job with a fixed plan in mind. The plan was nearly always flexible, dependent upon the circumstances of the day, and dependent too upon any discussion that preceded the work. Growing up, one of his greatest pleasures had been working with his father, and with neighbours, listening to them talk a problem through and come to a solution. Even if the job required several days' work, it was necessary to reconvene each morning, and often after lunch, to discuss how things were progressing and to decide whether anything needed to be done differently. As he got older, he would try to contribute, and they would listen to him, never dismissing his ideas but nodding silently, as if they were seriously considering the merits of whatever he had to say.

Those discussions of practicalities, roles and techniques taught David much of what he knew about work. They taught him too that, on a croft, there is rarely a solution that can simply be taught or imparted. Each problem is slightly different from those problems that have come before, and each solution has to be worked at. As he got older and took on his own croft, David had to work more on his own, but he preferred, always, to work with others. Even when his father and his neighbours were too old to take part, he would often consult with them before he began, talking through what needed to be done, involving them. It made them happier, and it made the job more enjoyable. When Willie was still alive, living at the Red House, David would often stop by there on a Saturday morning to seek some advice, whether he needed it or not. And Maggie herself was always keen to be asked. Sandy, so far, was not much more practical than David had been aged nine or ten, and his contributions weren't much more helpful. But the discussion was still necessary. It made it clear in both of their minds what needed to be done.

'We'll hae ta drain as much o dis waater aff as we can, ta start wi, does du think?' David asked.

'Aye, that soonds aboot right.'

'Mebbie een o wis should clear da ditch alang da edge o da park, and da idder can dig a channel fae da pool ta da ditch. No too deep, just enoff ta let it run aff.'

'Okay. And where do you think the water's comin fae?'

'Well, if we're lucky hit'll be somethin simple. Dere's a pipe at runs fae da end o dat ditch by da road. As far as I can mind, hit goes under da turnin circle and meets up wi yon ditch, ower beside da fence. Hit could easy be dat pipe at's broken, in which case we juist hae ta fin da brak an repair it. Ah'm got a length o field drain in da pickup we can use.'

'An if it's no that?'

'If it's no dat, it micht be da waater mains.'

'Where does that go?'

'I havna a clue.'

'And how would we fin it?'

'We'll figure dat oot if we come tae it.'

Sandy nodded. 'And what do *you* think it is?'

David smirked, just a little. 'I haed a look at da ditch by da road when I cam doon. Hit seems ta be runnin fine. I dunna think dat pipe is blocked.'

'Right, okay. So it's probably the mains?'

'Aye, likely.'

'Okay, so if we can clear the park a peerie bit, we might see more clearly where the water is risin?'

'Exactly.'

David sent Sandy to the bottom of the ditch, where it ran into the burn. 'Work dy way up,' he told him. 'Cut in fae baith sides, den lift oot da mud. Let's get him runnin ageen.' David himself stood beside the pool and ducked his head, trying to see where best to cut a channel towards the ditch. As it was, he didn't have to look too hard. The water was making its own way through the park. David marked a route with his spade, pressing a shallow line into the dirt, and once he reached the ditch he began to dig.

The dog, Sam, was halfway up the hill, peering into rabbit holes. He'd barely given a glance to the sheep gathered at the other side of the park. He seemed to know without being told, David thought, when his skills were required and when they were not. Today was a day off, and he was making the most of it.

The channel didn't take long to cut. It was only twenty metres or so from the pool to the ditch, but he left the last few metres undone until the ditch itself was clear. No point running the water down until it had somewhere to go. Sandy was making slower progress, so David went to join him, starting a few metres upstream. They would leapfrog as they went.

Ditching used to be one of David's favourite jobs. Satisfying, it was, to see it done properly, to see water running away where previously it had stood still. There were few tasks so straightforward or so effective. But as he'd got older, the pleasures of ditching were accompanied by increasing pains, and every ten minutes or so he'd have to straighten himself, pressing his lower back inwards to stretch the muscles the other way. It brought relief, briefly, but he knew he'd be hurting this evening. And for several days to come, most likely.

'You should have left it to Sandy,' Mary would chide him later.

'But I canna stand by an watch someen else wirk,' he'd say. And he couldn't, that was true. He'd rather feel sore than feel lazy.

'It's days like this I mind how unfit I really am,' Sandy said.

'I'm buggered, and it's only eleven. Mebbie I'm no cut oot for this croftin nonsense.'

'Hit'll git easier.' David shook his head. 'Dis is da warst part o da job, an we're nearly by wi it noo.'

'We'll see. I'll mebbie hae a sleep in the ditch this afternoon.' Sandy looked towards the gate, his smile fading in an instant.

David turned and saw Liz coming down the park, with two cups of coffee and a packet of biscuits in her hand. She had a black raincoat on, and her hair was pulled back in a ponytail. She looked younger than she had the day before.

'Coffee time?' she shouted, raising the mugs a little.

'Perfect,' David replied. 'Du's read me mind.'

Liz passed one cup to each of them, then pulled a plastic bag off her wrist. 'I brought milk and sugar, David, as I wasn't sure how you took your coffee.'

'Oh, a peerie splash o milk is perfect, thanks.' He opened the carton and poured, clouding the black liquid, then wiped a muddy finger on his boilersuit and dipped it briefly in to stir.

'You guys have been working hard.' Liz looked down at the ditch. 'Nearly finished too, by the looks of it.'

'Nearly feenished this part of the job, aye.' David turned and pointed at the pool behind them. 'We're got ta sort oot dat lot next.'

'Aha, I see. Well, rather you than me. I think I'll leave you to it.'

Sandy snorted. 'That could be your motto really,' he said. '"I'll leave you to it."'

David hadn't asked Sandy about his mother this morning, though Mary had insisted he try to find out something. He'd been shocked to find Liz in Gardie yesterday, knowing as he did a little of Sandy's past. Now he felt himself caught between the pair of them, and he wanted to escape. But Liz settled it for him. She didn't seem to flinch at her son's words at all.

'Well,' she said, 'I'll let you get on. I'll make some lunch for one-ish though, shall I? David, you can eat with us, right?'

David wanted to say no, to go home and eat with Mary, but he didn't feel he could refuse. 'Aye, dat'd be splendid. Ah'm a vegetarian, though, mind.'

'Oh, right, okay.' Liz nodded sincerely until David, then Sandy, laughed out loud.

'Ah'm only pullin dee leg,' he said. 'Ah'll eat onything. Ah'm even pitten up wi Sandy's cookin, an dat's sayin somethin.'

Coffee done, the two men continued digging until the ditch was cleared back up to where the channel came in. Walking back over to the pool, they began slicing the last few metres out of the channel, until just one turf remained, holding the water in place. 'Does du want to do the honours?' David asked.

'Aye, I'll take this one,' Sandy replied, pressing his spade down, first one side, then the other. He dug in, felt the suck and squelch of resistance as the sodden earth clung to itself, until, with a rush, the turf turned and the water ran.

These were the moments you worked towards. Like the elaborate dams of sand David had once built on the beach near his grandmother's house, only to break them down again and see the water spill, this was a moment to admire. Gravity and hard labour combined to make a miracle. A gush of soupy brown liquid pushed down the channel like a worm through a hole. It funnelled its way at running pace, and the two men followed, watching the first of the water spill into the newly cleared ditch, then race onward towards the burn and the sea. When they turned back, the pool had already changed shape. It hadn't shrunk yet, but had come to life. Rather than sitting, stagnant, it now seemed poised, ready to push seaward. It had been stirred into action.

'And noo we wait.' David thumped his spade into the ground and leaned against it, watching the water go. 'Time fir lunch?'

When they returned after a short break, in which the numerous silences were perhaps the least awkward moments, there was just a large puddle in the lowest slump of the land. As they crossed the space where the water had been, their boots slurped in the mud. The earth was saturated.

'Where do we start?' Sandy asked.

'Hmm, well, if we can fin da weetest part, dat micht help wis.'

'It aa feels pretty wet to me.'

'Aye, I ken.'

The two men walked around the park more or less at random, lifting their feet high with each step to try to avoid getting stuck and falling over. They stared at the ground. From a distance, they must have looked ridiculous, like giant blue birds, hunting. But neither of them was entirely sure what exactly they were hunting for. Some sign or clue, perhaps, as to the origin of this quagmire.

'Right, hit's drier up here,' said David, standing on a piece of higher ground, closer to the house, 'an da weet starts juist below. Ah'm pretty certain at waater runs *doon*hill rather as *up*hill, so if we dig a trench roughly alang dis contour we'll hoopefully fin sometheen.'

'Lik what?'

'Lik a pipe.'

And so they began digging again, across the park this time, a line of about ten metres, just above where the mud began. They dug down a foot or so and turned the turfs over. They found nothing.

By mid-afternoon, they were no nearer to a solution. Both men were streaked with mud, from their boots to their hair, and the banter that had knocked back and forth between them for most of the day had drifted into silence. David felt the irritation rising in himself, too.

'In da aald days, dere'd be someen wha could fin a pipe wi divinin sticks at times lik dis,' David said. 'Maggie's fedder used ta dae it, if I mind right.'

'Well, I can find you a couple of auld coat hangers if you want to gie it a go. Or I can see if his ghost is hangin aboot.'

'Hmph.' David kicked at the ground.

Both of them looked around then, as though a solution might be there, floating in the valley, or on the hill across the burn. Sam had long since become bored of the rabbits, which all remained, very sensibly, beneath the ground. After lunch, he'd lain curled up a few metres away, but for the past half-hour he'd been pestering David, lingering close to his feet, looking for something to do. He, too, was covered in mud.

'Oh, fir fuck's sake, Sam, go hame, will du!' David pointed up the road, and the collie sloped away, looking back just once to check he'd understood correctly, then trotting silently up the park, under the gate and back towards the house.

When five o'clock came, the park was crisscrossed with ditches and channels of various depths, some dry, some saturated, and both David and Sandy were leaning on their spades, exhausted, frustrated, but reluctant to give up.

'It shouldn't be this bloody difficult,' Sandy said.

'No, hit certainly shouldna. But Ah'm no sure my back'll let me carry on da day. Mebbie we should see if we canna git some mair help da moarn. Or nixt weekend.'

'More help? Like who?'

'Like Terry, I suppose. Or Ryan.'

'Ryan?' Sandy said. 'Aye, that'll be right.'

'Whit? He's a fine enough fellow. No datten practical mebbie, but neither was du when du first arrived.'

'A fine fellow? Ryan? Aye, well, he's certainly got you fooled.'

'What does du mean by dat?'

'Oh, nothin.'

'Well, du meant *somethin*!'

Sandy paused.

'He's cheatin you. Did you ken that? Well, sort of, anyway. Makin out they're in need so they can get the hoose fae you for cheap. He has a big hoose in toon he's rentin oot. He's makin a fortune fae you.'

David looked straight at Sandy. 'Is yon true?'

'Aye, he telt me himself.'

'Hmm.' David went back to digging. He felt a rush of anger, as if he'd just been humiliated, by Sandy as well as by Ryan.

Sandy stabbed his spade down into the ditch he'd been digging, as though struck by that same rush of anger. Then he paused. He lifted the blade then pressed down again, more gently this time. He kneeled. David looked over, noticing the change, as Sandy began clawing at the mud with his fingers, staring intently at the ground beneath his feet.

'Fucking yes!' he shouted, looking up at David. 'I'm found a blue pipe!'

* * *

'Will you help me get this chest of drawers in from the car?' Jo shouted, leaning her head in through to the hallway from the front door. She waited a few seconds, then went back to the open boot and tried to lift the chest out. If she manoeuvred the legs upward, then slid the back over the edge of the car, it should tilt smoothly down onto the driveway. But she was struggling. It was heavier than it looked, and fitted snugly into the back of the car, its seats folded down, so there wasn't much wiggle room. She needed another pair of hands.

'Come on, Ryan!' she called.

He appeared in the doorway in a pair of football shorts and a T-shirt, a half-eaten apple in his hand. His hair was sticking up at the side. He didn't look like he'd showered. He didn't look like he'd been out of bed more than ten minutes, in fact, though it was past five o'clock in the evening.

'Why do we need a chest of drawers?' he asked, not moving from the threshold. 'We're aaready got een.'

'Yes, we've got one. And we need another one. Plus, I like this one. I saw it in the charity shop, and I liked it. I wanted to have it in our home. Is that okay?'

'I guess so.'

'And the man in the shop was kind enough to help me put it in the car. So would you be kind enough to help me get it out?'

'Ah, but du paid him, didn' du?'

Jo continued to struggle with the chest. She had the legs up on the lip of the boot now and took one in each hand, ready to pull. She wasn't confident she could do it without either scraping its back or dropping it on the ground, but she refused to stop what she was doing. She didn't want to allow Ryan to feel he was necessary, though right now he probably was. Or at least *somebody* was. He loved to feel essential, she thought, as she leaned back into the weight. And not just in the way that someone might enjoy being valued. It was more that he liked it when she couldn't do something without him. He liked seeing her weaknesses. She pulled again. It shifted an inch, then wedged tight. It was strange – when they first got together, he had spoken appreciatively about how competent she was, how practical. But now he'd stand there watching her struggle with something as though it were a form of entertainment. Jo wondered if, sometimes, the things you appreciate first in a person could also be the things you came ultimately to resent.

'Fuck*sake*!' She pulled harder. Nothing.

Ryan padded out in his sock feet. 'Careful,' he said, 'you'll damage it.' He eased the chest back inside the boot, then adjusted the angle. Between the two of them it came out easily. They sat it down on the driveway, and Ryan examined it, pulling out drawers, rubbing his hands over the varnish, as if inspecting it for quality. 'It's fine,' he said. 'Whar's it goin?'

'At the top of the stairs, on the landing.'

'Hmm, I was hoopin du wouldna say that.'

'Sorry, but that's where it's going.'

'Aye, okay.' Ryan took one end, shuffling backwards, his head swivelled as far round as it would go, while Jo took the other. He edged himself through the doorway, his elbows brushing the jambs, and she followed, trying not to trip. Once inside, she kicked the door closed behind them, and they began, slowly, to climb the steps, Ryan first, Jo following.

Halfway up, he grinned and stopped. He put his end down and let go, then continued up the stairs without a word.

'Hey! Where are you going? Ryan, come back! I'm going to fall.'

She wasn't going to fall, and she knew that. The chest was heavy, but she could support it without difficulty. Resting as it was, it didn't take much effort. But she couldn't move. She could feel the weight of it against her hands. If she let go of her end, it would tumble or slide down on top of her. And so she was stuck, immobile, on the stairs.

Ryan went into the bathroom. He didn't close the door, but

made a big deal of what he was doing, making as much noise as possible, unzipping, pissing, then flushing. He didn't wash his hands, but returned to the chest, taking his time, then grasped it again.

'You are a fucking arsehole!' That was all she said. Then they continued, up the seven steps to the top.

'Looks good,' he said, once it was in place. 'I wouldna a picked one as wide as that, but, ken, it's dy choice. It's dy furniture.'

'*Our* furniture.'

He laughed. 'Okay, *our* furniture.'

In truth, they didn't really need another chest of drawers. The first one, in the bedroom beside the window, was not entirely full. It was doing its job sufficiently well that Jo had not felt any need for more space until she saw this one for sale. But she knew even as she bought this one – even as she admired it in the shop, commenting to the assistant what good value it was and how useful it would be and how pleased she was that she'd come in that afternoon when she hadn't intended to come in – that her purchase was not really about making more space for her jumpers and jeans. She didn't buy the chest of drawers to contain a surplus of belongings.

When Jo was sixteen, her mother developed a habit of buying flowers every Friday night. After work, she would go to the florist and pick up roses or carnations, something colourful, something bright, something beautiful, then take them home. She'd cut them in the sink, throwing the handful of stalk ends into the compost, then arrange the flowers in a tall crystal vase in the living room, beside the television. There they would stay until the following week, when they were removed and replaced. Though the habit began without warning – Jo couldn't remember flowers being in the house before that time, except on special occasions – their sudden arrival did not prompt any particular discussion in the family. Jo did recognise their increasing importance though, not just as a weekly ritual but as a presence. Sometimes, when she looked over at her mother in the evenings, Jo noticed she wasn't watching the TV at all, but gazing instead at the vase on the sideboard, as though entranced by its contents.

The flower buying lasted for about a year. It began to peter out shortly after Jo's seventeenth birthday. The first stage was when, one Thursday, her father brought home a bouquet and put it in the vase. He made no big deal of it – there was no announcement and no jokes – he merely arranged them, then waited for his wife to notice. When she came in to the living room later that evening, once dinner and dishes were done, she stopped, looked at the flowers, walked over and bent her head to smell them.

'Did you buy these?' she asked Jo, who was slumped on the armchair, watching *EastEnders*.

'No!' Jo snorted, as though the idea were preposterous, which it was.

Her mother left the room, clearly unconvinced that her husband could be the one responsible for such an act. But he was. And over the coming months he bought more. Not every week, certainly, and not always on a Thursday. Once, both of them bought a bouquet on a Friday, and that week there were two bunches in the living room, one on either side of the television. After that, she stopped buying flowers herself so regularly. She seemed buoyed by her husband's occasional, unpredictable thoughtfulness, and sometimes a bouquet would sit there for almost a fortnight before one or other of them would replace it. And then, sometimes, the blooms would fade and droop before either of them had had a chance to go to the florist. Once the first petals fell, she would pick them up and dump the whole lot, and the vase would sit empty beside the sink for a few days in expectation of the next delivery.

Finally, one Friday, almost six weeks after the last petals had curled and fallen, Jo's mother put the vase back in the cupboard and closed the door. She didn't buy any more flowers, and perhaps she didn't feel the need. Six months later, Jo left home. It was years before she thought about the flowers again. One weekend, after she and Ryan moved in together, he brought home a clutch of tulips from the supermarket. And though she hated tulips, and always had, she put them in a tall glass and set them on the dining-room table. Still, she'd had no cause to buy a vase.

Standing there in front of the empty chest of drawers, Jo had an unexpected thought: it would look good with flowers on top. Nothing showy or ostentatious, just a few bluebells or primroses, something like that. They'd look perfect as you ascended the stairs, sitting bright and inviting. They'd make the whole place more like a home. Perhaps tomorrow she would go and ask if she could pick something from Mary's garden.

And then she remembered, and a knot of guilt tightened inside her.

Jo had pushed the memory of the party away for the past week. She had tried her best to forget it. There wasn't much to feel sorry about, after all. Only a moment's thoughtless embrace. But still, she did feel sorry. She felt sorry not just for what she'd done – that was nothing, really, nothing – but because, having been caught, it didn't *feel* like nothing. Indeed, the very fact she felt guilty seemed proof of her guilt. And the fact that it was Mary who'd caught them made it worse.

She wondered, then, if she should go and explain. The thought that Mary might judge her, that she might think Jo had been doing what it looked like she was doing, was painful. Almost as bad, in fact, as the fear that Mary might tell someone else what she thought Jo had been doing. It wouldn't take much to explain, if she made herself do it. The truth would be convincing enough: she was drunk, she was sad, she was confused, *it was only a hug, for goodness sake!* But somehow she couldn't imagine that conversation actually happening. She couldn't imagine herself confiding.

Jo sat down at the top of the stairs. Ryan had long since returned to the living room, and she could hear the murmur of the television through the closed door. He was watching the news, it sounded like. Watching the world happen, far away. She couldn't face him again just yet, with this guilt so loud inside her, so she waited a moment, then went back outside, into the quiet of the early evening. She turned left and walked up the road, past Kettlester, then past Bayview. She carried on until she was at the top of the road, then turned back and looked over the valley.

She stood there for a long time, just watching, leaning for a while against a strainer post in the fence. No cars came. No people either. Only the sheep, the birds and the burn moved between her and the sea. Beyond, a shallow curtain of fog lay on the water as though in wait, and the air was getting chilly.

She tucked her jacket tight around her, then walked back towards the Red House. In the field opposite Kettlester, lambs were pronking and galloping back and forth in gangs. At this time of the evening, they'd leave their mothers' sides and career around the park, euphoric, ecstatic, unbridled. Jo stopped to watch, unable not to smile, then carried on towards the house.

'Whit's fir denner, love?' Ryan shouted as she stepped in and closed the front door. The television was still blaring, and Jo didn't reply. Instead, she went halfway up the stairs and sat down again, on the same step she'd left twenty minutes before. 'Hello?' He tried again, but she said nothing. She wrapped her arms around her knees and tucked her chin in, like she used to do as a teenager.

Eventually, Ryan came out of the living room and stepped up to sit beside her. He put his arm around her and squeezed. 'Sorry,' he said. 'I'm a dick sometimes. Even when I dunna mean to be.'

Jo leaned her head over onto his shoulder. 'Yes. You are.'

'I'll cook tonight,' he said. 'Whit would du like?'

WEDNESDAY, 25TH MAY

It was the first truly warm morning of the summer. Terry was outside, on the green, half-rotten bench beside the front door. The sky was clear, and the sun hung lazy over the valley. He could feel it on his face, on his cheeks and his eyelids. He could feel it in his hair and among his fingers. He focused on those places, on the edges of his body, where the warmth held him as tenderly as if it were willing him to sleep. He took a drag on his cigarette, then stubbed it out on the flagstone at his feet.

A breeze lapped against his ankles but came no higher. Sheltered by the house as he was, the air around him seemed almost perfectly still. There were never many days like this in a year, never enough. He'd intended to go to town this afternoon, to run some errands, but he wouldn't go. Why be anywhere else when the weather was like this?

With his eyes closed, Terry focused on the sounds of the valley. He'd never learned the names of most of the birds, the way others seemed to learn them. But if he concentrated he could recognise a few. The piping that rose behind him, from the beach, was oystercatchers. And the sweet, fluting song from down the road must be a blackbird. There was a skylark hovering some-where over the valley, though he probably couldn't have seen it even with his eyes open. And that was some kind of a gull, or maybe a bonxie, that guttural *skwaw* from the hill above the house. The rest, he had no idea. The air was threaded with songs and calls he could not untangle.

From further up the valley, there was the sound of sawing – most likely David – and a voice, though he couldn't tell whose. There was, too, another insistent noise, and with his focus elsewhere it took a while to identify that noise as footsteps, coming up the road. He waited until the steps were close to the gate, then opened his eyes. He was surprised not to know the owner of the feet. A woman of about fifty: short hair, slim, smiling. He'd seen her somewhere before, he thought, but he wasn't sure when.

'Hello,' he said, squinting into the sun.

'Hi there,' the woman said. 'You must be Terry.'

'Aye, that's me. But I'm no sure wha you are.'

'I'm Liz. Sandy's mum. I'm staying with him at the moment.'

'Ah, okay. That explains it. I thought Ah'd seen dee afore. The idder day, oot walkin.' He leaned back. 'It's a boannie day.'

'Yes, it's amazing. I don't think you get days like this anywhere else. Or at least they don't feel like this anywhere else.'

'No, I think du's right. Mebbie it's juist that you dunna feel as grateful for the sun in ither places. You tak it for granted. You certainly canna tak it for granted here.'

'No, you can't.' Liz laughed and shook her head. 'Feeling grateful. Yes, you might be right. There's a lesson there.'

Terry yawned, stretching his arms upwards, then, too late, covered his mouth. 'Is du goin onywhere in particular,' he asked, 'or just wandering?'

'Oh, I'm just wandering. I thought I might go and say hello to Mary. I've been here more than a fortnight, and the only person I've met so far is David.'

'Well, du's no met me afore, and I was just aboot to mak coffee. So, if du's time to stop, du's very welcome to join me.'

'Thank you. I don't need any coffee at the moment. But if you've a glass of juice or something that would be great.'

'I can manage water. Will that do? Or beer?'

Liz laughed again, a kind of shallow snort, her lips pulled tight. 'It's a bit early for beer, I think. But water is perfect.'

'Aye, du's probably right. Water it is.' He stood and went inside, boiled the kettle and made coffee. He looked for biscuits but found nothing. The house seemed dark and cold after the brightness outside. He went back to the garden.

'So,' Terry said, sitting down on the bench again, where Liz had already settled, 'how lang's du visiting for?' He handed her the tall glass of water and set his mug on the ground beside his feet.

'Oh, I'm not quite sure yet. I've been going through a bit of a tough time recently, and I needed a break. I'm thinking though, if I can find a job, that I might move home again. I've been away too long.'

'Home?'

'Yeah, well, we moved up here when I was thirteen. Hence the accent. My dad worked at Sullom Voe, and I was here for fifteen years or so after that. So, it's kinda home, but it's kinda complicated. My parents moved away years ago, and I've not been back in a long time.'

Terry nodded. In the three years he'd known Sandy, this was the first time he'd even heard about Liz. It struck him as peculiar. He hadn't ever asked Sandy about his family directly. They didn't have that kind of a friendship. But mothers are the kind of things that come up in conversation, like jobs, like politics, like music. Terry had assumed, without really thinking about it, that Sandy's mother was dead. And now here she was, fully alive and present.

'So how long have you lived here, in the valley, I mean?'

Terry sipped his coffee. 'Ah'm had this hoose for a while,' he said. 'Mebbie twelve years. But Ah'm lived atween here and the toon until recently. Noo Ah'm maistly here.'

Liz nodded. 'So you like the valley?'

'Today I do.'

'I can understand that. It's a beautiful place.'

'Sandy liks it too, I think. Well, I ken he does.'

'He hasn't really told me what he thinks about it.' Liz sighed. 'He hasn't told me much of anything.'

'Hmm, I suppose he's no a big talker.'

'Certainly not with me, he's not. I can hardly get a word out of him.'

Terry remembered then it had been almost a month since he'd spoken to his own mother, and three months since he'd seen her. Maybe even longer. They used to talk and visit all the time when Jamie was younger. His parents lived a few streets away and loved to spend time with the boy, loved to be involved. But these days he just couldn't muster the will. He had nothing new to tell them, really, and he didn't want to hear how disappointed they were that his marriage had fallen apart. He didn't need to hear that.

The disappointment of his parents was a burden Terry found impossible to shake off. Impossible, since it was assumed more than it was spoken. His own disappointment pre-empted theirs, was shaped by the knowledge of their expectations and their hopes. When he was unhappy, the thought that they desired his happiness added guilt to his melancholy. When he made poor decisions, he cursed himself in their name. When he lost those things he ought to have cherished, the whole world seemed to shake its head at him under their direction. His parents' unfaltering care seemed, in those times he needed it most, outrageous and unjust. And so he did his best to evade it.

When he saw his mother's number on his phone, calling, he didn't answer. Most often he'd text her back a few minutes later to say he was busy but fine, knowing she would struggle to reply. Her fingers had never become fluent on a keypad, so when she did write it rarely amounted to more than a few words: *Ok love. Spaek soon.* He read them, then deleted them. It was not just an act of sabotage, this silence he'd imposed. It was an act of self-harm.

'It's good that du's here,' he said to Liz. 'It's a good thing, I think.'

'Thank you, Terry.' She turned in the seat and smiled at him. 'I hope Sandy will come to see it that way, too.'

Terry nodded. 'Ah'm sure he will.' It was a stupid thing to say. He had no idea of their situation, no idea if what he said was true. But it sounded comforting, and Liz looked like she needed comforting words.

Silence settled between them, then refilled with sound. The valley was humming with life.

'The birds are beautiful, aren't they?' Liz said. 'I hardly notice them when I'm south, but here they're like a layer you can't peel away.'

'Aye, I was thinking that, too. I dunna notice them most o the time, to be honest. Mebbie I should try and learn mair of the names, so I can recognise them.'

'Oh, but that might spoil it. Maybe it's better not to know, to keep the mystery.'

'How so?'

'Well, sometimes things lose their magic when you know how to take them apart.' She laughed, then sipped at her water.

Liz reminded Terry of someone. To begin with he'd not been able to think who it was, but he realised then. Christine, a girl he'd known years back, just after he left school. They hadn't been friends, exactly. She was friends with people he knew, but he was never once alone in her company. He remembered her talking sometimes like this, in riddles, with a kind of vague certainty, as though the ambiguities of the world had added up to something resolute, which she knew but was too shy to share.

Terry had always liked Christine. He liked the confidence with which she spoke and shared her opinions, and he liked the way she carried herself. She listened to bands that nobody else had heard of, read books they didn't know. She dressed differently, wore clothes that were baggier, more colourful than what was fashionable at the time. She even used to wear a beret sometimes, which, if he remembered right, she'd bought on holiday in Paris. It looked ridiculous here in Shetland, and she was teased often, but she continued to wear it. He admired her for that, too. She was braver than him. He had always felt hemmed in by other people's expectations. Not only his parents, but friends and colleagues too. He tried to be the person others wanted him to be, because, in the end, he was terrified of being anyone else.

Terry had mostly kept his distance from Christine at the time, as unnerved by her independence as he was attracted by it. In the years since, he'd sometimes wondered what she'd done with her life. He thought of her more often than he did most of his school friends. A few years ago he had searched for her on Facebook, but she wasn't there. Somehow he had not expected her to be but was disappointed nonetheless.

Liz reminded him of Christine not just in the way she spoke. There was also something else, something *unfixed* about her, as though she were still uncertain of who she wanted to be. It was charming, in a way, as it had been back then. But it was unusual in a parent. It made Liz seem younger than she was. It made her seem younger than *he* was.

Terry closed his eyes, focusing on the sun against his skin once more. 'This is wonderful,' he said. 'I think I might just sit oot here aa day, get burned, then lie on the sofa and watch the news aa evening. My perfect day.'

'The news?' Liz screwed up her face. 'That doesn't sound like much fun.'

'Oh, it is! I love seein aa the chaos oot there in the rest o the world, while Ah'm here, far awa fae aa that nonsense. It maks me feel lucky or somethin. I havna got much else to feel lucky aboot.'

'Are you serious?'

'No. Well, aye. Sort o.' He smiled. 'I dunna ken. I dunna ken what I'm spaekin aboot really, Ah'm just spaekin.'

'I think I know what you mean,' Liz said, after a pause. 'Even if you don't mean it. I think I understand.'

'Feeling grateful. That's what I mean. Like I wis sayin afore. My lesson for the day.'

'Yes, that's right. I didn't think you were talking about getting pleasure from other people's misfortunes, but . . . you know . . . I reckon you have to take it where you can get it, right?'

'Exactly.' Terry laughed. Then, straight-faced, 'Ah'm no a horrible person, du kens. No really.'

'Well, I'll take your word for that.'

'That's kind. Mony folk wouldna tak my word for onything.'

'That I can definitely believe.'

Terry felt a hum of pleasure. It was not quite flirtatious, their exchange. But it felt good.

'Thanks for the water,' Liz said, standing up. 'I'm going to head on up the road now. But it was good to finally meet you.' She smiled again, a curious, tight-lipped smile.

'Well, drop by onytime,' he said. 'Ah'm rarely busy.'

She laughed. 'I will do. I'll see you soon. Enjoy the sunburn and chaos.'

He lifted his hand and waved.

Mary glanced up through the small window beside the oven. She had seen Liz before, several times, going up and down the road while Sandy was at work. She'd known at once that it was her. Something in the way she walked, the way she carried her body, reminded Mary of him. Something in the slope of the shoulders and the swing of the arms. Now, here she was, striding up the driveway towards the house. Mary washed her hands, clenched them into the tea towel beside the sink and took off her apron. She readied herself.

'Hello,' she said, opening the front door. 'Come in, come in.'

'I'm so sorry to come empty-handed, but I was just passing and thought I should drop in and introduce myself.'

'Oh, nonsense, no need to bring anything. It's very nice to meet you. David told me you were here, so I was hoping I would get to meet you soon.'

'I've been hiding myself away the past couple of weeks. Just settling in, really.'

'That's understandable. It's a long while since you've been back to Shetland, isn't it?'

'Yes, it's been years. I can't remember how many, actually. Now that I think of it, I really can't remember. Twenty maybe.'

'A lot has changed since then, hasn't it?' Mary said. She didn't notice any embarrassment from Liz about the implications of what she'd said.

'I'm glad to be back, that's for sure. And it's lovely to see Sandy, of course.'

'Yes, it must be. I can just imagine.'

In fact, Mary could not imagine. She could not imagine at all what it must feel like for Liz to be here now with the son she walked away from; the son in whom, according to Emma, she had shown almost no interest ever since. Mary felt protective of Sandy, and she felt, too, a shudder of outrage at the woman who now sat smiling in her kitchen. She tried to smother that feeling with generosity, but it wasn't easy. She thought of her own daughters then, and was struck by a sense of relief. Neither of them would ever once have doubted her love, she knew that. Neither of them would ever once have questioned it. Then she thought again of Sandy.

The two women chatted for fifteen minutes or so, about the valley, about the island. Mary was polite; Liz was enthusiastic. Then Mary tapped lightly on the table. She stood up. 'I'm really sorry. I promised David I'd make bread today, and if I don't get started now I'll never get it done.'

'You bake your own bread, that's wonderful!'

'Not always, no. Mostly we just pick it up at the shop, but I try to make a few loaves now and then. David prefers it. So do I. And I've got the time for it now I'm not working, so . . .' She shrugged.

She'd expected, then, for Liz to leave. The bread had not been a lie, but it was an excuse. She could easily have worked around her, of course, but by making a show of it, by making an announcement, she assumed Liz would take the hint: one must work, one must go. But that wasn't what happened.

'Oh, would you mind, Mary,' Liz asked, her face brimming with eagerness, 'if I stayed and watched? I could help too. I've never made bread myself, and I'd love to learn. Now that I'm back home, I feel I want to learn some of these skills I should have learned when I was younger. My mother wasn't a very good teacher. At least, that's what I thought at the time. But you're never too old to learn, are you?'

Liz didn't wait for a response. Instead, she went to the sink, rolled up her sleeves and began washing her hands.

'So, where do we start?' she said. 'Sorry, I'm hopeless. I can cook just fine, but baking, well, there always seemed to be something else I had to do.'

'She was like a little child,' Mary said later, when David came in for his lunch. 'So eager, so giggly, I didn't know how to speak to her.' David nodded, though he wasn't paying much attention. He looked up from the newspaper when Mary spoke, but his eyes weren't focused. Still, though, she needed to tell him.

'I thought maybe she'd just watch, but no, she needed to do it herself. She insisted. "Let me try," she said. Well, what could I do? I let her mix the dough, then she tried kneading it, and she was hopeless, obviously. Never done it before in her life.'

'Hmm, well dat's no her fault, I suppose,' David muttered from his chair.

'No, I know that's not her fault. That's not what I'm saying. She was just so . . . so *strange* with it. I felt like she wanted me to pat her on the head and give her a gold star once she'd managed to get it right. She was clapping her hands together in excitement by the time we got the dough into the bowl to prove. And she wanted to stay to finish it, but I had to explain it would take hours. She asked me to bring a loaf down to her later.'

'Sandy certainly dusna git his way fae her den. I canna imagine him clappin his hands in excitement.'

'Well, we should be grateful for that, I think.'

David looked up properly from his paper then. 'Mary, mebbie we need to gie her mair o a chance. I ken why du dusna lik

226

her, and I canna say Ah'm datten enamoured wi someen at wid abandon a bairn lik dat. But, du kens, shu's here noo, and shu's tryin ta mak amends. An I dunna think we should stand in da wye o dat. She's dere wi Sandy noo, an wi ony luck dey'll sort things oot atween dem.'

'But she can't just stride in like this, after all this time, and expect him to welcome her with open arms. It's not right! You can't just pretend things never happened.'

'I ken you canna. But sometimes you hae a chance ta repair some damage, an du haes ta tak it. Sandy haes a lot o forgivin ta dae. We dunna hae ta forgive on his behalf. We should gie her a chance.'

'I feel like I *do* have to forgive her.'

'Well, mebbie du does den, and mebbie du should.'

'I just don't want her taking advantage of him.'

'Takin advantage how? If he dusna want her ta stay, he'll no let her stay.'

'It's not as simple as that.'

'How no?'

'Well, she's his mother. It's never going to be simple. She's got the upper hand, coming back without warning like that.'

'I dunna think Sandy is da kind ta let onybody hae the upper hand. He'll decide whit he needs ta dae. I trust him. Du should as weel.'

'I do trust him. I just don't trust her.'

'Du dusna hae ta trust her. No juist yet. Du haes ta be polite, be friendly. Let Sandy deal wi his situation an juist respect his choices.'

Mary stopped arguing then. She knew David was right, or almost right, but she'd felt the need to express her resistance out loud. She needed to explain why she didn't like Liz, why she didn't *want* to like her. Now that she'd done that, perhaps she would feel able to forgive, or at least to accept the situation. What she wanted though, now, was to go and give Sandy a hug, remind him that they cared for him and were thinking of him. But she wouldn't. There were too many reasons not to.

'By the way,' David said, 'Ah'm still no decided whit ta dae aboot Ryan an Jo.'

'What do you mean?'

'Well, du kens. Aboot da hoose.'

'Have you made sure it's true yet, what Sandy said?'

'No. I wanted ta figure oot whit ta dae first.'

'Well, that seems a bit backwards, but okay.'

'It's no backward at aa. I dunna want ta go an spaek ta him an no hae a response ready if he says hit's true. An if Ah'm no goin ta dae onything aboot it dere's nae point in me even askin, is der?'

'I suppose not.' Mary smiled. Sometimes her husband's logic could be both strange and perfect at once.

'Ah'm no happy, though.'

'No, I know that. And you're right, it definitely seems cheeky.'

'Bloody right hit's cheeky. Ah'm chargin a pittance fir dat hoose. He'll be chargin a fortune fir his een. Dey're makin a fool o me.'

'Well, they're hardly doing that. Being generous is not foolish.'

'But dey're exploitin my generosity. I wid nivver a charged sae little if Ah'd a kent.'

'Well, chuck them out if you care that much about it, but don't do it unless you're sure.'

'Sure o whit?'

'Sure that it's the right thing to do.'

'Ah'm no sure o onythin, dat's da problem.'

Mary, likewise, was unsure. She'd been shocked when David first told her about the house in town. It seemed so brazen and so wrong. And yet, perhaps it wasn't. Perhaps it was their attitude – Mary's and David's – that was out of date and out of place. They'd been naive; Ryan had been smart. The fault was theirs, not his.

What had shocked her almost as much, though, was to know it had been Sandy who brought the news. He seemed an inappropriate messenger somehow. She'd thought again about what she'd seen at the party, and what it might have meant. She'd thought again about the hug. Things right now were complicated, that's all she knew. And she wanted them to be simple.

'I think you should just ask him. Call him up and ask directly. If he says yes, you can just end the conversation, whatever, then we can talk about it again. If he says no, then you don't have to think about it any more.'

'Unless he's lyin.'

'I don't think he'd lie, love. He's not stupid. It'd be too easy for you to find out from someone else.'

'Aye, mebbie.'

'And there's other options, too. If he says yes, you could just tell him you're increasing the rent, to whatever he's getting in town. Then they'd surely leave anyway.'

'I dunna think I can juist hike da rent lik dat. It's no alloo'd.'

'No, it's not. But nor is chucking them out. Not yet. You can just say it'll go up at the end of the first six months, if you want. He won't argue with that.'

David's quietness suggested he'd assented, as she thought he would.

'You can call him later on, if you like,' Mary said. 'But I'm going to phone Emma first, from the other room. Do you want to speak to her once I'm done?'

David looked up again, his face changed entirely. 'Aye, certainly.'

Hearing Emma's voice allowed Mary to push aside the complications of Ryan, Jo, Sandy and Liz. It made the day seem even brighter. She put the bread in the oven after its second proving, then went outside into the sunshine. She sat for a few minutes on the bench beneath the living-room window, until the weeds distracted her.

The garden looked beautiful now. The lupins were blooming – deep pink and blue spires huddled against the house – and the crimson peonies, too. They had toppled as they came into flower, too heavy to support themselves, and she'd propped them with wooden stakes and bound them with twine. Now they were lolling like wedding guests, drunken and splendid. Everywhere though, among the flowers and between the flagstones in the path, the weeds were rising. They seemed to come almost overnight. Each time she cleared them, they'd return, fresh and vigorous. But she kept clearing them, because there was nothing else she could do. To leave them, for a week, a month, would be to give up on the garden, and she couldn't do that. Not for as long as she was able.

Mary knelt and plucked at dandelions and silverweed, at willowherb and lady's mantle. She heard bumblebees among the flowers and felt the sun resting on the back of her neck. She pulled and piled the weeds into a bucket, until a broad stretch of earth in front of her was clear and clean of intrusions. She sat back and admired it for a moment, then returned inside and opened the oven. The kitchen overflowed with the hot, dry smell of bread.

'Ah'm beginning to wish I nivver gave those things tae Alice,' said David, stomping into the room, the telephone in his hand.

'What things, love?' Mary asked.

'Maggie's things. Shu seems obsessed noo. Shu wis pesterin me aboot dem when I saw her da idder day, and noo shu wants ta meet up an ask me mair questions aboot her.'

'Well, why did you give her them then, if you didn't want her to ask anything?'

'I dunna ken. I didna think dey'd be muckle use. I haed a look an it aa seemed dry as onything.'

'So you gave them to her because you didn't think she'd be interested?'

'Pretty much, aye.' He grinned. 'I juist wanted rid o dem.'

'Well, it serves you right, then, I'd say.'

Mary smiled to herself as she continued to work. Her husband's ways of thinking had always made her laugh. He could be infuriating sometimes, too. But funny, always funny.

'Well, as lang as shu dusna ask onything too personal. If those diaries had been personal, I wouldna a geen dem tae her. Surely shu understaands dat.'

'I'm sure she does, darling. She's just curious. It's understandable.'

'Well, I canna see hoo shu's going to write onything aboot Maggie. Whit's der ta say?'

'I have no idea. Did she not tell you what she was planning?'

'No really. Juist at shu wants ta tell Maggie's story. But I hae nae idea whit dat means.'

'Well, when you meet her, ask her to explain. Then you can decide how much you're wanting to say. Does that sounds sensible?'

'Aye, mebbie so.'

'So when are you meeting her, then?' Mary asked.

'Next week sometime, probably. I said Ah'd let her ken. Ah'll leave it a few days an mebbie shu'll forget.'

Mary didn't answer.

'Okay. Ah'm goin oot ageen. Is du needin me ta dae onything dis eftirnoon, or am I free ta use me time wisely?'

'No, I don't need you. We'll eat late, I think, so don't worry. Go out and wander.'

He stood behind Mary then, placed his hands on her shoulders and kissed the top of her head.

'Did you phone Ryan?' she asked, as he walked towards the door.

'No, no yet. Ah'm still thinkin.'

FRIDAY,
3RD JUNE

'Come in, come in.' Mary stood clear of the door to let Alice through. 'David's just out the back, but he's expecting you, I know, so he'll be here any minute. Do you want a cup of tea?'

'Yes, that'd be lovely, thanks.' Alice leaned over to scratch the dog, then followed Mary through to the kitchen and they chatted as the tea was made, then went down the hall to the living room and sank into the wide, blue armchairs, one on either side of the fireplace. The room was comfortable, carpeted, with pictures on each wall. Kate and Emma were everywhere.

David came in then, his shirt creased and half-untucked. He nodded a hello and looked from Alice to Mary.

'Your tea is beside the sink,' she said. He nodded again and went out, returning a moment later with a mug and a packet of biscuits.

'Right, Ah'm ready. What's du wantin ta ken?'

Alice wondered if she ought to have compiled a list of questions, or something solid to begin with at least, and she was glad when Mary excused herself and returned to the kitchen. 'Well, it's mostly pretty general stuff I'd like to hear from you. I've read all the diaries and so on, but I'd really like to get a better idea of what kind of person Maggie was. I mean, what was she *like*?'

'What was shu lik?' David raised his eyebrows, as though he'd been asked a particularly tricky question. 'Well, I dunna ken. Shu wis juist Maggie, really. It's hard to say it better as dat.'

'Can you try?'

He hesitated, spoke slowly. 'I guess Ah'd say shu wis friendly, generous – at least shu aalwis wis wi me. If Ah'm honest, Ah'd say mebbie shu could be stubborn, but can't we aa?' He smiled briefly. 'A strong personality, really. Du aalwis kent whar du wis wi Maggie.'

'What do you mean by that?'

'Well, shu wis . . .' He seemed to clutch for the word. '*Consistent*, I suppose. Shu wis da sam wan day as shu wis da next.'

Alice wrote down what he said in her notebook, though so far it hardly seemed worth recording. 'Anything else?'

'Shu haed a braaly good memory, dat's fir sure. Used to tell stories at went way back. Things at happened afore shu wis even born. Folk at used to bide aboot here, shu could tell dee aa deir connections. Shu haed somethin ta tell aboot aabody. Amazin.' He shook his head. 'I used ta think sometimes I must o heard aa her stories, at wan time or anidder – shu wisna above repeatin herself, certainly – but den, noo an ageen, shu'd come oot wi somethin Ah'd nivver heard, aboot me ain faither or mither, even. Amazin! And dat's aa gone noo, of course. I canna mind even a tenth o whit shu kent.'

'That's a shame. And did nobody ever write down any of the stories? It sounds like they should have done.'

'Write them doon? No. I canna think onybody wid be interested idder as me. They widna o kent wha shu wis even spaekin aboot. Juist a list o names. Micht as well o been med up. Mary didna ken half o dem, and shu's lived here mair as thirty years.'

'I'd have liked to have heard the stories.'

David shrugged. 'Du coulda done. Shu wisna shy.'

Alice looked down at her notebook. The chair sagged deeply in the middle, and she tried to move sideways, edge herself higher.

'So, whit exactly is it du's needin to ken aboot her? I mean, whit exactly is du writin? If I kent dat, mebbie I could be o mair help.'

'To be honest, I'm still not quite sure. My book is nearly finished now – about the valley, I mean – but I just thought there was something missing from it. And I think Maggie might be it. I want to get that real human side in there.'

'Aye, well, shu wis a real human, dat's fir sure.' He smirked, but Alice pretended not to notice.

'I mean I've written about history, about plants and animals and birds and so on. But I thought maybe telling Maggie's story would help bring the human side of the valley to life in the book.'

'Even though shu's dead?'

'Yes.' Alice felt frustrated, as much by her own inability to explain what she was thinking as by David's refusal to understand. She tried her best to continue. 'What I mean is that, by writing about Maggie, I think I could say something about the community here in the valley.'

'Say whit aboot it?'

'I don't know yet.'

'Okay.' David nodded, paused. 'Well, mebbie du could. But would dat no be lik writin aboot a hen's egg in order ta say somethin aboot a cake?'

'No, I don't think it would be like that at all. Maggie was more important to the community than that, wasn't she?'

'Well, shu's gone an we're still here.'

'I know, I know, but that's not what I . . . I mean, I just don't think that's a good analogy.'

'Fair enough.' David leaned back and took the last swig of his tea. 'Well, if du's read aa her letters an dat,' he said, 'surely du can git somethin oota dem?'

Alice fished in the bag she'd brought with her and pulled out two of the diaries. She opened them at random and read aloud, one day from each, then looked up again at David.

'That's it,' she said.

'Dat's whit?'

'Exactly. That's it. That's all she writes. Work, food, weather. But that can't be all there was to her life.'

David shrugged. 'Mebbie it wis. Dat's whit wis important tae her.'

'I can't accept that. There must have been more to her than that.'

'In whit sense?'

'She must have had thoughts, had feelings. She wasn't a robot.'

'No, shu wusna. But what business o dine is Maggie's feelings?'

Alice stopped and looked at David again. His face was serious, but not angry.

'I'm not looking for deep secrets or anything. I'm just looking for something human.'

He shrugged again. 'I dunna ken whit ta say. Yon seems pretty human ta me.'

'Does it not trouble you at all that after eighty-eight years, this is all Maggie left behind: piles and piles of nothing much?'

'No, no at aa. It's mair as maist fok. I winna be leavin onything lik dat when Ah'm gone, I can assure dee.'

'No, okay. But you have two daughters, two grandchildren. That's what you'll leave behind. They're real. They mean something.'

David nodded slowly. 'Aye, dey do. Dat is true.'

Alice paused, then asked, 'Why did Maggie and Walter never have children?'

'I hae nae idea,' he said, stretching the words out as though they were elastic, ready to snap back into shape. 'It wasna somethin shu ivver spak aboot. No ta me onywye. An I nivver asked.'

At that moment Mary put her head round the door. 'Do either of you want more tea?'

'No, I'm fine, thanks.' Alice smiled politely.

'Me too. Ah'm fine.' David looked up at his wife. 'Did Maggie ivver spaek ta dee aboot bairns?' he asked. 'Aboot why dey didna hae ony?'

'No,' Mary said, quietly. 'She didn't. I always assumed it was just something medical. There wouldn't have been much help back then. If a baby didn't arrive, it didn't arrive. That was that.' She thought about it a second, then continued. 'She always loved looking after our bairns when they were little, so, you know, I can't imagine it was a choice they made themselves. But I don't know.'

'No, dat wis likely it,' agreed David. 'I'm hardly even thoght o it afore.'

Alice felt something gently tighten inside her, like a hand clasped around her heart. She saw Mary turn and leave again, then listened to her footsteps go down the hall and into the kitchen. She gazed at the open doorway.

David leaned forward and looked directly at Alice then. He waited until she turned back to him, then began to speak. 'Look, Ah'm no meanin ta be difficult wi dee. Well, I am in a wye, but . . .' He glanced to the floor, then corrected his gaze. 'I dunna ken hoo to say dis exactly. I dunna want to offend dee. But, it juist seems to me . . . Ah'm no sure du understaands whit du's writin aboot.'

Alice's mouth fell open, as though his words had fixed themselves to her jaw. She couldn't think how to respond. His judgement was like a slap on the cheek, and she felt a surge of indignation. But she didn't get up and leave. She sat, silent.

In the end it was David who spoke. 'Ah'm sorry, Alice. I shouldna o said yon. Mebbie it's juist me. I hae to admit I dunna really get whit du's lookin fir.' He shrugged. 'Maggie wis juist Maggie, and if du wants to write aboot her, I think du'll fin aa du needs in da diaries. I ken dey dunna soond lik much ta dee, but dey soond lik da Maggie I kent. Wark an wadder: dat wis her.'

He stood up, then, grabbed his mug from the mantlepiece. 'An if du wants to write aboot da community, well . . .' he smiled. 'Mary kens mair aboot cake as me.'

He led Alice down the hall towards the porch. 'Thanks for comin,' he said. 'An Ah'm sorry I canna be mair use ta dee. Honestly.'

'It's okay,' she smiled. 'You've been helpful, really. And you might be right, in what you said.'

'Which bit o it?'

'About me not understanding. I suppose I don't. But I'd like to. I'm trying.'

'I ken du is, I ken.' He put a hand on her shoulder then. Not a hug, not even close. But enough to lift the weight of what he'd said before, to absolve her. It was an intimate encouragement.

'Oh, Alice, would you like to look at these before you go? Or you can borrow them if you like.' Mary came down the hall, then, a folder and a frame in her hand. 'I forgot to show you earlier. It's just a few photographs. Some from Maggie's house, some we had already. I thought you'd maybe like to see them.'

'Yes, I would, absolutely. Thank you.'

Alice took the thick, dark-stained frame in her hand. She turned it the right way. A man and woman in their forties, dressed well – he in a baggy suit, she in a long, patterned dress. They stood facing the camera, close but not quite touching. The man was smiling, the woman doing her best to smile. Her expression looked forced, as if she were impatient to move on, to escape the photographer's attention.

'That was our wedding day,' said Mary. 'You can't tell from the photo, but she told me later it was one of the happiest days of her life.' She looked up at her husband. 'Maggie was always very fond of David.'

'And dee, love.'

'Yes, and me, fortunately. Once she'd made her initial assessment.' Mary grinned, and handed the folder to Alice. 'You can borrow these,' she said, 'but look after them. We miss her.'

'I will. I promise, I will. Thank you, again.' Alice looked at Mary, then at David. She felt enclosed in the moment, somehow. Held by it, and by them. And then she turned for the door.

'I'd like to hear some of those stories sometime, David,' she said, leaving. 'If you can remember them.'

He nodded. 'Aye, certainly. Dere's aalwis stories.'

★   ★   ★

Sandy parked and switched off the engine, then sat, listening, as the car returned to silence. The cooling metal ticked to nothing, and the day faded behind him. He opened the door.

He wasn't dressed for the croft but wasn't ready yet for the house. Life at Gardie had become, for Sandy, a full-time exercise in self-control. It took considerable effort now to avoid arguments and confrontations, and often he did not succeed. What made things worse, though, was that his mother seemed to require no such effort. Almost without fail she was cheerful and relaxed, as though there was nothing odd about their current situation at all, as though she was just a normal mother visiting her son, as she did each summer, as she always had done.

It was not easy to impact on Liz's cheerfulness. She seemed impervious to the anger and irritation that rose up regularly within him. When he turned on her, as he did often in those first few weeks, she barely responded. She would smile, patiently, and wait for his irritation to subside. It made him sick to his stomach to feel that *he* was the bad person, that *he* was the irrational one. Sandy was like a teenager in those weeks, pushing his mother, testing her limits, waiting for the moment she would explode, shout, scream, do *something* that would make his own fury feel righteous rather than petty. He'd never really had the chance to test those limits before.

For half his life, he had longed for his mother to take an interest in him. He had longed for her attention, for her love, and she never gave him what he wanted. Now, here she was, and he still couldn't get the required response. His anger bounced off her, just as his affection had done years earlier. She seemed immune to the world around her, immune to what other people did, what they said, what they wanted. Sandy wanted his mother to disappear again. He knew how to deal with her absence. He wanted her to be gone, but he could not, yet, insist on it. The part of him that still craved her love would not allow it.

He stood, leaning against the car, watching the ewes and lambs in the beach park. One sheep stood eating, oblivious, as four starlings hitched a ride on her back. Another was lifted almost off her feet by the enthusiasm of her twins, which galloped and grabbed hungrily at her teats. They fed for just a few seconds before she stepped away, leaving them on their knees behind her. Unfazed, the pair wandered off side by side, apparently happy. Sandy was tempted sometimes to envy the animals, with their short, contented lives. They never wanted for anything, except maybe some warmth in the winter, and these lambs would never see winter anyway.

He looked at his phone – there were two missed calls from David – then went inside to change his clothes. It looked almost ready to rain.

'Are you serious?' Sandy gripped the back of the chair and stared at his mother. She was standing in front of the stove, stirring with a wooden spoon. 'Are you *actually* serious?'

'Yes, of course I am. Why not? You missed out on having us both around when you were younger, so it seems only fair to try and do something about that now. I've spoken to Jim, and he's happy to come round for dinner some time. It's just a case of when suits you.'

'Dad's *happy* to come roond? He said that?'

'Well, he said he was willing to give it a try. That's as much as I could hope for now. Give it a few months, though, and I reckon we can all be friends. I'm planning to stay around for now, so I think it would be good if we could spend time together. Make up for what we missed out on before.'

Sandy didn't know where to start with that. He didn't know which bit of it to argue with first.

'I know that me leaving hurt both of you,' Liz said. 'I know that, and I'm sorry it had to be that way, but it just did. I've tried to explain before. And anyway, it was a long time ago now. I think we're all capable of acting like adults and learning to get on.'

Sandy turned away from his mother then and towards the kitchen window. As a teenager, he used to dream of a moment like this – a reconciliation, a truce, a reunion – but that dream was too old to resurrect. It had festered, impossible, for twenty years. Yet now here she was ordering him to bring it back to life. He couldn't do it, but nor could he refuse.

'If Dad wants to come roond and visit, he's welcome to do

so.' Sandy didn't turn back to look at his mother. He kept his eyes on the window. 'He's welcome ony time. He kens that. You can invite him, and you can cook for us. I'll be here. That's aboot as much as I can say. And it's no even a promise. I'll let you ken if I change my mind. Which I might do.'

'Thank you, Sandy. I know this is all a bit of a shock for you, but I really think it will be worth the effort.'

'I winna be making any effort, believe me. I'll just be eating me denner. The effort is all yours to make.'

Liz smiled weakly, or tried to smile. 'It might even be fun,' she said. 'We'll all enjoy it, I promise.'

Sandy shook his head then and walked away, into the living room. He lay on the sofa and closed his eyes. Tears swelled beneath his lids, and he clenched them tighter, his chest quivering as he pushed back his hope, his fear, his grief. He took his phone out and wrote a text. *What am I supposed to do about her?* He sent it to Emma. She was the only person who might know what to say.

Liz watched her son go and returned to the stew on the stove. She didn't hear him cry. She didn't think him capable of tears. His crankiness, she thought, was a kind of hardness in him. Not a shell or a scab, but a kernel, long since formed. He was more like her than he imagined.

She had not been a good mother, she knew that. She had been a bad mother, in fact; there was no point trying to water it down. She had walked away from her responsibilities and abandoned her son. ('Abandoned' was not the word she would use. She had left Sandy with his father, not on a convent door-step. But it didn't really matter what you called it.) Liz had never felt guilty for that decision. Not really. Guilt was corrosive, like regret. It set you looking in the wrong direction. 'I regret nothing except regret,' she had announced to a room of friends one Saturday night, after a bottle and a half of wine. 'I regret nothing except regret.' She had said it again, the words sounding so perfect.

'You should remember that,' Trevor had nodded. 'Write it down. It's good.'

'I will. I fucking will.'

And she had, though the words didn't sound quite so perfect the next morning, when she found them scribbled on a Post-it note on the carpet, amid bottles, cans and trampled crisps. It was hard to push aside regret on a morning like that.

You can't be good at everything, though. It's just not possible. People are good at some things, and they are bad at other things. That's the truth of the matter. Liz was a pretty good cook. She was a good listener, as well. All her friends said that. And Trevor, too, in the beginning. She was good at finding solutions to problems. She was clear-headed, logical, consistent.

On the other hand, she was a bad mother. And she was bad at sports, always had been, even when she was young and fit. Her limbs just didn't seem to work in unison. Each on its own was fine, but together they were a mess. She was bad at music, too. She'd tried to learn guitar as an adult and never progressed further than four laborious, buzzing chords. Aged ten she'd played piano, or at least tried to. Her father played well, and he wanted to teach her. But her fingers were no more coordinated than her legs. They flopped and stumbled over the keys, clumsy and slow, until, shuddering with frustration, he slammed the lid down onto her hands, then walked away. She never played piano again.

It was hard now to see Sandy the way he could be, and to wonder if that was where it came from, that seething anger – from her father. Liz would prefer for it to be her fault. She'd prefer for it to be learned rather than ingrained. She didn't mind taking the blame for the way he was. But if the blame lay behind her, in the man who had, for years, taken his anger out on her, and whose anger she still felt inside herself sometimes, like a foreign body, that was unacceptable.

She had never wanted children. Her own childhood had not been happy, tainted as it was by fear. Childlessness seemed a way of escaping that time, freeing herself from it. But that wasn't how it went.

It was an accident, of course. A mistake. Not thinking, not making sure. That's all. It happened. It was done. She never suspected. And then she did. It was certain. Liz was twenty, and she insisted on getting rid of the baby when she found out. She talked it through with Jim, and she insisted. She would go away, get it done. It was her body, her choice. And so he took that choice away.

Jim told both their parents that she was pregnant. He told all their friends, too, made it sound like a joyous announcement, and the congratulations came in. It was a perfect trap. She couldn't help but respect him for his ingenuity, and for knowing her so well. He understood she could have gone through with the abortion. No regrets. But he understood, too, that she could not have faced the shame of everyone knowing, of her parents knowing. He understood her, and he abused that understanding. She respected him for that, and she hated him for it. Their end was made inevitable by Sandy's beginning.

The stew was ready. It had been ready for an hour or more, but Liz continued to stir, the heat purring through the food. She wasn't quite able to face her son again, to bring him back to the table. This wasn't easy for her either.

It was not as if she was looking forward to seeing Jim. It was for Sandy's benefit that she'd invited him. She knew he'd resist at first, but she was sure it was the right thing. Her hatred of Jim had long since passed. She pitied him now, and the life he'd led since she left, which didn't seem to be much of a life at all. He must have loved her more than she ever imagined. Falling apart like that without her, it wasn't what she'd expected. She thought he would meet someone else within a year – a better mother for Sandy. That was honestly what she expected, and what she thought was for the best. It wasn't like he was an old man, after all. He was only just in his thirties, then. But crumbling like that, giving up, it was weird. There were moments when she figured she'd have to come back and take her son away from him, and there were moments when she was almost tempted. But still, as mediocre a father as he turned out to be, Jim was still a better father than she could ever have been a mother. Until now, anyway.

And if she was honest with herself, that was what this whole trip was about. Not making up for missed time. She knew there was nothing she could do to ever make up for the years she'd been gone, and it wasn't worth trying. But now she was older, maybe even wiser, she thought perhaps she could be a mother after all. Some kind of a mother. Trevor throwing her out like that was just the prompt she needed to do something about it.

'Sandy, come and eat,' she shouted, almost surprising herself.
Silence.

She called again. 'Food's ready, Sandy. I'm just putting it on the table.'

There was no sound at all from the living room. She waited a moment longer, then went through to look. Sandy was lying on his side on the sofa, one hand beneath his head, the other against his chest. His legs were bent and tucked up close into him. His mouth was open, and he was breathing heavily. He was fast asleep.

'Sandy, darling.' Liz kneeled down on the floor beside his head and whispered. She gazed at him there, this man who was her son, and she thought of something she'd not thought of in years. She remembered when he was young, five or six, he would come down to the living room at night, an hour or so after he'd been put to bed. 'I can't sleep,' he'd say, rubbing his eyes, like a bad actor pretending to be tired.

'Why can't you sleep, Sandy?' Liz would ask.

'I don't know. I want to sleep here with you.'

And so he would lie on the sofa and rest his head against her. Sometimes they tucked a blanket over him, and sometimes he just lay in his pyjamas. They'd turn back to whatever it was they'd been watching on the television before he came in. Nothing more would be said between them. Very little ever was. Sandy would be quiet, knowing that if he made too much noise he'd be sent straight back to his room. Sometimes he'd lie with his eyes wide open, not watching the TV but watching one or other of his parents, as though terrified they might leave him there alone. But usually he would turn and fall asleep, curled as tight as he could manage, and he would stay there until his parents went up to bed. His father would carry him in his arms and lay him, still sleeping, on the mattress. When he woke in the morning, he would never ask how he'd got there.

Liz thought of that, then. It seemed such a long time ago, like another life; it seemed strange that she could even remember it now. It seemed strange, too, that this sleeping man had been that sleeping little boy, with his mop of brown hair and checked pyjamas. It seemed impossible. All of it seemed impossible.

'Come on, Sandy.' She rested her hand on his head and stroked his cheek, her finger brushing the edge of his ear. 'Come on, son, it's time to get up. It's time for supper.'

SATURDAY, 4TH JUNE

Each of the photographs she had scanned, carefully, making sure not to leave so much as a fingerprint. She held them by their edges, placed them face down on the machine and watched as the images appeared on the screen in front of her. A few were in black and white. The oldest were printed on thick paper, with an ivory border half a centimetre wide. One showed Maggie in her early twenties – 1949, according to a note on the back. Ina, a few years younger, stood beside her. Their brother Gilbert would have been five years dead. No photographs of him, in or out of his uniform, survived.

Ina was shorter than Maggie – or perhaps she stood a little less straight – but other than that the two of them looked entirely alike. The way they stared at the camera, as if in defiance of its gaze; the way their heads were tilted, just a touch; the way they pressed one hand against their hips and held the other at their sides. They could almost have been twins.

The two, though, must have been quite different, despite appearances. Not long after this picture was taken, Ina had left the valley and moved to New Zealand. She had removed herself from the place in which her sister would live and die. Alice wondered whether Maggie too had been tempted to go. A better life must have been promised to them both. An easier life, together, far from the hardship their parents had known.

But Maggie didn't go. She dug in her heels and remained.

There was another photograph that showed the two of them together, in colour. This one must have been taken in New Zealand, perhaps in the 1980s. The garden in which they were pictured was lush, almost luminous green. The pair stood, arm in arm, with a younger woman beside them. Lynette, presumably, with Ina's husband behind the camera. Here the differences were more apparent. Ina looked much younger than her sister, more relaxed and comfortable. Maggie smiled stiffly. She seemed dressed for different weather than the other two women, and Alice could detect a hint of discomfort in her face. A flush. She was too hot, but too stubborn to change her clothes.

Flicking through the rest of the pictures – two dozen in all – Alice saw Maggie grow old. She saw her face soften, her hair fade from brown to grey, her shoulders grow slack and her back begin to stoop. She saw a life that leapt from one caught moment to another, and yet which only truly existed in the space between those moments.

Among the photographs, two in particular stood out. One was the most recent image, taken just a few years ago by the looks of it. In it, Maggie sat on the bench outside Gardie with Emma beside her. This time she smiled, though her expression was somehow as defiant as ever. One hand rested on a stick held out in front of her. The other was on Emma's knee.

Emma smiled too, in the picture, and something of the same look was on her face. The same unyielding confidence that Maggie had. The same certainty. She was also beautiful, and Alice wondered why she had never noticed that before. It was as though she were illuminated – her freckled skin, her hazel eyes – by the woman beside her on the bench.

The other photograph was older. Taken in the late 1970s, while Walter was still alive. Here, neither of them was facing the camera. They were together in the pen in the beach park, surrounded by sheep. David – young and bearded then – was leaning on the wall, watching or talking, it was hard to tell which. All of them were looking at the animals, not at each other.

The picture was badly composed. Walter was only half in the frame on the left side, while a view of the road down to Gardie took up space on the right. The focus wasn't great either. Nothing quite looked sharp, and a movement of Maggie's arm had left a blur on the page. But her face was clear enough. Though she wasn't looking towards the camera, her expression had been caught. She was laughing – a broad, open-mouthed, unself-conscious laugh.

All of the pictures were now stored on Alice's computer and the originals placed back in the folder and frame. She wanted to return them as soon as possible, to thank Mary for sharing them. She'd intended to go to Kettlester this morning, just after breakfast, but had seen Mary's car go up and out of the valley so had decided to wait. She wasn't yet ready to face David on his own again. His words were still rasping inside of her from the day before. His accusation – his underlining of her ignorance – still stung. More so because she knew that he was right.

It seemed odd to Alice that there were so few pictures of Maggie and Walter, so little evidence of their life together. Her own marriage had been recorded from start to finish. Scores of photographs, hundreds even, in albums, on CDs and in digital folders. She'd kept everything. There were two framed pictures from their wedding in the house – one on the mantelpiece in the living room, the other beside her bed. And on the desk in her office, a picture taken a few months before Jack died. In it, he is stood by the doorway of their house in York, a warm coat on, though the sun is shining. His face is thin, but not yet drawn, as it later would become. Alice is beside him, her arm around his waist, holding him as tight as she can manage, which was never tight enough.

She realised then that since his death no one had taken a photograph of her. Not one. It was almost as though she had ceased to exist on that day, or simply disappeared from view. And in a sense, by coming here, that's exactly what she'd done. She had exited the life she once led, erased herself after Jack had been erased. Her life here in the valley, the one she was still trying to create, had been unrecorded.

★   ★   ★

David wasn't smiling when he arrived at the front door. He was dressed in his boilersuit and wellies, and looked impatient. He had a shovel in his hand.

'Is du ready?' he asked.

'Aye, Ah'm just puttin me boots on.'

David turned and went out to the gate, leaving Sandy to catch up with him.

'What's the plan today, then? Not mair digging, I hope.'

'Well, dere'll be some diggin, but nothin lik last time. It'll no tak lang, hoopfully.'

'That's a relief.'

They walked from the gate at the turning circle down through the beach park towards the burn. The little bridge crossed just above a pool, where fingerling trout scattered at their approach, bolting for cover beneath the banks. From there they headed up towards the big park on Burganess. The grass had been gnawed low by the sheep. It looked bright and healthy. The air was damp, but it wasn't cold. The low clouds pressed down on the land. In front of them, a snipe burst from a ditch, like a faulty rocket, twisting one way then the other before careering east up the valley.

'Where are we goin exactly?' Sandy asked.

'We're going up to that ditch that runs along the edge of the big park.' David looked up and nodded in the general direction.

'Okay, is he needin cleaned oot? I shoulda taken me own shovel. We'd've gotten it done quicker.'

'No, I doot wan'll be enough fir dis job.'

David was striding faster than was comfortable on the steep side of the valley. He knew exactly where he was heading, and Sandy felt strange about it. Usually their work together had a relaxed, convivial feeling. This was different. It didn't feel like they were travelling together. It felt like he was being led.

They crossed from the beach park into the big park, then followed the fence northeast up the valley a little way. Up ahead, a gang of hooded crows were loitering, heads down, like street-corner hoodlums. Then David stopped, and Sandy saw why.

Lying in the shallow ditch at the corner of the field was a lamb. Its eyes were scarlet holes dug by the crows, but otherwise it was intact. Intact, and dead. The animal was lying on its front, splayed out as though it had bellyflopped in, but its head was caught inside a broken square of wire in the fence. One end of the wire had stuck into its neck, but there wasn't much blood, so it hadn't punctured anything vital. There was mud splashed around on the grass, from the struggle, and its back legs too were filthy. The lamb had died trying to escape. Once it had exhausted itself, it must have lain down, terrified, in pain, and been suffocated by the fence.

'Shit!' Sandy said.

'Aye. Shit.'

'How did you ken it was here?'

'I could see it fae da road. *Du* should o seen it too. A big white blob in da park, no movin. *Du shoulda seen it!*'

Sandy felt like a child being scolded. He wanted to argue and defend himself, but he had no argument, no defence.

'Well, at least du'll no hae ony mair problems wi him.' David lifted one of the legs to check, then corrected himself. 'Wi *her*, I should say.'

'What do you mean?'

'Dis is da een at wis gettin oot onto da road afore. Da wan du wis askin aboot. Sometimes dey just tak a notion and den keep takin it. Ony fence'll dae.' He shook his head. 'Made a bad choice wi dis een, though. Got through an couldna git back. Shu was probably lyin here fir quite a while, though. Makkin a lot o noise, Ah'd o thoght. Her mither tae.' He nodded towards a ewe lingering nearby. She was feeding, with another lamb at her side, but she was apart from the other sheep. Still waiting for this one to come home.

'How lang has she been dead?'

'A day, mebbie. Less probably. Da craas is pecked oot her een afore shu was deed.'

Sandy flinched. There were two crows still lingering in the park, preening themselves.

'Right, I guess we need to bury her then. That's what the shovel's for, isn't it?'

'Nope, *we* dunna need to bury her. *Du* needs ta bury her.' David handed the shovel over.

'Where?'

'Onywhar du can dig a big enoff hol. Keep her awa fae da ditch an awa fae da burn. Towards the cliff a bit, mebbie. Git doon at least a metre. Dat's da rules.'

David turned his head and pressed a finger to his nostril. He blew his nose onto the ground, then wiped it with his sleeve. He turned and walked away, back down and across the fence. Sandy watched him striding toward the burn, with the gait of a much younger man. He watched him, and he felt a clutching in his gut. It was a feeling of abandonment and of guilt. It was an old feeling. He bent down and took the animal's back legs in one hand and its front legs in the other, and lifted. It was a big lamb for the time of year, but there still wasn't too much weight in it. It was stiff and awkward. He let go with his left hand and it swung, head down, just above the ground. He grabbed the shovel again and walked up the headland a bit, then laid the lamb on the grass.

The digging wasn't easy. The hole didn't need to be wide, but it needed to be deep, and every bite the shovel took hit stones just beneath the surface. After a few moments, the point hit a rock large enough to send a shudder through Sandy's whole body. He stopped, replaced what he'd dug, and moved on. He wasn't going to get deep enough there.

Further up the hill the ground looked even shallower, with stones protruding from the grass. Nowhere did the earth look soft enough to dig a grave. Eventually, Sandy was standing close to the cliff, the shovel in one hand and the dead lamb dangling in the other. He crept towards the edge and peered over at the churning sea below. He could, without difficulty, hurl the animal out into the water, and no one would be any the wiser. Except David. He would ask, and Sandy wouldn't be able to lie.

He sat down. The morning wasn't warm, but in his boilersuit he was comfortable enough. The dampness had eased off, and it looked like the afternoon would stay dry. Fulmars and kitti-wakes patrolled the banks around him. He watched them, and they watched him.

He thought, then, of a story Emma had once told him about her father. David was not religious, though he didn't make a big deal of it. He'd gone to church when he was younger, then at some point he'd stopped, as most people here had. One evening, shortly after the family finished eating together in the kitchen, there had been a knock at the front door. Emma wasn't sure if her father had seen the two Jehovah's Witnesses coming up the driveway in their black suits or whether he could tell, somehow, by the nature of the knock, who it was, but he stood, a comfortable smile on his face, and went to the door.

Emma didn't pay much attention to the beginning of the conversation – she could hardly imagine anything less interesting, aged seventeen – but when she went to the bathroom half an hour later and saw that the three were still there on the doorstep, she did notice. And when, after another ten minutes or so, she saw her father march the men to the park at the back of the house to admire his ram, she started to laugh.

'Jesus was a shepherd?' she heard him ask, through the open window. 'Funny, we were always told in school he was a carpenter. I suppose it's hard to be sure after so long.'

David knew how to act like a stupid man when it suited his purpose, and on this occasion his sole purpose was to amuse himself. He was speaking English too, which he almost never did. 'Well, if he was a shepherd, then I've obviously made the right career choice,' he said. 'Jesus was a man who knew what he was doing, right?'

The men did not look troubled by the welcome they were receiving. They were glad, perhaps, that someone was taking an interest in them. Most doors would have closed in their faces. But after almost an hour they surely wanted to leave. David had talked to them, been enthusiastic, but he wasn't showing any signs of conversion. And so eventually they departed, with David's best wishes roared out behind them.

Sandy shook his head. It was a story about David, but he was thinking now of Emma. He missed her. Last night she'd responded to his text. Not straight away, but later in the evening. Mary must have told her about the situation, as he'd guessed she would. Emma, then, must already have been wondering. *I dunna ken*, she'd written. *I'm sorry, it must be difficult. We can spaek aboot it if du needs to. It's okay. Call me.* He needed to speak now. He needed to hear what she thought, to hear her reassurance, her voice. But there was no signal on his phone.

If anyone had come up behind him at that moment, they might have wondered at this strange pair: the man and his dead companion, looking out to sea. He felt like leaning over and petting the lamb, then, stroking its tight, greasy wool and rubbing his thumb across its nose, as if he could revive it, a day too late. But he refrained. There wasn't much comfort to be found in a carcass.

The smell of salt rose and filled his nostrils as he stood again, lifting the body and the shovel and looking around. He set off back down the hill, trying not to think of how visible he was up here. He thought of Jo then, and wondered if she was watching him. He felt ridiculous. Like some kind of macabre joke had been played on him, and he now had to be humiliated in front of everyone. He felt annoyed with David for doing this to him. He must have known the ground was no use here for digging.

In a patch of darker green at the bottom of the big park, Sandy stopped and plunged his shovel into the earth again. It felt softer, and he lay the animal down beside him and started to dig. He had almost enough time to feel relieved when, a foot beneath the surface, the blade struck a rock, which turned out to be a boulder.

'For fuck's sake!'

He threw the shovel. The point of it struck the lamb's face, then bounced off beyond. Sandy lay down and looked up at the sky, a patchwork of greys, embroidered in white thread. A cold breeze swiped the left side of his face, pawing at his lashes until his eyes began to water. The digging had left sweat prickling on his back and the insides of his legs. He stretched out there on the grass, letting the day surround and enclose him. Turning his head to one side he saw the lamb looking over at him, its empty red sockets pointed in his direction.

'I'm sorry for throwin the shovel. I didna mean it to hit you.' Sandy twisted his mouth into an apologetic smile. 'An I'm sorry for lettin you die. I shoulda seen you earlier an helped you oot.'

Sandy reached his arm and stroked the animal's head, his hand cupping its muzzle as if it were a dog. 'I'm sorry.' He closed his eyes, cradling the lamb, listening to the sounds of the valley and of the sea.

When he woke, he wasn't sure how much time had passed. It couldn't be long – it still felt somewhere close to lunchtime, and a glow behind the clouds showed the sun was not far from its peak – but he felt groggy and stiff. His hand was still tucked beneath the lamb, and there was still a half-dug hole at his feet. Lying here, Sandy was entirely visible to anyone down on the road, especially anyone with a pair of binoculars. He didn't get up. If he had been spotted, he reasoned, somebody would have climbed the hill, thinking something was wrong. But there was no one around. The valley was strangely still, as though there was no one down there at all. Sandy lay on his side, just watching, waiting for something to happen. He was waiting for a door to open and someone to emerge, or for a sound to come ringing through the air. But there was nothing. The valley seemed as dead as the lamb.

Sandy imagined for a moment that it might be true. He imagined that, while he was sleeping, everyone in the valley had died. He imagined himself a kind of Rip Van Winkle, fallen asleep for decades and woken to a valley empty of people. How long would it be, he wondered, before no one was left living here? David had sometimes mentioned his fear that the place would empty. It was a recurring nightmare of his, and there were times when Sandy thought it might not be so fanciful or unlikely. There was no one left now except David whose ties to the place were any deeper than circumstantial. Only Kate and Emma shared that connection, and they were already gone.

But what if the valley *did* empty? What if all these houses were sold to people who only wanted to live in them a few weeks a year? Or what if they were abandoned, and crumbled into piles of stones, like the two houses at the far end of the big park? What would it matter, really, if another valley was deserted? Sandy thought, somehow, that it did matter, but he could not explain why.

He sat up, filling the hole back in, kicking the earth with his boots, then moved a few metres down the hill. He began again to dig, and sure enough the ground here lifted without difficulty. Before long he had a hole about a metre deep and wide enough to fit the lamb. He didn't throw it in but instead placed the animal gently at the bottom, arranging it as comfortably as he was able in the space. He stood up, looking at it curled up beneath him, nodded, then began to fill the earth in again, pushing the soil down on top of it, covering the hole again with turf. He tapped it all down with his boot, then turned and headed back towards the house.

Closing the gate at the turning circle, Sandy heard a car come down the road. It was David's pickup. He didn't want to speak to David, didn't know what kind of mood he'd be in now. But he stood and waited.

'Aye aye,' said David, leaning out of the window, not turning off the engine. 'Du get her buried?'

'Aye.' Sandy nodded.

'An du's been diggin graves fir aa da rest o da animals too, wi da time it's taken dee?'

Sandy didn't smile. He said nothing, then turned as if to continue home, but David spoke again.

'Juist so du kens, Jo and Ryan are movin oot o da Red Hoose.'

Sandy stopped. 'How come?'

'Dey were takkin da piss, exploitin me lik yon. Du wis right ta let me ken. Ah'm geen dem a month's notice.'

'That seems a bit extreme.'

'Aye, mebbie. But I giud ta discuss it wi dem an Ryan juist wouldna accept at he wis don onything wrang. I thoght at we could sort it atween wis, but he wasna interested. So I sorted it mesel.'

Sandy looked at him for a moment. He shook his head, but not enough that David might notice, then walked back towards the house. He took the phone from his pocket, found Emma's number and dialled.

★   ★   ★

Mary smiled to herself. She stood up from the wooden chair in the hall, then stepped through to the kitchen. Everything was tidy, everything was done. There was nothing that needed her attention. And yet her attention needed to settle somewhere. The thought of sitting down again, reading or watching television, made her feel immediately restless. She had to do something with the afternoon. She felt that old, unshakeable niggle.

Maybe flapjacks. David would like that. He was out working with the sheep, so he'd missed Emma's call, but he'd be back soon enough. And hungry, no doubt. She took the oats and raisins from the cupboard, and the scales from the bottom drawer. She didn't need the recipe. She knew it well enough.

Mary had spent the morning in Lerwick, performing grandmotherly duties. Kate had called last night. She had some kind of appointment – a massage or something like that – and Callum, her husband, had to work, so would Mary mind coming in for a couple of hours? And no, of course she didn't. Not in the slightest, though a bit more warning would be nice. She preferred to have them here when that was possible. It was easier to entertain the children at the house than it was in town. Cheaper, too. But they were no trouble anyway. Charlie was quiet. A little uptight for a six year old, perhaps. But happy, for the most part. And Beth was great fun. Chatty, engaged, just perfect. Exactly as Emma and Kate had been at that age.

The three of them drank hot chocolates in a cafe first of all, then walked along Commercial Street, looking in the shop windows, Beth pointing, Charlie striding ahead. Then round the Knab and out on the footpath to the Sletts to see the seals, the two young ones chattering all the way, hardly bickering at all. It was almost a shame to have to give them back.

But no matter how good they were, the children always left her drained of energy. When she'd got home at lunchtime, she'd sat in the living room and closed her eyes, just for half an hour or so. As close to a nap as she could manage. She felt better after that.

She and David usually took Beth once a month, sometimes twice, while Charlie was at school. On those days they could pace things better. David would take her outside to see the animals, then she'd come in to help Mary. Often as not they'd end up making biscuits, or sometimes a cake. The little girl would stand atop a stool sieving flour, weighing sugar, counting eggs, stirring. Kate had been a good baker herself when she was younger, as had Emma, but she didn't have the energy for it now, she said. Not by the time work was done. She bought biscuits, bought cakes, bought bread.

Mary had no problem with that. She knew what it was like to come home after a day at work and be faced with hungry children, dirty dishes, a full laundry basket. But still, when it came to Beth – and Charlie too, when he was here – Mary felt an urge to pass on some of this stuff she'd carried with her, this knowledge. Baking, sewing, gardening: it all felt like some kind of inheritance. And as she watched the little girl standing there, reaching up from the stool, trying to copy her grandmother, she felt her heart rise and swell and warm inside. She saw her own daughters as they'd been at that age: bright, curious, eager to please. And she saw herself, too, looking up at her own mother, waiting for instructions.

It was funny, she thought, how these things could change over time. Something as simple as baking biscuits started out as fun, then became a chore, then became something else entirely, some sort of gift to pass on to the next generation. In another two or three decades, Beth would be feeling guilty for not having enough time to bake for her own children, and then it would be Kate's turn to teach. Maybe, maybe. Who knew?

The flapjacks were nearly done when David returned, and by the time he was out of the shower they were cooling on the rack beside the window.

'Your timing, as ever, is perfect.'

'I try me best,' he said, sitting down at the table with a cup of tea. Mary set out a plate of flapjacks and sat opposite him, smiling. She had hardly stopped smiling for the past hour, in fact.

'What's up wi dee?' he asked. 'Du looks like du's won da lottery. Or else been stealin me whisky.'

'No, not that,' she said. 'But I've got good news.'

'Okay, well, is du goin ta tell me?'

'Emma's coming home.'

'Comin hame? As in back to stay?'

'No, David! For goodness sake! Just for a holiday, later in the summer. She phoned this afternoon to say she'd booked a flight.'

'Well, dat's great news.' He bit into a flapjack and nodded, then grinned. 'Ah'll mebbie let her ken the Red Hoose is free again though, juist in case.'

Mary laughed. 'Aye, you let her ken that. See what she says.'

SUNDAY,
26TH JUNE

Sandy leaned back against the wall, on the road side of the pen, and sighed. This was, in some ways, one of the more pleasurable tasks involved in keeping sheep. Removing the winter coats, cutting the year's growth away, felt like an achievement. It brought relief to the animals, who were beginning to look distinctly uncomfortable. But it also brought a tangible outcome, with a great mound of greasy wool left over at the end of the day. Not that the wool was worth much – it certainly didn't pay for the time it took to collect it – but it had a use, and that was something.

Those few dozen fleeces would be folded, rolled and packed in hessian bags, then taken to the brokers in town. There, they would disappear into that mysterious system that would turn them, eventually, into something else. Sandy had once expressed out loud his desire for the whole process to be brought closer to home, for the benefits to be more tangible. The expression on David's face told him how naive and romantic he was being. A few days later he'd found a pair of knitting needles on the kitchen table. 'Dad brought dem,' explained Emma. 'A present for dee, he said.' There was no one left in the valley now who knitted.

Sandy smiled to himself, then, as he thought of Emma. They had spoken several times over the past few weeks. Mostly about Liz, of course, though she'd ask about the croft too, about how he was enjoying it, this life they might have had together. Sometimes Sandy would complain about David, about the way he was always there, looking over his shoulder.

'Now you ken what it was like growin up wi him,' she'd laugh.

'Aye, now I ken.'

He'd felt something opening inside himself as they talked, some physical echo of the space she'd once occupied. He missed her, but he hadn't told her so.

David had come down first thing this morning with Sam to round up the sheep. It hadn't taken long. The dog was used to this park, and the sheep were used to this dog. It seemed they dawdled only out of stubbornness. As soon as the dog jumped over the fence, with the men close behind, the animals understood what was required. Their refusal to cooperate was just part of the game, in which every player knew their roles. The dog would crouch, cocked like a rifle, awaiting instructions it didn't really need. David yelled those instructions – *Away! Lie doon! Come by!* – and the dog would obey most of them. The sheep, for their part, would go where they were meant to go, bunching together, then splitting at the last moment. Sandy would chase those that escaped, while David and Sam held the others as steady as possible. With a bit of luck the fugitives would turn around again, deciding, after all, to choose the safety of the flock over the freedom of the field. And then they were in.

They dosed the lambs first, squirting creamy-white worming fluid into each of their mouths, then daubing red paint on their heads so they knew who'd been done. Then the lambs were lifted out and the pen gate brought tighter, to keep the sheep together. David went home, leaving Sandy behind to clip.

The ewes were bunched close in the pen, but they milled around as Sandy took one then another aside to shear. In the park, the lambs would lift their heads from time to time and call, forlornly, to their mothers, who in turn would call back, assuring them that everything was more or less okay. None seemed overly concerned by their incarceration. They knew it was temporary.

Sandy clipped as he'd been taught, with hand shears rather than electric clippers. 'Yon electric eens is juist too noisy,' David had told him, by which Sandy understood him to mean too easy. David always had an idea of the proper way to do things, and that didn't always equate to the simplest way. But Sandy had to admit that, while slower, there was a pleasure in doing it this way, taking as long as it needed to take, and hearing the morning unfold, without the buzz of an electric motor.

When he got hold of a ewe, Sandy would turn the animal until it was sitting on its backside, then he'd stand behind, gripping its body between his legs. 'Be firm wi dem an dey willna struggle. Let dem ken du's gotten a good grip,' David had told him. Which sometimes turned out to be true.

Leaning forward, he would start with the neck, holding the fleece away from the skin, looking for the rise, that thin layer of new growth beneath last year's wool. By cutting through that layer the old fleece would, in theory, hold together, and come off in one piece. On some ewes, it was easy. Their wool had already begun to slough away, like old wallpaper, and the shears were hardly needed at all. On others, though, it took longer. The wool had to be teased back to find the rise, close enough to the skin to keep the fleece intact but not too close to cut them. A can of purple antiseptic spray stood at his feet in case of such accidents. When the sharp blade slipped, exposing a pink triangle of flesh, he felt the sheep flinch, and he flinched too. A squirt of the spray covered up his mistake.

The one he held now was a wriggler. He hadn't cut her so

far, but she was in danger of causing herself harm, twisting beneath him as though offended by the indignity of her position. Sandy stood up and straightened. He would suffer for this tomorrow, he always did. There were other methods, of course – he could have lain the sheep down and tied her legs, which would have allowed him at least to kneel. But David seemed to regard such tactics as cheating, or at least highly undesirable in some vague and inexplicit way. And so Sandy continued like this, bending then straightening, bending then straightening, doing his best to calm the fidgety ewe as he removed her tightly fitted winter jacket, clip after clip.

'Hey, Sandy!'

He looked up, surprised. He'd not heard anyone approaching, so for a second it seemed as though the shout had come from the animal between his legs. He turned around and tried his best to keep his expression neutral. Jo was standing at the gate just behind him.

'Hello,' he said, raising the shears in greeting. 'How're you doin? I'm no seen you in a while.'

'No, I've been lying low. Or hiding maybe.'

Sandy couldn't think of how to respond. He opened his mouth, but she cut him off.

'Actually, I've come to say goodbye, really. I suppose David told you he's chucked us out.'

'Well, he didna put it like that, but aye, he mentioned it.'

'I don't blame him, I suppose. We should have been honest from the start. But I am sorry. I liked it here. I don't really want to go.' She turned her eyes away, clenched her jaw.

'I ken,' Sandy said. He looked down at the ewe again, which had remained still since Jo arrived. 'So where're you goin noo?'

'To my mum's house, in the short term. Ryan's flat is let out on a six-month lease, so we can't go there. In theory, we were on the same agreement here, but . . . Well, Ryan wanted to argue, or go to the Citizen's Advice or something. But I persuaded him not to. It wouldn't make any difference. We couldn't live here if David didn't want us to.'

'No, you couldn't. None o wis could.' Sandy raised his eyebrows and gave a sympathetic half-smile.

'I don't know what the long-term plan is, though. Well, there isn't one. We'll probably just wait until Ryan's place is free, then move back to town. But who knows? At the moment I have no idea what I want to do. Part of me feels like just jacking my job in and moving away.'

'And Ryan?'

'Yes, I feel like jacking him in too,' she laughed, then paused. 'I wanted to say sorry, though. About the party. I know it's a while ago now, but I haven't had a chance. I was very drunk. I'm not sure what else to say about it. I'm sorry if I was confusing.'

'Well, yeah, you were confusing. But then I'm easily confused. You're the least of it, to be honest.'

'Drink's a dangerous thing,' she smiled.

'Aye, it can mak you tell the truth to strangers.'

'You're not a stranger, Sandy.'

'No, I guess no.'

Sensing a moment of weakness, Sandy's sheep came suddenly to life, writhing then wrenching herself out from between his legs and back among the others, trailing a white woollen cape on the muddy ground beneath her.

'Shite!' He dropped the shears and dived after the animal.

'Sorry,' Jo said. 'That was my fault for distracting you.' She paused. 'Do you want a hand, though, since I'm here? I've never clipped a sheep before, but I'm willing to try.'

Sandy grabbed hold of the half-shorn ewe. Her fleece had shredded and was covered in mud and shit. He looked up. 'Well, you're no really dressed for it, but if you want to grab a boiler-suit and shears fae the shed I'll no stop you.'

Jo nodded. 'Okay, boss.'

She returned a few minutes later in a pair of overalls several sizes too big. The sleeves were rolled back and the legs hung down over her boots, dragging on the ground. 'Right,' she said, 'so what do I do?'

'Climb in,' said Sandy. 'I'll show you.'

For the next hour, the two of them stood side by side, hardly speaking. For her first sheep, Sandy tied the legs, instructing Jo to kneel beside it. But afterwards, she did as he did, standing, leaning, legs clasping. He'd look over at her now and then, watching her hands move, seeing how careful she was, how considerate with the blades. She was good. She picked it up easily, seemed confident with the animals and unfazed when they tried to escape.

'You're a natural!'

'I know!' she laughed. 'I'll have to get some of my own now. Maybe this is the life for me, after all.'

'Mebbie so. It's a shame you're leavin, then.'

'Yes, it is,' she said. 'It is.' She gave a smile that seemed to carry a heavy burden of regret. He wished he'd kept silent.

When all the sheep were done, Sandy opened the gate to let them go. The ewes jumped and ran the few metres into the park, then bowed their heads again to the grass, as though nothing had ever happened. He saw the skin on their backs quiver as they adjusted to the temperature. Lambs followed the calls of their mothers and hurtled to meet them, thrusting their heads hard beneath, eager for a feed. Everything was back as it had been.

'Thank you for your help,' Sandy said. 'You made that job go a lot faster.'

'No, thank you for letting me join in,' said Jo. 'I enjoyed it.' She unzipped the boiler suit and drew her arms from the sleeves, letting it fall from her shoulders to the ground. He watched as she slipped her muddy boots off and stepped out of the overalls. They faced each other.

'I'm really sorry,' he said. 'I wish you were staying.'

'I know. And it's okay.'

Sandy wondered if she knew it was him who'd told David about the house. She and Ryan must have suspected, they must have guessed. But then, this was Shetland. It could have been anyone. Ryan wasn't exactly secretive about it. He'd almost boasted. Perhaps she had no idea.

'Well, take care,' he said.

'Yes, you too. And you've got my number, so just text me if you fancy meeting up in town sometime. It would be nice to see you. Really.'

He nodded. 'I will do,' he said, though he knew that he wouldn't. There was surely something else to tell her, but he couldn't think of it.

Jo leaned forward and put her arms around him. Two seconds, maybe three. That was all. 'See you, Sandy,' she said, then turned and walked away.

Sandy put all of the fleeces into a hessian sack, aside from the torn muddy one, which he rolled up under his arm. The sack, slung over his shoulder, he set at the back of the shed, and the shears, paint and spray on the work bench. The dirty fleece he threw in a corner to be dumped. The shed was cool and overflowing with shadows, and he stood in the doorway for a moment, looking up into the valley, before returning to the house. He carried Jo's boilersuit in to be washed.

★　★　★

Liz heard the front door close and footsteps on the stairs. She heard the lock on the bathroom click, and she heard the shower fizz into life. Jim was due in half an hour, and everything was almost ready. The table was set, the lamb had not much longer to go in the oven, the vegetables were on. Nothing much now needed to be done. But still, she was panicking. It was, in part, the panic of the expectant host. But it was more than that.

She had spoken to Jim twice on the phone since she'd returned. Both were brief, somewhat tense conversations, and not at all enjoyable. Prior to that she had not had any communication with him for many years. They were estranged entirely. That had suited her fine then. Now, it needed to change, and she was nervous.

Several times this past week she had considered cancelling their lunch. Once, she had even picked up the phone and started to dial his number. But she couldn't do it. Too much rested on today. She imagined Jim doing the same thing now, sitting at home, stewing over old resentments, lifting his car keys then putting them down again, changing his mind. She felt anger at the very thought of it.

The day that she and Jim met, she was eighteen and less than a year out of school. She was working up at Sullom Voe, serving food in the canteen. Those were long days, but the job paid pretty well. Well enough to put up with the whistles and the nudges and the come-ons, at least. She was carrying dirty plates down the corridor from the dining room to the kitchen one lunchtime when two men – boys, really – emerged from behind double doors, bringing deliveries in from a van outside. The two of them stopped and waited for her to pass, then continued down the corridor to the store room. When she returned from the kitchen, this time with plates of mince and tatties, they were coming the other way, their hands now empty. She smiled at them, and both men smiled back.

'Hi aye!' Jim nodded as he passed, and then he turned, as she'd already guessed he would, and smiled again. 'Ah'm Jim,' he said. 'Pleased to meet dee.'

'You haven't met me yet.'

'No, du's right. Well, is du free on Friday? We could meet properly den.'

She hesitated, then decided. He was handsome, and he'd made her laugh. That was enough. 'Sure, okay.'

He waved and turned to go.

'I'm Lizzie,' she called after him.

'I ken wha du is.'

Their date, if you could call it that, did not go particularly well. They had a few drinks, and he didn't seem to have much to say for himself. Then his friends joined them, and they were loud and leery. She didn't like any of them very much, but he seemed sweet. He paid attention when she spoke. He didn't let her become excluded. He walked her back to her house late in the evening, though he was the drunk one, but she turned away before he had a chance to try to kiss her. She closed the door behind her and expected that would be the end of it. But the next day there he was at work again, the same cheeky smile, the same cockiness. She gave him another shot.

Liz insisted from the very beginning that there would be no marriage. Anything that felt like a boundary, like tying down, she would not accept. I won't cheat on you, she said, but if you tell me I can't cheat, then I will. I need to be able to run if I have to. I need to be free to go.

Probably he never quite believed her. Everyone says things like that when they're young, don't they? Probably he assumed that, sooner or later, some kind of 'biological clock' or 'home-making instinct' would kick in, and there she'd be, begging to get married, for him to make a good woman out of her. But she always knew it wouldn't happen. She didn't have those instincts, or at least if she did they weren't strong enough to cancel out her instinct to leave a door open in case she needed to flee.

For that reason, she never saw their relationship as anything other than temporary. It lasted a month, then six months, then a year, so it was fair to call it long term. But she knew it would only last until she wanted something else, someone else, somewhere else. She thought, perhaps, that he liked her flightiness, her unpredictability. It made her, for as long as she stayed, more of a catch. It made him value her presence. Men become bored when they know women are going to stay, that's what she thought. So she ought to be the perfect partner.

Naturally, though, while this quality did help to maintain Jim's attention – his infatuation, even – it also created problems. It created anxiety in him, a sense that he was teetering always on the edge of panic. When they were out in company, he would watch her. She saw him, though she tried not to meet his eyes and acknowledge that gaze. She felt it on her like the heat of a lamp, and it both warmed her and made her want to retreat. He watched, she thought, not because he didn't trust her with other men; it wasn't jealousy that made him stare. He watched because he wanted to make as much of her as he could. He watched because, she assumed, every time she left the room to go to the toilet he feared she wouldn't return. She was both flattered and appalled by his gaze.

So Sandy, when he arrived inside her, must have seemed to Jim like the anchor that Liz needed, the anchor that would fix her where he wanted her to be, always nearby. And for Liz, who recognised immediately what it meant, it was an anchor that, in the end, she had no choice but to cut free.

She managed seven years. That was better than she ever

imagined. It was better, in truth, than Jim should have hoped for. Looking back, it was hard to say for sure whether she had always *intended* to walk away, always known she would abandon her partner and her son. It wasn't as simple as that. All she had known for certain was that the situation Jim had engineered, the cosy family unit he created, was not one that could last indefinitely. She didn't foresee the exact outcome, but she always knew that *something* would happen.

'You know, nothing lasts forever,' she said to Jim on the phone, a few weeks after she left. 'I could die tomorrow. You wouldn't be angry at me then, but the result would be the same.'

'If you killed yourself, I'd be angry,' Jim replied.

'I'm not going to kill myself, so maybe you should be grateful for that.' She tied him in knots deliberately, bound him up in never-ending coils of illogic.

It had never occurred to her, since coming home, that Jim would not want to see her again. Hate, like everything else, was surely temporary. And even if he did still hate her, he must at least be curious. When someone disappears from your life like that, you must always wonder who they actually are, what part of them it is that would make them go. Jim, it seemed, had spent more than twenty years wondering who she was, so he could hardly say no to Sunday dinner.

'Do you need a hand?' Sandy was standing, wet-haired, at the bottom of the stairs.

'No, I think everything's under control. You can go and sit down, or pour yourself a glass of wine, if you want. Pour us *both* a glass of wine.'

'I'm okay for the moment, thanks. I'll hae something when Dad arrives.' He looked up at the clock on the kitchen wall. 'Shoulda been here five minutes ago.'

'I'm sure he'll be here any time now. Are you nervous?'

Sandy raised an eyebrow and screwed the side of his mouth up. He didn't answer, just went back upstairs until a knock at the front door brought him down again.

'Hey, Dad, how're you?'

Jim stood in the porch, dressed like a man who wasn't sure what was required of him. He had on a smart grey shirt, tucked in to a pair of faded jeans, with a pair of work boots below. Put together, they made him look more like an off-duty cowboy than a lonely, late-middle-aged council employee.

'Ah'm okay, son. Quiet weekend. Quiet week. Ah'm okay.'

Sandy nodded. 'You didna have to come oot today. I wouldna hae been offended.'

'I ken, I ken. It's fine. It's aa fine.'

Liz stood listening to them talk, until, when the pleasantries were done, Jim turned to her.

'Hi aye, Lizzie.' He extended his hand hesitantly. She could see in his face that he regretted it. A handshake wasn't right at all. But she took it and smiled, squeezing his palm between both of hers, then let go.

'Thank you for coming, Jim,' she said. 'And I mean that. Thank you. It means a lot to me that we can all be together. And to Sandy, too.'

'Don't bring me into it.'

Jim nodded, then grinned, just slightly. He looked into the kitchen. 'Ah'm gaspin fir a drink, if du has wan.'

'Wine or beer?'

'What's du drinkin, Sandy?'

'I'll hae wine, I think.'

'Ok, well, Ah'll go wi dat fir a change. A glass o wine'd be good.' He clasped his hands together and gazed around the room, taking the place in.

Looking at this sagging man, Liz wasn't sure quite what she felt. It wasn't guilt, anyway. Jim had always been a good man, and she thought he probably still was. Not in any particularly admirable way. He just didn't have much badness in him. He didn't mean anyone any harm, except perhaps himself. Liz realised that any anger she might once have felt towards him had long dissolved. The anger she felt over her pregnancy had gone as soon as Sandy was born. For, despite everything, it wouldn't be fair to say that she didn't love her son. She did. Just not in the way that was required of her.

No, she felt no anger and no guilt. It was more a kind of pity. This man, who was a good man, more or less, had not enjoyed the kind of life he deserved to enjoy. He had not had the happiness he ought to have had, that he probably thought he'd have when he first met Liz.

The three of them sat around the little table in the kitchen, its two side flaps lifted to accommodate the meal. Liz carved the lamb and served it out, together with the roast potatoes, peas and carrots. She poured the wine and poured the gravy and said 'Cheers' and was the perfect host, and the two men went along with it, not saying much at all.

'How's your mother, Jim?' Liz asked, trying hard to find a suitable conversation.

'Well, still living, just aboot. Shu's in a home noo, thank goodness. Her body still works fine enough, but her mind isna up ta much. Dusna ken wha I am half da time. Mebbie dusna care. I go an visit, but it's hard wark, du kens.'

'I'd hate to end up like that. Makes me shudder.'

'Aye, well, it's worse if du haes naebody to look eftir dee, I suppose.'

She took the jibe in silence. Then, after a pause, 'Did you ever think Sandy would end up a crofter? I could hardly have imagined it. I was surprised enough when he came back to Shetland, but crofting! Sheep!' She laughed.

Jim nodded, chewing a mouthful of lamb. 'Well, onybody can be surprisin if dey want to be. An if he's happy, well, dat's fine wi me. Croftin is fine wi me.'

'Yes, I mean, I didn't say there was anything wrong with it. I just didn't expect it, that's all.'

Jim shrugged, then spoke again. 'So, how lang is du plannin on stayin?' he asked, swigging back the last of his wine.

Liz raised her eyebrows, then looked at her plate, where a half potato lay in a puddle of gravy. She saw Sandy turn to her, waiting for her reply.

'Well, I've been thinking about that. I wasn't sure when I came back if I'd feel like being home for more than a month or two. It's been so long, you know, I just wasn't sure. But I'm enjoying it. More than I thought, anyway. I've started looking for jobs.'

'So is du goin to rely on Sandy's hospitality indefinitely?'

'No, not at all. I'll be leaving soon, I think.'

'Uh huh?' Sandy said. His mouth was full, but the question mark was audible.

'No, in fact I think I'll be out of your hair in a week or two, all being well. I was going to tell you later on. I've spoken to David. The Red House is going to be free from next weekend, and I asked if I could move in, on a trial basis anyway. He was delighted, said it saved him the trouble of advertising and interviewing and all that. Suits us both, it seems. And you, Sandy.'

Sandy's chewing had slowed as she spoke, and now it stopped entirely. 'How does it suit me, exactly?'

'Well, you can't want me sharing the house with you much longer. I'm getting under your feet here.'

'Aye, you're right there, onyway.'

'So I thought that moving up the road would be good for us both.'

'No, it'd be good for *you*. No for me.'

'I don't understand. You don't want me to go, but you don't want me to stay?'

'No, I *do* want you to go. An I dunna care where you go, particularly. I just dunna want you stayin *here*, in the *valley*. This is *my* home, no yours.'

'So what am I supposed to do, then?'

Sandy shrugged, then stood. 'Start lookin for somewhere else. Find your own home. There's plenty of other places to live in Shetland. Just pick one and stick wi it.'

He left the table then and went to the front door. Outside, he drove the car up the road to Kettlester, parked next to the house and went in without knocking. David and Mary were sat in the kitchen, either side of the table, two mugs in front of them. David nodded as Sandy came in.

'Aye aye, boy. Is du wantin to join wis? Da kettle's juist boiled.'

'You canna help it, can you?' said Sandy. 'Interferin in folk's lives. You canna help tryin to control everythin and everyone in this valley.'

David didn't speak, just waited for Sandy to continue.

'Ah'm sick o it. Ah'm sick o you tryin to choose my future for me. It's no dine to decide. Ah'm sick o it.' His voice trailed off, and he stood beside the door, no words left to throw, his anger gone.

It was Mary who rose from her seat and came towards him then. She put her arms out, and he allowed her to encircle him, to hold him, as he leaned into her shoulder.

'Come and sit doon,' she said. 'Come and sit doon.'

SATURDAY,
16ᵀᴴ JULY

This was the first time Alice had been to Gardie since Maggie died. It was, in fact, the first time she'd been here in almost three years, and only the third, or perhaps fourth, time ever. The house was not familiar to her in the way that David and Mary's was, or even the Red House. Standing at the front door, she tried to conjure an image of the place as it had been, before stepping into it as it now was. She struggled to picture the space inside. A vague, incomplete memory of the living room – the shape of it, the colour of the walls. Maggie's chair huddled in a corner. That was all she could manage.

Alice paused, knocked, then opened the door.

Sandy was expecting her. She'd told him she'd be here at noon, and her watch said 12.01. 'Tea? Coffee?' he called from the kitchen, as she hung her jacket in the porch.

'I'm okay, thank you.' Alice pulled her shoes off, one then the other, pushing her toes into the heel of the opposite foot.

'Aaright, come on in. I'm just makin mesel a coffee.'

The entranceway was narrower than she remembered. The right wall extended full height most of the way across the room; the left one just a couple of metres, then it opened out into the kitchen. Ahead was another door, leading to the bathroom and the staircase, she assumed, though she'd never been through it before. The walls were white on all sides.

Sandy was leaning against the counter in the kitchen, waiting for the kettle to boil. He smiled and nodded. His hair was a mess. He looked tired.

'How're you, Alice?'

'I'm well, thank you. Very well. It's really kind of you to let me come and visit. I know it must seem like an odd request.'

'Well, I guess it does, a little, but that's aaright. You're very welcome. I'm glad you asked me rather as just comin to look while I was oot.'

She laughed. 'Yes, that would have been a bit rude, wouldn't it? Can't say I wasn't tempted, though. I was just worried your mother would catch me.'

Sandy looked away. 'Well, she's gone noo,' he said. 'She left last week, so you dunna need to worry aboot her.'

'Oh right, well . . . Did she have a good holiday?' Alice knew that Liz's visit was not a holiday. Mary had told her more than a month ago. But she didn't want to let on she'd been gossiping.

'I dunna ken, really.' Sandy poured the coffee from the cafetière into his mug, then turned back to Alice. 'So, you want the tour?'

When she first thought of it, the idea had seemed like a good one. Her biography of Maggie was floundering, particularly since her discussion with David. She'd written several thousand words now, and they were decent words, good enough. They told some kind of story. But still Maggie did not feel present in them. Still she was vague, elusive, almost ghostlike, as though Alice had failed to pin her down. Which was true. She *had* failed. What she'd done was join the dots, fact to fact, date to date. And that wasn't enough.

The house, really, was her last hope. It was a long shot, perhaps, but it was worth a try. This was the place Maggie had spent almost every day of her life; the place where she woke each morning and went to sleep at night; where she ate and laughed and watched television and wrote, before bed, in her diary. Surely, after all that time, after all that living, there would be some part of her left, some memory in the house itself that Alice might, by being here, be able to access. Yes, it was a long shot.

'The tour would be great. I've been in before, but only a few times, and only here, in the kitchen and the living room.'

'Well, it's aa been decorated since Maggie died, an a lot o the furniture is new. But other as that . . .'

Alice followed him into the living room. Again, it didn't look as she remembered it. The coffee table was familiar, and the bookcase in the corner. The layout was pretty much as it used to be, too, with the sofa facing the window, and two armchairs – one facing the television in the corner. But it was different somehow. It seemed bigger, more open. And less lived-in, too. Which was obvious really, yet she hadn't quite expected it. It was like an old person in a very new coat.

'Do you want me to leave you alone for a minute or somethin?' Without turning her head, Alice sensed him smirking. She knew he thought what she was doing was silly, but it was okay. He was probably right. She smiled.

'No, you're all right. How about you show me where everything is, then just leave me to wander for a moment, make a few notes? If that's not too much of an intrusion.'

'That's absolutely fine. I'll show you aboot, then go ootside an drink me coffee in the gairdin.'

'You don't have to leave!' She laughed.

'That's okay. Drinkin coffee ootside is one of life's luxuries. At least it is livin here.'

'Yes, that's true. Okay, we can do that, then you can leave me. I won't be long, I promise.'

'You can be as long as you like. Just dunna go hawkin through me dirty laundry.'

'Okay, deal.'

The tour took only a few minutes. Sandy led her through the door to where the downstairs bathroom and boxroom were, then up the stairs to the first bedroom, then the second, then the little toilet at the end of the corridor.

'And that's it! It's no a big hoose, really. Fine big rooms, but no many of them.'

'Thanks, Sandy, that's great. I'll let you go then, and just note a few things down.'

'Fine, fine. See you in a moment.'

She stood there, still, waiting for him to go out to the porch. She listened as the sounds of the house rose around her. She closed her eyes. There was hardly any wind today, so it was quiet. There was no sucking noise at the window, no creaking or tapping. Just a faint hum from the fridge, and beyond that a hiss, unsteady but insistent. Waves on the beach. Here, the sea would always be present.

Alice didn't look in the bathroom. Instead, she went first to the smaller bedroom, at the back of the house. This was the room, David said, where all Maggie's diaries and letters had been kept. Since she hardly ever had overnight visitors – the last time Ina came from New Zealand was more than a decade ago – it had served mostly as a store. Now it looked like a bedroom. Sparse, but obviously used recently. The sheets on the bed were not fresh. Sandy hadn't changed them since his mother left, Alice guessed. In fact, now that she looked, there was still a half-drunk glass of water on the bedside table. Perhaps he'd not been in here at all.

Sandy's mother had seemed an odd woman. She'd come to visit Alice one afternoon, unannounced, when Alice was trying to work. She invited her in, of course, and made her tea, but she hadn't been as hospitable as she otherwise might have been. Her mind was still on her writing.

Liz had asked all kinds of questions, personal questions, that Alice had tried her best to answer. At the time she found it almost intrusive. But later, when Mary told her more about Liz, she felt even worse about the encounter. There was something manipulative about it, she thought. As though Liz wanted to know the neighbours better than her son did. Or maybe she was just imagining things. The woman made her uncomfortable, that was all, really, and she wasn't sorry she was gone.

There was nothing to see now in this room. The half-made single bed, the wardrobe, the little bookcase and bedside cabinet. That was it. Not even a picture on the wall. It felt empty and anonymous. Sad, even.

Alice turned around and went into the other bedroom, just across the hall. This one had been Maggie's, and now it was Sandy's. But there wasn't much more in here than in the first room. Another wardrobe, identical. A little table on either side of the bed – this one a double. A chest of drawers in one corner, with a mirror and a few other items on top. A jar filled with copper coins. A stick of deodorant. A wallet. A little wooden box. The room was tidier than she'd expected. She looked around, then felt guilty for looking. These things were all Sandy's. They had nothing to do with Maggie.

She wasn't sure what she'd expected, really. Some lingering sense of what had been before. A presence, maybe. Not like a ghost, just some hint of the past. Like when you paint a coat of white over a dark wall and it doesn't quite disguise it. The old remains visible, a shadow beneath the new. But there was nothing. Even the carpets had been changed, so the scuff marks of Maggie's slippers were gone.

The chest of drawers had been hers, Sandy said, so Alice took a closer look. It was a dark wood – she couldn't say for sure what type – and despite some scratches on the corners it looked good for its age. She ran her hands down the side of it, feeling the smooth varnish against her skin, then tugged at the top right drawer, the old wood resisting, then grumbling outwards. A pile of coloured boxer shorts was inside, thrown in together, and one stray sock on top.

'Everything okay up there?'

Alice jumped. She hadn't heard the front door at all. She pushed the drawer back in as quietly as she could, then stepped back across the room.

'Yes, everything's fine. I'll be down in just a second. Sorry for taking so long.'

'No problem at aa. I'm just back in for the last o the coffee. See you ootside.'

She took a long breath. What the hell was she doing, creeping around like a burglar? Looking through Sandy's underwear, for God's sake! What on earth did she expect to find in there?

Alice went out of the room, took a last look, shut her eyes to try to memorise the space, then walked away. Downstairs, the porch door was lying open. She looked around the living room again, but she'd lost her enthusiasm for the task. Whatever she'd hoped to find here she wasn't going to find. Maggie was long gone. She had vanished.

Outside, Sandy was stooping in the flower beds around the edge of the back lawn. He had a mug in one hand and a bucket beside him for the debris. He looked up.

'Any good at weedin?' he asked.

'No. Useless. It just always seemed like too much effort. You should get Mary down here, though. She seems to love it.'

'Aye, she certainly does,' he nodded. 'Well, I hate it. I dunna mind the vegetable patch so much, but this . . .' He waved his free hand around him, indicating the garden. 'This seems like a waste o time. It's no like we get much o a chance tae enjoy it.'

'I know what you mean. My mother always said I'd come to appreciate gardening as I got older.' She grinned. 'But I'm older now, and it still seems like a chore. Maybe once I'm fifty. Or sixty.'

Sandy wandered towards the house, where a bench sat against the wall. It wasn't quite warm enough for sitting out, but both of them had their coats on.

'Did you get what you needed, then?' he asked.

'I think so. I don't really know what I needed, though, to be honest. Like I said, it was just an idea. I'm trying to write about someone I hardly knew. I thought maybe seeing her house would help, but I'm not sure if it will.'

He nodded. 'Well, maybe it's just her. I kent Maggie for three years, and I'm no sure I kent her at aa. She was just . . . Maggie.'

Alice laughed. 'That's exactly what David said: "She was just Maggie." But Maggie must have been someone.'

'Aye, she was *someone*.' Sandy looked away. 'We're aa someone. Even if we dunna ken wha.' He looked at the ground for a moment, then spoke again. 'You know I taught her to send emails?'

'No, I did not know that.'

'Aye, well, Ina was nagging her to learn how to use a computer for years, so I gave her wir auld een. She took to it fine, actually. Better as I expected anyway. She was slow, but . . .' He shrugged. 'Auld folk are always slow wi that stuff, aren't they?'

'I suppose so.' Alice nodded, then drew a long breath as the understanding clicked. 'So *that* explains why the letters from Ina dried up a couple of years ago,' she said. 'I assumed the most recent ones must have been thrown out or something, but obviously I was wrong. There weren't any recent ones.'

'Aye, that'll be it. Once she got the computer, she hardly wrote anither letter, I reckon. Took her half the day to send an email, to begin wi, but she persevered.'

'That's funny,' Alice said, slowly. 'I kind of wish she hadn't, though.'

'Why's that?'

'Oh, I don't know. No reason really. I'm just sentimental about letters.'

'Aye.' Sandy nodded. 'Lots o folk are. It's a lang time since I got a handwritten letter. I'd probably keep it noo, if I did. Just for the novelty.' He took a swig, though the coffee must have been cold.

'Did you keep anything of hers?' Alice asked, after another pause. 'I mean, other than the furniture. This is probably sounding desperate now, but I suppose maybe I am.' She laughed.

'Um . . .' Sandy clenched his eyebrows downward. 'I think there might be a few things up in the loft that we couldna decide what to do wi. We put the figurines up there, and mebbie some photos, if I remember right.'

'The figurines?'

'Aye, she haed a collection o peerie dolls. I dunna ken what you'd call them. Made of china. Animals mostly. Sheep an dogs an bears an things. They were hanging up in the living room in a display case.'

'Oh yes, I think I remember that. Beside the big window?'

'Aye. David took the case away. He made it when he was at school, he said. But I kept the animals. He wanted to throw them oot, but I thought someone would mebbie want them. And by the look on your face you might be the very person.'

Sandy laughed again and stood up. He shook his mug upside down over the grass. A few last drops of coffee fell. 'I'll look them oot for you later,' he said. 'I'm goin in to the toon this eftirnoon, then Terry is comin over for a drink later.' He raised his eyebrows dramatically, so Alice understood what that meant.

'I'll try and get up to the loft afore he gets here, then bring them roond to you da moarn.'

'Oh, no need for that. I can come down at some point and pick them up.'

'Okay, you do that.'

Alice stood then and followed Sandy to the front garden and out to the gate. She turned. 'Thank you, Sandy. I'm really sorry for intruding, but it was very kind of you to let me look round.'

'That's no problem at all.' He raised his hand. 'Cheers! See you soon.'

Back at Bayview, Alice sat down in the office and leaned back in the chair. The trip to Gardie had not provided her with a great deal of material, but enough, perhaps, to be going on with. There wasn't much left now to do: just write up what she had, accept the fact that Maggie was still something of a mystery and be done with it. She was too close to the end of the book to get caught up and delayed. She was too near to pause. If she worked hard, it could be finished in a month. Two, at the most. The thought excited her, made her feel almost giddy. It had taken so long to get to this stage.

She pulled her phone from her pocket. She felt like chatting to someone, sharing her excitement, so she found her brother's home number. He probably wouldn't be in − Saturdays they'd be out with the kids doing family things, tennis, picnics or some other wholesome activity − but she'd not spoken to him in weeks, and so she dialled.

It was her sister-in-law who answered, sounding oddly formal, as she often did. 'Hello, Jenny speaking.'

Alice had always liked Jenny, always wanted to know her better, to be *friends* with her, but somehow it had never quite happened. Jenny was nice to her, asked her all the right questions. But she seemed distant, as though she felt it wasn't appropriate to be friends with your spouse's siblings.

'Hey, Jenny, it's Alice. How's things?'

'Oh, hi, Alice. I'm fine, thank you. I take it you've heard, then?'

There had been a change of tone before Jenny's question, and Alice struggled to translate the meaning of it. Sympathetic, perhaps? Understanding? Something like that. She felt a tremor of panic. 'No. What do you mean? Heard what?'

'Oh, I assumed that's why you were calling.'

'What's why I was calling? Sorry, I don't understand.'

'No, that's okay. Don't worry. It's nothing really. Simon wasn't going to tell you, but it's all right. He's with your mother now. She's fine, just a bit shaken up.'

'Jenny, sorry, you're going to have to start a bit further back. Simon wasn't going to tell me what? Why is Mum shaken up?'

Jenny took an audible breath, trying to resolve a situation she had, without intending to, created.

'Your mum had a fall. A couple of days ago. But *don't* worry, she's fine. She broke her arm and bruised a couple of ribs. It looked bad to begin with, but once they got her all cleaned up, you know . . .' She seemed about to add something, then changed her mind.

'But, I mean, how did she do it? Where?'

'She was out at the supermarket – the one near the house. So there were lots of people round her, fortunately. Someone saw her fall and called the ambulance. He said she just slipped on a kerb in the car park and went down sideways. Just one of those things, when you get to that age.'

'Okay. Okay.' Alice felt her panic pushed aside by a gust of anger. 'But why did no one tell me? Why the hell didn't Simon call me straight away?'

There was a delay as Jenny chose her words. She tried to explain Simon's thinking but didn't sound entirely convinced as she did it. 'Well, your mum didn't want him to worry you. You're so . . . far away, she just didn't want you rushing back here when there was nothing you could do and nothing really to worry about.'

Alice didn't know what to say to that. She wasn't even sure whether to believe it had been her mother's choice rather than her brother's. Had he even tried to argue?

'Well, he agreed there was no point in you coming down, and he knew if he told you when it happened that's what you'd have done.'

'Of course it's what I'd have done.'

'Well, yes, exactly. But she's fine, you see. She's fine now. So there was no need, no need to come rushing. She's at the hospital this afternoon, just getting it checked out again. But it's all okay. She's staying here with us for a few days while she gets used to the cast. See how she gets on with it, that's all. Everything's fine. We just didn't want to worry you, Alice. We know how everything is.'

'What do you mean, "how everything is"?' She almost shouted the question, too loud, too angry.

'Sorry, I mean we just didn't want you to be upset, love.' Jenny had never called her that before.

'Well, I'm upset now. And I'm even more upset because you didn't tell me. Is there anything else you've been hiding from me? Is Dad still alive? Are the kids okay?' She was sounding irrational now, but she couldn't help it.

'Alice, everything is fine. Of course we don't hide things from you. It's just this once, and it wasn't meant . . .' She stopped. 'Listen, maybe it would be best if Simon called you once he gets back. I mean, I'm not really . . .' She didn't finish the sentence.

'Yep, get him to call me. And tell him I'm fucking furious.'

'Okay, I'll tell him that. But, Alice, don't worry about your mother. She really *is* fine.'

Alice put the phone down, then lay back on the sofa. She slept.

When Simon called, late that afternoon, he repeated much of what Jenny had said. Mum was fine. He was sorry, he said, that they hadn't told her at once. But they didn't want to worry her unnecessarily. Specifically, they didn't want her jumping on a plane at huge expense when there was nothing she could have done to help.

'I'm not a child, for goodness sake,' Alice said. 'I don't need you to protect me from bad news.'

'I know, of course not. And it's not about *protecting* you. Not really. Look, I'm sorry you had to find out that way. That wasn't the plan. Mum and I were intending to just leave it a few days, then it wouldn't have seemed such a big deal. And really, it *isn't* a big deal. Mum is seventy-five. That's not really old these days. She slipped over and hurt her arm . . .'

'*Broke* her arm,' Alice corrected.

'Yes, *broke* her arm, and now she's on the mend. It's just one of those things that seems worse than it is.'

'So are there other things you've not told me, other things you're hiding from me?'

'No, of course not. We, I mean, look, Alice, I *am* sorry. Genuinely. It seemed like the right thing to do at the time, for your sake, to save you the worry. But I understand why you don't feel that way. It's just, you know, we're *here* and you're *there*, and it's easy to judge things wrong sometimes.'

'What do you mean? Do you think because I live in Shetland I don't care about what happens to you and Mum?'

'No, that's not what I mean. Of course not. I just . . . Alice . . . you're a long way away, that's all I mean.'

He was right. Alice had never felt so far away from her family. She had never felt so excluded from their world, their lives.

'I'm not here because I want to be distant from you.'

'No. I know. But to be honest I'm not really sure why you *are* there any more. I mean, I understand you wanted to get away for a while after . . . I mean, you know, after Jack. I get that. But now . . . I'm not sure I get it now, four years later.'

'I like it here. What's not to get?'

'Well, *do you*? Are you actually *happy* there?'

'Of course. Why wouldn't I be?'

'I don't know. You just don't sound very happy most of the time. All your friends are here. All your family are here. *Everything* is here. What do you have there except . . . except distance?'

'I have friends here.'

'Do you? I never hear you mention anyone except your neighbours – Dave and Mary, or whoever.'

'*David*. And yes, they are my friends. What's wrong with that?'

'Nothing's wrong with it. I'm just not sure I believe you. I'm just not . . . I mean, I just feel like everything is here and you are there, and I don't get it. That's all I mean. I don't get it.'

Alice ended the call. She put the phone back in her pocket and went through to her desk. The pile of papers in front of her needed sorting and editing. All that she'd written about Maggie so far was there, waiting for her. She picked up a red pen, clutched it between her fingers, and began to sob. There was no warning, no whimper or sigh. Just a welling of grief that rose from her guts, her lungs, her throat, as if to drown her. The tears came, and kept coming. Her body shook. Everything came at once – Jack, her parents, Maggie, Simon, the girls – everything she missed or had lost, everything that was far away. She cried until there were no more tears left within her, until the paper in her hands was wet, the ink smeared and smudged. Then she was quiet.

When the house phone rang an hour later, Alice had calmed. Her grief had faded, though a knot of hurt was still tangled at the back of her thoughts.

She answered sternly, expecting her brother. 'Yes, what?' But it was Sandy's voice that greeted her.

'Alice?' He sounded confused.

'Yes, Sandy, hi, sorry, I was miles away. The phone startled me.'

'Oh right, I didna mean to disturb you. Sorry aboot that.'

'No, no problem. Don't worry, it's just me being peculiar.'

'Okay, well, I winna keep you. I just wanted to say that I'm been up in the loft just noo. I found the box wi the peerie animals, and a few framed pictures we decided to keep. It's no much, really.'

'Oh, that's okay. Thanks, Sandy, that's very kind of you.'

'And there was anither notebook up there. A diary, I think. It was awa in a corner, but I brought it doon, in case you wanted that too.'

'A diary?'

'Well, I think so. I'm no looked through it to check. Do you want me to?'

'No, that's okay, I'll read it, whatever it is. Thank you again. Thanks for letting me know.'

'That's nae problem. I'm brought them doonstairs so they're lyin here for you, in a box in the kitchen. You can stop by and get them tomorrow if you lik. Dunna make it too early though,' he laughed. 'Terry is just on his way doon wi a bottle o whisky, so, you ken, I'd advise leavin it until the eftirnoon.'

Alice laughed. 'Sure. That's fine. I'll see you tomorrow then. Have a good night.'

SUNDAY,
17TH JULY

He was conscious of something. A pressure in his eyeballs. A swelling. A widening space, somewhere behind his forehead. Terry forced his eyes open and felt the pressure ease, then twist and buckle into pain. He winced.

The lights were still on in the room. The tall lamp in the far corner and the small one on the table beside Sandy's chair. Sandy himself was sleeping, his mouth agape, with a half-empty bottle of beer beside him. One arm was tucked around his body, the other hung limp beside the seat.

Terry turned his thoughts around. He remembered arriving, a bag of bottles in his hand. Swinging, clinking. He'd been drunk already. Then he was drunker. Sandy followed, taking swigs of whisky, swigs of beer. He'd been purposeful about it. Not quite himself somehow.

Things grew dim after that. Then gone. Swallowed by sleep and by drink. Only patches of light remained. Some joke about David — he remembered the laughter but not the line. Then a conversation about Jamie. The usual stuff. Terry poured out his guilt, his self-pity, as if, like the whisky, it could be shared between them and used up. But Sandy only nodded, listened, said nothing. He couldn't do what was required of him.

The boy was supposed to be staying this weekend. It was Terry's turn. But they'd agreed, he and Jamie, to postpone. A phone call on Thursday night. There was a birthday party, or something like that, Jamie said, and he wanted to attend. The son held up an excuse, and the father grabbed hold of it – glad to shed his duties, and disgusted by his own relief. Last night's alcohol was his punishment and his reward. This morning, only the punishment would remain.

There was no clock in the living room, and the pale sky outside gave no indication of the time. He pushed his hands down against the side of the chair and lifted himself to his feet. He felt unsteady. Crushed. Both drunk and hungover at once. His muscles didn't work. His eyes didn't work. His brain fidgeted, lurched, coiled, crouched. He needed a cigarette.

The packet was in his coat beside the door, and he stumbled in that direction, leaning momentarily against the wall. He needed to get home. He needed a cigarette. He needed to get home most of all, but he needed a cigarette in order to get home. He found one and put it between his lips. Sandy was still sleeping. He wouldn't notice if Terry smoked this one in the house, and by the time he woke, Terry would be back in bed, just up the road.

Terry thought about his bed. He felt a heavy longing to be there, sleeping, dreaming, without fear or nausea. He closed his eyes, wishing it true, wishing he might wake up in a few hours, his son in the next room, the pair of them excited for the day ahead. Terry could see the boy then, tucked up and drowsy, as perfect a thing as could be possible in this world. Smiling, he reached down to kiss Jamie's forehead, to cup his hands around the boy's face, and to hold him, tight, against his own body. Terry leaned forward, tipping, until he lost his balance. Jolt. Back. He pulled himself against the wall.

'Fuck!'

Too loud. Too loud. He stopped, looked. Sandy was still sleeping.

Terry reached into his pocket for the lighter, but it wasn't there. Just a few coins and a set of keys. No phone either. Where had he left it? It didn't matter. The phone didn't matter. He could find it tomorrow. No one would have called him.

No phone. Okay. No lighter. Not okay. Where was it? He looked around but saw nothing. Outside? He'd been smoking at the doorway all night, so maybe it was there. It must be there. He didn't feel like looking. He would check on the way out. He would find it.

Pushing himself away from the wall, he stumbled forward through the hallway to the kitchen. He tripped on a cardboard box beside the table. His feet tangled, stumbled, but he grabbed the countertop and stayed upright. He'd find a light in here. Matches. Top drawer? No matches. Second drawer? No matches. He turned. Sandy hadn't stirred. He had to get home. No matches. The cigarette was wet now. He was drooling. He wiped his mouth with his sleeve and put the cigarette back between his lips.

A fog of exhaustion descended. Terry needed to go. He needed to be horizontal. The stove was the last resort. He stood, hands on the counter, and gazed at the dials on the front. Squinted. He pressed and turned one, anticlockwise, smelled the gas, then pushed the igniter button. A ring of blue light. He looked at it for a few seconds, half-hypnotised, forgetting why he'd made it dance like this. He felt the warmth rising. Then he remembered, leaned forward, sucking as the tobacco touched the flame. Smoke rushed into his mouth, his lungs, and he closed his eyes. He felt himself wobble, felt his arms slacken. Then a wall of heat against his face. For a second, only, it was pleasant. Comfortable. Then it wasn't.

His lashes singed first. He smelled them, acrid, and opened his eyes, as his face dropped into the flame.

Everything found him in that moment. A fist of searing pain.

A stabbing. A shuddering. It was like a hole had opened up in his head and the world was forcing itself inside.

'Jesus!' He threw himself backwards into the room. He jumped, stepped, tripped again on the box, then fell, his skull finding the ground.

'Jesus!' He cupped his hands over his clenched eyes. He wanted to shout to Sandy for help, but he didn't want Sandy to know how stupid he'd been. He didn't want anyone to know how stupid he had been.

'Jesus!' He tried to look upwards, but everything was tight and sharp and hot. He saw something, a light perhaps, a flicker, a shadow. Then nothing. He closed them again, kept his hands to his face, kept everything shut, lay waiting for it all to subside. Waiting.

Time was strange. Terry might have slept, though he couldn't possibly have slept. The pain was too much. But he felt himself drifting, swaying, cradled, as though it were pain itself that could comfort him. All thoughts were banished and blank.

It can't have been more than a few minutes, though perhaps it was more, when he woke again. This time it was the smoke that brought him back. He felt it inside himself. He thought at first it was the cigarette in his mouth. But the cigarette was not in his mouth. It was somewhere else. And the smoke was different.

He tried to sit up, but his eyes still wouldn't open. They were raw and swollen now. 'Fuck! Sandy!' He coughed. His lungs wouldn't let him shout. He couldn't fill them properly, couldn't pull the air in or push it out hard enough. He didn't have the strength.

He tried to crawl, moving sideways first, then forward, until his head hit against a cupboard door. He put his hand out and felt around, but couldn't tell exactly where he was. He tried to call again. 'Sandy! Help!' There was no reply.

310

Terry pulled himself along the ground, keeping his left shoulder against the cupboards until something stopped him. He put his hands out again, felt around. To the right, something was standing against the wall. Cold plastic. The fridge. Fuck. He was going the wrong way.

He turned his body round and went back again, his other shoulder to the cupboards now, trying to remember the room, to picture the place as it was. He saw it as it had been hours ago, when he first arrived – the surfaces clean, the air clean. Behind him was the fridge, to his right were the cupboards, so up ahead he would reach a wall, beyond which was the hallway and the living room.

He stopped and coughed. The smoke was inside him now. He was panicking. He kept going until he found the wall, his head, then his hands.

'Sandy! Sandy! Wake up!' He shouted again, though it seemed hardly more than a whisper. It wasn't loud enough.

Whatever was burning was close now. When he tried to turn left, to move round the wall, he felt the heat of it against his face. He started to choke and moved back again. He crouched in the corner, pressing his cheek to the cool of the painted plasterboard, pulling his legs in close.

Terry thought about Sandy, just a few metres away in the living room. He thought about his own house, cold and empty, just up the road. He thought about Jamie, asleep in town, and he wondered what would happen next. He felt himself at an edge from which it was impossible to go back.

He might die. That thought came to him whole and simple. He might die. It wasn't what he'd expected to happen tonight. It seemed so peculiar a thing to die. To cease being, when everything else continued. There was something un-right about it, something ridiculous. It was almost a joke.

He huddled in against the wall, tucked his head into the crook of his arm, breathing through the fabric of his sleeve. He coughed again, felt a sharpness in his lungs, digging deeper.

* ★ *

It was hopeless. For hours she'd lain awake, turning and stretching and curling up, her body exhausted, but her mind refusing to rest. Alice knew before she went to bed that this would happen. Since Sandy had rung in the evening she'd thought of nothing else. She had almost convinced herself several times to go, to pick up the box from Gardie and read what she had waited months to read. But each time she talked herself out of it. Each time she imagined herself arriving, with Terry and Sandy half-drunk or worse. She would feel a fool. Her impatience would seem ridiculous. And despite it all, she still cared about such things. She cared what people thought.

And so Alice went to bed as usual, with a glass of water and a book. She tried to read but failed, then tried to sleep and failed. She lay, eyes closed, assailed by questions, longing her thoughts to be quiet, to leave her alone, at least until morning. But the noise continued. The churning and wondering went on, until, a little after four, she gave in and got up. She stood, put on her dressing gown and slippers, and went to the window.

Rising early could be a pleasure. The hours before others woke were flavoured with a sweet, illicit tang, especially in summer. In Shetland, daylight stretched its arms almost fully around the clock; and now, early as it was, the day's thin sliver of darkness had faded to a twilight. It was hard though, woolly-headed and deprived of sleep, to find pleasure this morning. Alice looked out on a valley dawn into which sunlight soon would spill. But she thought only of the hours that divided her from Maggie's things. The pictures, the figurines, the diary.

What might actually be in that diary, she had, as yet, no idea. She had wondered, with only a little hope, if it might be the missing volume, from after Walter's death. But it was hard to imagine. The contents of the other notebooks had been so dull, so lifeless, that the thought of Maggie recording her own grief no longer seemed possible. Perhaps it no longer even seemed desirable.

From the bedroom window, Alice could see down to Gardie. The house was as she'd always known it, settled snugly just above the beach, as though it were left there by some long-receded glacier. It looked inevitable, somehow, like a circle of standing stones. Without it the valley would be incomplete. The white stuccoed walls were in shadow still, offset by the reflection of the sun glittering in the kitchen window.

Except that . . . no. If the walls were in shadow, it couldn't be the sun. Alice looked harder, trying to understand what her eyes were seeing. There was a flickering on the glass, and a glow. That was certain. She could see it now. But it wasn't a reflection. The light was not on the glass. It was behind it.

Alice reached for her phone but didn't dial. She wasn't confident enough in her tired eyes. What if they were fooling her? What if she was wrong? She needed to be sure. She dressed, quickly, warmly, grabbed a coat from the porch and ran for the car. The distance between her house and Gardie seemed further than it ever had before.

The morning was close to silent as she pulled up and turned off the engine. But inside, everything was noise. She had not been wrong. The house was on fire. She could see the flames through the window, and wavelets of smoke lapping against the glass. She rang, then, fumbling for the numbers. 'Fire. And ambulance. I think there's someone inside.' She struggled, through her panic, to get the words out, the address. 'Yes, that's it,' she said. 'The house at the end of the road.'

Half an hour it would take for the fire brigade. At least. And the same for the ambulance. She called David. No answer on the mobile. She called the house. It rang six times before the click. Mary answered. Her voice was quiet, muffled by sleep. Alice could hear a tremor of concern in that single word, 'Hello?' A call at this time of the morning is almost never good news.

She said it quickly. She didn't pause to let Mary speak. She just said it. 'Gardie is on fire.'

When Mary answered, it was with a calm, efficient urgency. 'Is Sandy safe?'

'I don't know. I've just got here. I saw it from the house.'

'Okay. Have you called the fire brigade?'

'Yes, they're on their way.'

'Right. I'll wake David. We'll be down there in a moment.'

Alice looked up the road, then back towards the flames. She couldn't wait. She couldn't stand, helpless, and do nothing as the house burned, with Sandy still inside. It wasn't possible. The fire didn't yet look out of control, at least from where she stood. It was visible only in one window. There was still time.

She took off her jacket and jumper, and ran to the front door. The air bit cold at her bare arms. She put the jumper over her mouth, turned the handle and went inside, through the porch to the hall. Smoke billowed thick and dirty around the ceiling, and the whole place was murky, half-visible, as though in the process of being erased. The flames were confined to the kitchen. Belches of light erupted from the countertop, reaching up over the far wall.

Alice squinted into the living room. Her eyes were sore, and she could see only vague shapes through the gloom. She was about to keep going, upstairs to the bedroom, when Sandy coughed from the far corner. She ran, almost tripped over the table, then went down to her hands and knees. Sandy was drooped over the armchair. She couldn't tell if he had passed out from the smoke or not yet woken from the drink. She grabbed his dangling arm. 'Sandy! Sandy! Wake up!' He shrugged and swivelled in his chair, pulled away from her, then coughed again. She pulled harder. This time he opened his eyes, drew the back of his hand across his lips and looked down at Alice, confused. Then he looked up at the fire.

'Come on!' Alice shouted. 'We've got to get out.'

Sandy leaned forward, tried to stand, then toppled. She helped him to his knees and turned, back towards the door. He followed then, slow crawling, spluttering.

'Terry?' he whispered, as they got to the hall.

'He's not here. He must have gone home already.' She opened the door to the porch just as David was coming in from outside. He grabbed at Sandy's collar and lifted him to his feet, but some doubt yanked Alice back. 'Take him!' she said to David. 'I just need to check.' She didn't wait for him to stop her. She turned, still clasping the jumper to her face, her eyes streaming now. There was no one in the living room, she made sure, checked each seat, one after another. But when she turned again, to the kitchen, she stopped.

She saw.

Feet. Legs.

'Terry!'

It was hot now, and Alice pushed forward against the will of her own body. She kneeled down and grabbed at Terry's clothes, tried to wake him. He didn't move. She tugged hard, fingers clasped around his belt. He was heavy. Nothing moved.

Alice didn't hear David come up behind her, she just felt his grip on the shoulder. 'We hae ta be quick,' he said. That was all.

The two of them slipped their hands beneath Terry's armpits and turned him round, shuffling together. Alice could feel the heat searing through her T-shirt, to her back. She stumbled once, then again, her feet slipping against the weight. David fell, too, cursed, then kept going. Alice wanted to shout, to scream at the body stretched out in front of them – *Wake up! Wake up!* – but she couldn't. It was taking all of her strength just to breathe and drag and think enough to keep moving.

The fire was growing quickly now. Part of the floor was ablaze, and the cupboard doors too. Flames gasped from the counter up the wall as high as the ceiling.

They pulled again, then paused. Alice grabbed the door in one hand and opened it. They hauled Terry into the porch, where the air was clearer, and continued, easing him through the front door, over the step and onto the path. They took him out as far as the gate, then stopped.

Alice put a hand to Terry's face. The skin around his eyes was scarlet and swollen. She leaned in and listened for a breath but could hear nothing over her own fierce panting and the wallop of her heart.

David stood. 'Sandy okay?'

'With any luck he'll suffer more from the drink than the smoke,' Mary said. 'They'll need to take him in, though, to make sure.' Sandy was hunched over beside the shed, retching. He didn't look up.

The ground was wet, and Alice could feel the damp creeping through her clothes to her skin. It was a relief after the heat. She leaned her head in close to Terry's, her hand on his chest. 'Can you check him, Mary? Please! I can't . . . I can't seem to . . .' She looked up.

'He's breathing,' Mary said. 'Not very well, by the looks of it, but he's definitely breathing.'

Alice rested against the concrete pillar of the gate. She felt herself shivering then, as if her body had needed to be reminded of how it felt. 'I think I'm cold,' she said. 'My coat?' Everything was indistinct now. Her focus had shattered.

Mary brought the coat from the car and wrapped it around Alice's shoulders. Alice felt the older woman's arms around her, and she leaned her head against them and closed her eyes.

* * *

The ambulance arrived first, hurtling down the valley to where its residents all were gathered. Mary stood as they approached, then watched as Terry was laid out on a stretcher, with an oxygen mask over his mouth. She hugged Sandy, held him tightly, then led him to the back of the ambulance.

'Ah'll follow on,' said David, before they closed the door. 'Ah'll see dee shortly, boy.' Sandy nodded, not looking up.

Alice hadn't moved from where she sat by the gatepost. She hardly even looked up until, a few minutes later, the fire engine appeared at the top of the road. Mary leaned over to her then, spoke quietly. 'We'll need to get out of the way,' she said. Alice rose to her feet, unsteady. Mary wondered if she, too, should have gone in the ambulance. She looked to be in shock. 'I'll take you home,' she said.

'No,' said Alice. 'Thank you. I'll wait till they're done.'

Mary was aware then of smoke billowing from the open window above the kitchen. Sandy's bedroom. And she could hear the rustle and gasp of it as the fire engine approached. She went and sat with Alice against the concrete wall of the shed, while David talked to the firemen. Then he, too, stood aside and came to join them.

The firemen did not take long. Mary heard the pump start

and then stop, she heard voices, she heard the door open and close again. David stood up and went to speak to them. He was gone ten minutes, maybe more. Then he returned. The fire engine drove away.

'Right,' he said, reaching out his hand. 'Come on. Let's go up ta da hoose, hae some brakfast afore we go ta the hospital. Is du hungry?'

Mary nodded, though she wasn't. Not even slightly.

'Alice. Du'll need ta join wis.'

'Thank you,' she said, her face streaked with tears. 'I will.'

'No, Alice. Thank you!' David put his arms around her then. 'I dunna lik ta think whit woulda happened if du hadna seen. If du hadna . . .' His voice quietened as he spoke into her shoulder, then stopped. He held her for a moment longer, then stood back, his hands still on her arms. His eyes were red. 'I telt dee there wis aalwis stories,' David said. 'This een belangs ta dee.'

SATURDAY,
20TH AUGUST

So that was that. Alice looked at the pile of printed pages in front of her and leaned back in her chair. She'd done everything she could with it. Four years of research and writing, and there it was: a stack of paper on a desk. A kilo and a half of paragraphs, sentences, words, letters, ink. *The Valley at the Centre of the World*.

It was not the book she set out to write. Nor was it the book she had imagined a year ago, or even a month ago, when she took a tour of the house at the end of the road. The fire at Gardie had changed everything. The box Sandy found in the loft had been the first thing to burn. The diary and photographs were destroyed, the porcelain figures all blackened in the blaze. Everything Alice had written about Maggie she discarded a few days later. The whole final chapter, in which the story of the old woman's life was supposed to illuminate the story of the community itself, she deleted in one twitch of her index finger. What she'd written, she realised, amounted to nothing, illuminated nothing.

Decision made, Alice found herself untroubled by doubt, calmed by the absence she had created in the book. What she'd done was to lay safe ground. Geology, history, natural history: those were the bedrock on which the place rested. Having fixed them in words, as well as she could, there was, perhaps, no need to do more. She had brought together the details from which a story could be born. She had created the possibility of a narrative. But that narrative could not be Maggie's. It would have to be her own.

This morning, Alice had driven to town, bought a couple of novels and some biscuits for Terry. She made the trip more often now, since Billy's shop in Treswick closed, back in June. Terry was staying with his wife, Louise, at least for the moment, resting up. He'd thanked her for the biscuits but refused the books. His eyes were still not fit for reading, he said. They ached when he tried to concentrate on anything. She brought them home. She would read them herself.

He'd been lying on the sofa when she arrived – Jamie opened the door to her – and though he sat up to speak, Terry maintained the appearance of a patient. He spoke quietly, almost whispered, and coughed often, wincing as he did so. He was still in pain and found it hard to take full breaths. He'd been lucky – they had pulled him out in time – but the smoke had done damage. When Alice asked if he'd be staying in town or coming back to the valley, he just shrugged. It wasn't up to him, he said. Nothing was ever up to him.

She felt sorry for Terry. He seemed so passive; not just today but always, as though his whole movement through life had been guided by decisions that were not his own. He was pushed this way and that, like a fictional character controlled by a malicious author. Had she invented him herself, Alice thought, she would probably have let him die in the fire. At least then he would have seemed tragic rather than pathetic. It was a terrible thought, and she regretted it as soon as it came to her.

For now, she just wanted a break. Simon and Jenny were coming to visit with the children in a fortnight, and Alice intended to take their holiday as her own. She would not be writing, would not be thinking about writing. She had already begun to make plans for the trip, to show them places they'd not visited before, to try to make them understand why exactly it was she stayed here, why she had to stay on. She was looking forward to it at least as much as they were. She would be host, tour guide, companion.

The only thing left to do now with her book was to decide what would happen with the manuscript perched on her desk. Alice knew it would be of no interest to her own, formerly loyal, readers. Everything those readers loved about her previous work was missing from this book; everything they wanted had been excised. In fact, it was hard to imagine anyone ploughing their way through it, other than the few people who already cared about this place.

Perhaps she would show it to David and Mary, to see if they approved. Perhaps Sandy, too. Or perhaps, in the end, she would just put the manuscript in a box and store it in the loft.

Alice flicked through the pile of papers in front of her, the tens of thousands of words she had spent these past few years producing. She was proud of it, proud to have written something that meant something. Even if nobody ever read it, that was all right. Everything was as it ought to be.

She turned the title page over and looked down at the very last few words she had written – the dedication. It read, in full: *For Maggie, who once lived here.*

Maggie, she thought, would have liked this book.

★ ★ ★

David sat in the truck outside the Red House and waited. He'd beeped the horn, so Sandy would be on his way. Looking down the valley, he could see the sun shattering the bay and the ocean beyond into a million bright pieces, each dancing on the darkness beneath. That's where they were headed now, out on the water.

It'd been years since he'd owned a boat. Since his father died, in fact, he'd been without one. They used to fish together, the two of them, until his father could no longer climb in and out safely. It was hard for the old man, giving up like that. But in the end he had to. Afterwards, David lost the inclination. He waited a few months after the funeral, then sold the boat. He didn't want to see it rot.

But this year he'd been thinking again about the sea. The thought had grown slowly – a vague notion, only gradually defined – until, surprising even himself, he acted. In a week of sunshine in early July, he'd scanned through the adverts in the *Shetland Times*, phoned a man in Scalloway with a fourteen-foot Shetland model for sale, gone to see it and brought it home, all in a day. David was not usually an impulsive man, but the boat felt right. The time felt right.

It had taken him another couple of weeks to find an engine, and by the time he did buy one – a little Yamaha outboard from an old school friend in Lerwick – the good weather had passed. Gales chased gales for day after day, and he began to wonder if he'd ever get a chance to try it out. But in late August an echo of summer returned. The wind died down, the temperature rose and the forecast was good.

The fine weather would coincide with Emma's visit. She was due to arrive this lunchtime. Mary would go to the airport to collect her, and Kate and the bairns were coming round later for their tea. So he and Sandy could have a couple of hours on the water this morning, and maybe bring home some fish for tomorrow too, if they were lucky.

The trip was not entirely for his benefit, though. It was Sandy who really needed it. He needed something, anyway. Since the fire, he'd not been himself. He'd gone back to work a few days later, no problem at all. But things weren't right. He wasn't ill, exactly, he just wasn't doing anything beyond the essential. He managed the bare minimum down at the croft. He could hold a conversation, without enthusiasm. But he just didn't seem entirely present.

A couple of days after the fire, they'd moved some of what could be salvaged from Gardie back into the Red House. All of it was heavy with smoke. Every now and then you'd still smell it on Sandy — a waft of dirty air from some piece of clothing that hadn't been through the wash enough to fully shed the stench. It'd been hard to see him that day, as they stepped through the house in their rubber boots. The fire itself had not spread much further than the kitchen before it was extinguished. But that was more than enough. That room was almost entirely destroyed — burnt, then soaked — and the ceiling and walls were blackened in the living room, too. There was a hole as wide as a silage bale in the ceiling, exposing Sandy's bedroom above. Only the spare room and the bathrooms were undamaged, though nothing had escaped the smell.

They were almost silent as they wandered from room to room that day, much as they'd done months earlier, after Maggie died. This time, though, there was no hopefulness to be found there, no sense of how things might be made better or renewed. Their thoughts were only on what was lost. It was lucky that the Red House had been empty then, so that at least was simple. But the insurance, it turned out, might not be. David was still waiting for word, but there were bad signs. The lack of a smoke alarm downstairs had been noted. The cause of the fire had been noted. The absence of paperwork for the rental had been noted. He wasn't confident.

Sandy emerged from the front door carrying a small rucksack and a jacket. He had on waterproof trousers and a pair of wellies.

He didn't look at David as he came out towards the pickup. He walked with his head turned down the valley, almost crablike.

'Morning!'

'Aye aye, Sandy. Is du got aathing du's needin?'

'Well, what am I needin?'

'No much. Extra gansie, sandwiches. Yon's aboot aa.'

'I'm fine then. Ready!'

'Okay.'

David took the handbrake off and turned the key halfway in the ignition. The pickup began to roll down the hill soundlessly. He pressed the clutch and put it in second gear, then lifted the pedal. The truck jolted and the engine caught. It wasn't necessary, this ritual, it was just habit. If he was on a slope, he would always bump start, as if he were saving the starter motor the effort. So much of his life was dictated by habit, he sometimes thought. Habit, punctuated by the uncontrollable and the unpredictable. That was the way it had always been.

'So, what are we expectin to catch da day?'

'Well, we'll juist see whit's aboot. Piltocks, ollicks, haddocks, cod, whitever. Somethin or nothin, I dunna really mind. It'll juist be good ta git oot ageen. It's been a lot o years noo.'

'Can you mind what you're doin?'

'Ah'm hoopin so. Wance we git oot, it'll aa come back ta me. Lik ridin a bike, I doot.'

'Well, I'll trust you on that. I've got nae idea though, so if you're wrong we're in trouble.'

'Ha! Dunna worry aboot dat. We'll no be goin far. If Ah'm wrong, I reckon we'll *still* be aaright.'

They were silent then as David parked the pickup outside Gardie. He saw Sandy look up at the black stain above the smashed kitchen window, but neither of them said anything. There was nothing to say.

David walked round to the back of the truck and lifted out the engine, cradling it in his arms. 'Could du tak da can o fuel an da rods? Ah'm got da rest o da gear in me bag.'

The pair of them took the track from beside the house, which curved down towards the beach. There, the boat lay in a noost in the bank, cut out, perhaps, by David's grandfather. At least that's what he'd been told. He could remember years back when there were more of these noosts still visible, but all of them had worn away with the winter storms. No one other than his father had kept a boat here for decades. Even Walter, who'd spent more than twenty years as a merchant seaman, never got himself a boat. Perhaps especially Walter.

The beach was neither quiet nor still. Though there was little wind, the waves unfolded themselves onto the rocks with a steady rush, an insistent whisper that seemed to swell the air. In the bank of seaweed at the high-tide mark, plovers ducked and prodded, and gulls floated close to shore. They put their things down on the rocks and stood either side of the boat. It was broad-bodied, painted blue, with white around the gunwales.

'Lift and walk,' David said. 'Keep da keel up.' It was heavy, but together they could move it, more shuffling than walking. David felt the ache in his back as he did so, and the stabbing between his shoulder blades, but he said nothing. They dragged it to the water's edge, then went back for the motor, the rods, the bags and the bucket. David fixed the outboard onto the stern, tilting it up to keep the blades high. Together they slid it a little further into the sea.

'Right, du jump in.'

'Okay,' Sandy said. 'But if we baith get in we can push off wi the oars.'

'Hmm, mebbie. But Ah'm no wantin ta scrape da erse aff her afore we're even got her fully weet.' He waited.

With Sandy onboard, David pushed until he was almost at the top of his boots. The bow was afloat, and Sandy held one oar up, ready to shove. David lifted his left leg and tried to pull himself aboard, but the boat rolled towards him and he slipped, almost falling backwards into the water.

'Shite! I shoulda taken me flankers. Ah'm gotten wet feet noo.'

'Dunna worry aboot your feet, just worry aboot gettin aboard.'

'Seems Ah'm no as limber as I wance wis.'

'No, I guess you're no.'

David gripped the gunwale tight again. 'Right, du lean back as I put me weight on it. Dat wye we'll no baith end up in da sea.' He lifted his leg again, pressed down on the side and pulled, performing something like a sideways roll into the seat at the stern. 'No elegant, but effective,' he grinned.

'Mair elephant as elegant, I'd say.' Sandy passed him the other oar, and together they pushed down onto the rocks, lifting the boat out from the shore. They both gave an extra shove as they felt it float fully. David turned around then and put the outboard in position. He primed it, pulled out the choke and set it to start. Then he pulled the cord. Though he'd practised this several times before to make sure it was working, he still felt relief when it started first time.

'Well, dere's a mercy.' He shook his head in wonder and grinned back at Sandy. He sat down again and led the boat out from the beach, heading towards the rocks beneath the highest point of Burganess. He could hear almost nothing above the sound of the engine, the calm roar of it, lifting them over the waves. Beyond the headland the boat began to bounce, and David pulled back on the throttle and pointed them south, into the breeze. When they were about two hundred metres off the cliff, he slowed the engine to a crawl and turned around. He lowered his head, checked the tallest of the skerries was aligned with the top of the hill beyond the valley, then he turned east-ward, but couldn't see what he was looking for at all. He continued slowly, keeping the skerry and the hill in line until the very top of the church in Treswick came into view. This was the spot.

His father had taught him the half-dozen or so fishing marks that lay close to their bay – close enough to be reached in a boat this size. To his shame, David had forgotten all but two of them. He'd hoped that being out here on the water the others would come back to him, the way a face you've not seen in decades will return at the very mention of the name. But for now he would stick with the ones he was sure of, beginning with this one. He cut the engine, and the silence poured back in like water into a sinking bottle. Except that it wasn't silence, and the sounds of the bay poured in behind it: the waves first, and the breeze against the land; then the birds – the kittiwakes and fulmars; and finally the sound of his own breathing.

'We'll try here,' David said. He told Sandy the mark – the formula of sightlines that had brought them to this spot. It was a kind of incantation, and he heard his father's voice as he spoke the words out loud. 'Try an mind,' he said. 'Fir next time.'

He'd strung the rods up with teams of brightly coloured flies and a lead weight. He handed one across the boat. 'Du kens how to use him, right?' Sandy nodded. David held his own out then, on the starboard side. He unhooked the lowest fly and hung the weight in the water, then flipped the lever on the multiplier reel, letting the line run out, his thumb slowing it, just enough to keep it from tangling. When it hit the bottom, he clicked the lever back and reeled in a few metres of line. Then he sat back and watched as Sandy did the same.

The boat drifted northeasterly, towards Burganess, but slowly. The tide was slack – half an hour from turning. Every few seconds David gave a stiff strike on the rod, then let it fall again, back towards the bottom. Fifteen minutes passed, then twenty. At one point he thought he felt something, a tug or a wobble on the line, but he struck hard and nothing solid happened. As they neared the headland, he reeled in, told Sandy to do the same, then brought them back to where they'd started. 'We'll gie it wan mair try, then go somewye else.'

They lowered their lines again and waited. They hadn't spoken at all on the previous drift, and no more was said this time. David's thoughts returned to land, to his house and to his wife. He thought of Mary, on her way south now, to the airport; he thought of his daughter, who was coming home; he thought of the limping ewe he'd seen that morning; he thought of the unhealthy rattle his pickup had developed; he thought of his father and the tobacco stains his fingers had carried; he thought about the fire. David's thoughts circled and swooped, yet were tethered, somehow, to that thin line that disappeared beneath him, reaching down into a world he could not see and could hardly even imagine. His thoughts were tied to that stillness below.

At the end of the second fishless drift, David turned and looked northwards, to the far side of the bay. There, a score of gannets were diving, one after the other, and he nodded to Sandy in their direction. 'Mebbie dey ken mair as we do,' he said, reeling up and fastening the flies in place again. 'I reckon dey likely do.'

The little boat crossed the bay, with the wind behind them. It was rising now, just a touch, but not enough to be uncomfortable. Both of them looked up at the valley as they bounced ahead. The Red House and Kettlester were visible; Flugarth and Gardie were almost hidden. Only their roofs and chimneys showed above the beach.

The gannets made space for them as they arrived, but

continued diving not far from the boat. David switched off the engine. 'Dunna drop it ta da bottom dis time. Juist a few metres doon, I reckon.'

Both of them swung their rods out and flipped the levers, let the weight fall, stopped, then struck. Once. Twice. Three times. They hit fish at the same moment, and David knew immediately that his guess was correct. Jerking and jolting like mad things, the mackerel came to the surface: two on David's line, three on Sandy's. Like blue and silver bullets, the fish were solid, muscular, shocking. The men unhooked them, threw them in the bucket and dropped their lures again. More came almost immediately, and were tossed in on top of the last. The mackerel flipped and leapt like popping corn.

For half an hour, they hauled fish after fish, until the bucket had overflowed and the boards around their feet were strewn with bodies and striped with blood. Then nothing. The shoal beneath them had moved on. The gannets were diving further north up the coast. David considered following them, but he didn't need to. They had enough fish to last them for weeks.

'Home,' he said. It sounded like a question, but it wasn't. Sandy just nodded, smiled. David turned around and pulled the cord on the engine. This time it didn't catch. He tried again. There was resistance, but nothing more. He took the choke out and hauled again at the cord. Nothing. Primed it. Nothing. He looked at the outboard then, hoping some solution might occur to him, but it didn't.

'Du ken onything aboot engines?' he asked.

'Nope. Nothin.'

'Neither do I, unfortunately. I aalwis meant ta learn, but . . .' He shrugged. 'Whit aboot oars?'

'I think I can just aboot manage those.'

'Ah'm aafil glad ta hear it.'

Sandy changed seats, and David watched as he set the oars in place and began, somewhat awkwardly, to row. David said nothing. He looked beyond, towards the shore, grateful that he didn't need to do this himself, grateful there was someone else to do the work. The quiet, too, was welcome. The splashing of the oars was louder than it needed to be, but it covered nothing. He could still hear the birds, hear the water and the air moving together, and he was glad, then, that the motor had failed. He was glad of everything the day had brought him.

Halfway across the bay, Sandy paused to take a break. He straightened his back and moved his shoulders, then turned briefly towards the shore.

'How's dy mither?' David asked.

Sandy looked back. 'I think she's fine,' he said. 'She's got a flat in toon and a job in the Co-op, stackin shelves or somethin.' He raised his eyebrows. 'Mebbie she'll stick it oot. I dunna ken.'

'And whit aboot dee? How's du?' David watched Sandy flinch, and waited.

'Ach, dunna worry aboot me,' he shrugged. 'I'll stick it oot, I reckon. If you still want me to.'

David nodded and smiled back. 'Aye. We do. We do.'

Sandy began to row again, heaving into the work. David could see the sweat shimmer on his forehead, and he knew that he was tired. But he wasn't going to take over. Not this time.

Two figures appeared on the beach then, arm in arm, walking slow over the rocks. David saw his wife and his youngest daughter, and he willed himself nearer. In the moments of their approach, Emma came down to the water's edge, and David watched, helpless, as she lifted her arm in the air and smiled. Sandy, turning, saw her too, and pulled harder at the oars, his body urging the boat towards home.

A NOTE ON LANGUAGE

It would be impossible to set a novel in Shetland and to ignore the question of language. The local dialect – sometimes known as Shaetlan or Shetlandic – is widely spoken in the islands. It is hugely important to the character and culture of the place.

Strictly speaking, Shaetlan is a variant of Scots; but these islands have a complex history, and the dialect reflects that. Many words are descended from Norn, the Norse language of Orkney and Shetland, which became extinct in the seventeenth or eighteenth century.

Today, the degree to which the dialect is used varies enormously between communities, between generations and between individuals. Its use also depends not just on who is speaking but on who is being spoken *to*. Some dialect speakers will moderate their language when communicating with people from elsewhere (this is known as *knappin*), while others choose not to do so.

All of this makes the novelist's job a little tricky, particularly when writing for an audience largely unfamiliar with Shaetlan, or even with mainland variants of Scots. In order to write effective dialogue, therefore, choices must be made, and compromises are necessary.

My own choice has been, firstly, to minimise the use of vocabulary that would be unknown to the general reader. To me, this seems preferable to explanatory footnotes, extensive glossaries, or awkward definitions shoehorned into the text.

However, I have tried my best to get the *feeling* of Shetland dialect and the local accents, by phonetically replicating, as best I can, the grammar, the rhythms and the sounds of the language. On the page this may, at first, look difficult to penetrate. But I hope the reader will soon find themselves able to hear the voices of the characters.

The results of my choices, I recognise, are not perfect. But I hope they provide an acceptable and comfortable balance between linguistic accuracy and general readability.

More information about the dialect, as well as a Shetland dictionary, can be found at shetlanddialect.org.uk. The site also contains many recordings of Shaetlan being spoken, and other educational materials.

ACKNOWLEDGEMENTS

Thanks to John Burnside, who, with great patience, helped me get this book off the ground. For their encouragement, reassurance and (necessary) criticism, I am grateful to Amy Liptrot, Jordan Ogg, Jennifer Haigh, Roxani Krystalli, Julia Smith Porter and Kerrie-Anne Chinn.

Thanks to Mary Blance for checking my dialect; to my agent Jenny Brown; to my editor Jo Dingley; to Debs Warner; and to everyone at Canongate. Thanks to Creative Scotland, who supported my writing with a bursary, and to Scottish Book Trust for awarding me the Robert Louis Stevenson Fellowship, during which part of this novel was written.

This book is entirely fictional. Its plot, characters and setting are not based on real events, people or places. However, what I know about crofting and community life I learned in Fair Isle, and my gratitude to that community – for these and other lessons – has not diminished.

RON RASH

SERENA

'A bloody – and bloody brilliant – story of passion and revenge . . .
There has never been a heroine quite like this'
The Times

'Beautifully wrought. The author's acute sense of
place is evident on every page'
Guardian

CANON‖GATE